The Female
of the Species

JOYCE CAROL OATES

The Female
of the Species

Tales of Mystery
and Suspense

AN OTTO PENZLER BOOK
A HARVEST BOOK • HARCOURT, INC.
Orlando   Austin   New York   San Diego   Toronto   London

Requests for permission to make copies of any part of the work
should be submitted online at www.harcourt.com/contact or mailed
to the following address: Permissions Department, Harcourt, Inc.,
6277 Sea Harbor Drive, Orlando, Florida 32887-6777.

www.HarcourtBooks.com

The Library of Congress has cataloged the hardcover edition as follows:
Oates, Joyce Carol, 1938–
The female of the species: stories of mystery and suspense/
Joyce Carol Oates.
p.   cm.
"An Otto Penzler Book."
1. Detective and mystery stories, American.   I. Title.
PS3565.A8F46   2005
813'.54—dc22   2005005068
ISBN-13: 978-0-15-101179-7   ISBN-10: 0-15-101179-6
ISBN-13: 978-0-15-603027-4 (pbk.)   ISBN-10: 0-15-603027-6 (pbk.)

Text set in Electra
Designed by Linda Lockowitz

Printed in the United States of America

First Harvest edition 2007
K J I H G F E D C B A

To Lisa and Otto

Contents

So Help Me God

1.

Phone rings. My cousin Andrea answers.

It's a pelting-rain weekday evening last April, just past 7 P.M. and dark as midnight.

Without so much as glancing toward me, Andrea picks up the receiver as if she's in her own home and not mine, shifting her infant daughter onto her left hip in a way that makes you think of a migrant farmwife in a classic Walker Evans photograph of the 1930s.

Phone rings! I will wish I'd snatched the receiver from her hand, slammed it down before any words were exchanged.

But Andrea is answering in her wishing-to-be-surprised high school voice, not taking time to squint at the caller ID my husband, a St. Lawrence County law enforcement officer, has had installed for precisely these evenings when he's on the night shift and his young wife is alone in this house in the country except for the accident of Andrea dropping by with the baby and interfering with my life.

"Yes? Who *is* this?"

Andrea laughs, blinking and staring past me. Whoever is on the other end of the line is intriguing to her, I can see.

I'm checking the digital code which has come up UNAVAILABLE.

Sometimes it reads NO DATA GIVEN, which is the same as UNAVAILABLE and a signal you don't want to pick up. At least, I don't. In Au Sable Forks, which is the center and circumference of my world, everyone is acquainted with everyone else and has been so since grade school. It's rare that an unknown name comes up; I can count on the fingers of one hand the people likely to be calling me at this or any hour, which is why ordinarily I'd have let UNAVAILABLE leave a message on the machine, figuring it must be for my husband.

UNAVAILABLE could be anyone. Like a hulking individual on your doorstep, wearing a ski mask—do you open the door?

I could wring Andrea's neck the way she's smiling, shaking her head, "*Which* one? *Who?*" opening the damn door wide. Wish I'd never called her this afternoon hinting I was lonely.

This pelting rain! The kind of rain that hammers at your head like unwanted thoughts.

Andrea hands over the phone, saying in a low thrilled voice, "It's this person won't identify himself, but I think it's Pitman."

Pitman! My husband. His first name is Luke but everyone calls him Pitman.

Andrea shivers giving me the receiver. There has been this shivery thing between her and Pitman dating back to before Pitman and I were married. When I'm in a suspicious mood I think it might predate my meeting Pitman when I was fourteen, an honors student vowing to remain a virgin all my life. I've never confronted either of them.

Pitman says my daddy injected my vertebrae with Rayburn family pride, why I walk like there's a broomstick up my rear. Why I'm so stiff (Pitman is just teasing!) in bed.

"Yes? Who is this please?" I'm determined to remain cool and poised, for Pitman and I parted early this morning with some harsh words flung about on both our sides like gravel. My husband is known as a man who flares up quickly in anger but, flaring down—which can be just a few minutes later—he expects me to laugh, forgive and forget, as if nothing hurtful passed between us. Pitman is a longtime joker and this wouldn't be the first time he has played phone games with me, so I'm primed to hear him in this deep-gravelly male voice so suddenly intimate in my ear asking: "Are you Ms. Pitman, the lady of the house?" Quick as Ping-Pong I say, "Mister, who are you? I don't talk to strangers."

You'd think that after living with a man for more than four years and being crazy in love with him for three years preceding you'd at least recognize his phone voice, but damned if Pitman hasn't disguised it with something like pebbles in his mouth (?) or a layer of some fabric over the phone receiver, and speaking with the broad *a*s of a Canadian! Also, he's making me nervous so I am not thinking as clearly as usual. The voice is chiding, "Ms. Pitman! You sound like some stiff-back old Rayburn," which convinces me that this is Pitman, who else? My face is hot and eyes tearing up as they do with any strong emotion, sweat breaking out on my body; I hate how Pitman has this effect upon me, and my cousin a witness. The voice is inquiring, "Is this 'Pitman' an individual of some size and reputation?"—a strange thing to ask, I'm thinking. So I say, "'Pitman' is a law enforcement officer of dubious reputation, a cruel tease I am considering reporting to authorities."

My teasing with Pitman is never so inspired or easy as his with me; it's like wrestling with Pitman on our bed: I'm a scrawny ninety-seven pounds, half his size. The voice responds quick, as if alarmed, "Hang on now, baby. What authorities?" and I hear *baby*—this has got to be Pitman: *baby* in his mouth and it's like he has touched me between the legs and any ice-scrim that has built up between us begins to melt rapidly. I'm saying, my voice rising, "He knows who! So he'd better stop playing games," and the voice says in mock alarm, or maybe genuine alarm, "What authorities? Sheriff? Police?" and I say, "Pitman, damn! Stop this," but the voice persists, "Is this 'Pitman' armed and dangerous at all times, baby?" and there's something about this question, a strangeness of diction. The sick sensation washes over me—*This isn't Pitman*—and my throat shuts up, and the voice continues to tease, husky and breathy in my ear, "Fuck Pitman, baby—what are you wearing?" and I slam down the receiver.

Andrea takes my hands, says they are like ice.

"Oh, Lucretia! Wasn't it Pitman? I thought for sure it was."

Andrea thinks that I should report the call and I tell her yes, I will tell Pitman and he can report it. He's a law enforcement officer; he will know best how to proceed.

Things you do when you're crazy in love, you'll look back upon with astonishment. Maybe a kind of pride. Thinking, *That could not have been me; I am not that person.*

When I married Pitman, my daddy disowned me. Daddy had come to believe that Pitman had cast some sort of spell over me. I was not his daughter any longer. I had not been his daughter for some time.

My father was a stubborn man, but I was stubborn, too.

Eighteen when I married Lucas Pitman, old enough to be legally married in New York State, but not old enough to be so coldly discarded by my father whom I loved. I'd come to believe that I hated Daddy and this was so, but I loved Daddy, too. I would never forgive him!

My mother disapproved of Pitman, of course. But knew better than to forbid me marrying him. She'd seen how Pitman had worked his way under my skin, cast his "spell" over me. She'd known long before Daddy had. Back when I was fourteen, in fact. Skinny pale-blond girl with sly eyes given to believe that, because she's conceded to be the smartest student in the sophomore class at Au Sable High, she can't mess up her life like any trailer-trash Adirondack girl.

I never did get pregnant, though. Pitman saw to that.

Luke Pitman was the youngest deputy in the St. Lawrence County sheriff's department when we first met: twenty-three. He'd been hired out of the police academy at Potsdam and before that he'd served in the navy. There were Pitmans scattered through the county, most of them with reputations. To have a "reputation" means nothing good except when it's made clear what the reputation is for: integrity, honesty, business ethics, and Christian morals. For instance, Everett Rayburn, my father, had a reputation in St. Lawrence County and beyond as an "honest" contractor and builder. Everett Rayburn was "reliable" — "good-as-his-word" — "decent." Only the well-to-do could afford to hire him and in turn Daddy could afford to hire only the best carpenters, painters, electricians, plumbers. Daddy wasn't an architect, but he'd designed our house, which was the most impressive in Au Sable Forks, a split-level "contemporary-traditional" on

Algonquin Drive. In school I hated how I had to be friends with the few "rich" kids. I got along with the trailer-trash kids a lot better.

There were Pitmans who lived in trailers as well as Pitmans in dilapidated old farmhouses in the area. Pitman himself was from Star Lake in the Adirondacks, but he'd moved out of his parents' house at the age of fifteen. He told me he had a hard time living in any kind of close quarters with other people and if our marriage was going to endure I would have to grant him "space."

Rightaway I asked Pitman would he grant me "space," too, and Pitman said, tugging my ponytail so it hurt, "That depends, baby."

"Like there's a law for you, but a different law for me?"

"Damn right, baby."

You couldn't argue with Pitman. He'd stop your mouth with his mouth. You tried to speak and he'd suck out your breath. You tried to get serious with him and he'd laugh at you.

How I met Pitman was quite a story. I never told it to anyone except Andrea.

I was bicycling back home from Andrea's house in the country. She lived about a mile and a half outside Au Sable Forks, which is not an actual town but a village. Summers, Andrea and I bicycled back and forth to see each other all the time; it was something to do. Andrea had more household chores than I did and my bicycle was newer and faster than hers and I was the one who got restless and bored, so it was usually me on my bicycle, slow and dreamy and coasting when I could and not paying much attention to cars and pick-

ups that swung out to pass me. It was late August and boring-
hot and I was wearing white shorts, a little green Gap T-shirt,
flip-flops on my feet. I wasn't so young as I looked. My ash-
blond ponytail swept halfway down my back and my toenails
were painted this bright sparkly green Daddy insisted I had to
cover up, wear socks or actual shoes, at mealtimes. I was
maybe smiling thinking of how Daddy got upset, or pretended
to, at the least "infraction" of household rules on my part,
when Pitman came cruising in the car marked ST. LAWRENCE
CO. SHERIFF. I wasn't paying too much attention to this vehicle
coming up behind me until a male voice came out of
nowhere — "You, girl: got a license for that bike?"

I didn't know Pitman then. Didn't know about what you'd
call Pitman-teasing. Almost crashed my bicycle, I was so
scared. For there was this police officer glaring out his car window at me. He wasn't smiling. His aviator sunglasses were
tinted so dark I couldn't see his eyes except they were not
friendly eyes. His hair was tarry black and shaved at the sides
and back of his head but grew long and tufted on top like a
rock musician's. How old he was, I couldn't have guessed. I
was so scared I could hardly focus my eyes.

What followed next, Pitman would recount with laughter,
in the years to come. I guess it was funny! Him demanding to
see my "bike license" and me stammering I didn't have one,
didn't know you had to have a license to ride a bicycle . . .
Fourteen years old and scared as a little kid, calling Pitman
"sir" and "officer" and Pitman had all he could do to keep
from laughing. He'd say afterward he had seen me riding my
bike on the Hunter Road more than once, looked like I was in
this dreamworld, pedaling along on an expensive bicycle

oblivious of other vehicles even when they passed close to me. He'd had a thought that here was a little blond princess needed a shaking-up for once.

I just didn't get it was a joke. The way Pitman grilled me, asking my name, my daddy's name and what did my daddy do for a living, what was my address and telephone number. These facts he seemed to be taking down on a notepad. (He was.) I was straddling my bike by the roadside trying not to cry, staring at Pitman who so captivated my attention it was like the earth had opened up; I was slipping and falling inside. Pitman must've seen my knobby knees shaking, but he kept on his interrogation with no mercy.

Daddy would say Pitman had cast a spell on his only daughter; when Daddy was being nasty he'd call it a sex spell and I concede that this was so: Pitman's power over girls and women was sexual, but it was more than only this, I swear. For there was this Pitman-soul you saw in the man's eyes when he was in one of his moods, or you felt in the heat of his skin — a soul that was pure flame, a weird wild happiness like electricity coursing through him. Just to touch it was dangerous, but you had to touch!

Can't take your eyes off him — he's beautiful.

"Well, now. 'Lucretia Rayburn.' Seeing as how you are a minor, maybe I won't run you into headquarters. Maybe just a ticket."

By this time most of the blood had drained out of my face, my lips must have been stark white. Trembling, and fighting tears. I was so grateful, Pitman was taking pity on me. But before I could thank him, he asks, as if the thought had only just occurred to him, how old is that bicycle, where had it been purchased, and how much did it cost? "Looks like a pretty expensive bicycle, Lucretia. One of them 'mountain bikes.' You got the bill of sale for that bike, girl, to prove it ain't stolen property?"

I did just about break down, at this. Had to say I didn't have any bill of sale but my father might have it, at home. Please could I go home? Pitman shakes his head gravely, saying he has no choice but to "confiscate" the bike and run me into headquarters after all—"See, they got to take your prints, Lucretia Rayburn, and run 'em into the computer. See if they match up with known felons. For all I know, you ain't even 'Lucretia Rayburn,' you're just impersonating her." And I'm stammering, No please, officer, please. But Pitman has climbed out of the cruiser to loom above me, frowning and severe seeming. He's six foot two or three, a hard-muscled youngish man in a uniform made of a silvery-blue material and I'm seeing that he's wearing a gold-glinting badge and a leather belt and holster and in the holster there's a gun, and a roaring comes up in my ears like I'm going to faint. Pitman takes my arm, not hard, but firm, and Pitman leads me around to the passenger's side of the cruiser, sits me down in the seat like I was a little girl and not this skinny-leggy girl of fourteen with a glamor ponytail halfway down her back. He notes the sparkly green toenail polish but refrains from comment. Takes from his belt a pair of metal handcuffs that are these adult-sized cuffs and says, still not cracking a smile, "Got to cuff you, Lucretia. It's for your own protection, too." By this time I'm sick with shame. I can't think how this nightmare will end. Pitman takes my arms that are covered in goose pimples from fear of him, gently draws them behind my back, and slips on the cuffs and snaps them shut. These cuffs twice the size of my wrists! Yet I still didn't catch on that Pitman was teasing. There wasn't much teasing in the Rayburn household, where I was the only child, born late to my parents and so prized by them you'd think I was sickly or handicapped in some secret way. Pitman would say afterward he was beginning to be worried, I was some poor retarded girl, only looked like a normal blond-princess type with the most beautiful brown doe-eyes he'd ever seen.

"You having trouble with them cuffs, Lucretia? Not resisting arrest, are you?"

This comical sight: I'm so scared of this uniformed man looming over me, I am actually trying to keep the damn handcuffs from sliding off my wrists behind my back.

Finally Pitman laughs aloud. And I realize he isn't serious, none of this is serious. Pitman's laughter isn't cruel like you'd expect from boys my age but a tender kind of male laughter that enters my heart with such suddenness and warmth, I think I began to love Pitman right then. This St. Lawrence County deputy sheriff who has scared the hell out of me has become my rescuer, hauling me up from drowning. Saying, "If them damn cuffs don't fit, how'm I gonna arrest you, girl? Might as well let you go."

For a moment I just sit there, dazed. It's like a bad dream ending; I can't believe that I am free.

The smell of the man (hair oil, tobacco, spearmint chewing gum) is close and pungent in my nostrils. The feel of the man (a stranger, touching my bare arms!) will remain with me for a long time.

Last thing Pitman tells me, deadpan, he won't be writing up his report—"Best keep it a secret between us, Lucretia."

Pitman climbs back into the police cruiser and drives off. But I know he's watching me in his rearview mirror as I get back onto my bike and pedal behind him, shaky and self-conscious. I can feel how my little Gap T-shirt is damp with sweat. I can feel the muscles straining in my bare legs as I pedal the bike, and I can feel the thrill of my quickened heartbeat.

Something has happened to me! I have become someone special.

Three years, two months and eleven days after the hand-cuffs, Pitman and I were married.

Daddy disowned me and good riddance!—I disowned *him*.

A wife cleaves to her husband and forsakes all else. I think so.

Mom was hurt, heartbroken, wet-hen-furious, but couldn't stay away from her only daughter's wedding. (In secret) she harbored a liking for Sheriff's Deputy Lucas Pitman herself.

It was hard to resist Pitman when he wished to make you like him. A man that size deferring to Mom, calling her "Mrs. Rayburn" like she was the most gracious lady he'd ever met. (Probably, Mom was.) Called her "ma'am" with such courtesy, like her own son, she'd forget objections she was trying to make.

Till finally Mom hugged me one day, conceding, "Your husband certainly adores you, Lucretia. Maybe that's all that matters."

"All that matters to me, Mom."

I spoke a little stiffly. In this matter of allegiance, a wife cleaves to her husband. She is reticent with her mother. Anything else is betrayal.

———

We had our honeymoon house. A rented winterized bungalow outside town. Pitman whistled, painting the outside
robin's-egg blue that dried a brighter and sharper color than
the paint sample indicated, and I made a mess painting the
rooms inside: pale yellow, ivory. The little bedroom was
hardly big enough for our jangly brass bed we'd bought at a
farm sale. This bed for one oversized man and one undersized
girl, I took pride outfitting with the nicest sheets, goose feather
pillows, and a beautiful old handmade quilt in purple and
lavender. This bed Pitman and I would end up in, or on, more
times a day than just nighttime.

Only a coincidence: our honeymoon house was close by
the Hunter Road. In the foothills east of Au Sable Forks, Mt.
Hammer in the distance. Our bedroom overlooked a branch
of the Au Sable Creek, which sounded like rushing wind
when the water level was high and like a faint teasing trickle
by late summer when the water level was low. Our house was
exactly 2.6 miles from my parents' house in town.

Some months after we came to live here, Pitman was assigned to a new shift. Later hours, farther away. Now he and
his partner patrolled little crossroads mountain towns like
Malvern, North Fork, Chapprondale, Stony Point, and Star
Lake. From his miffed attitude I had to conclude that Pitman
wasn't happy with this assignment, but he'd only joke: "That's
where a cop can expect to get it. Up in the hills."

It's cruel for a law enforcement officer to joke in this way
with his wife, but that was Pitman for you. Seeing tears in my
eyes, he'd turn repentant, brushing them away with his big
thumbs and kissing me hard on the mouth. Saying, "Never
mind, baby. Nobody's gonna get *me*."

This seemed likely. Pitman was fearless. But Pitman was also shrewd and knew to watch his back.

This night. It was a turn, I'd come to see later.

Pitman came home late from his night shift smelling of beer, fell into our bed only partly undressed, hugging me so tight my ribs were in danger of cracking. He hadn't wakened me from any actual sleep but I was pretending. Pitman disliked me to be waiting up for him and worrying, so I had a way of feigning sleep, even with the bedside lamp and the TV on. In those early months I was grateful my husband came home at all, wasn't shot down or run off the highway by some maniac; I'd forgive him anything, or almost.

Pitman hid his hot face in my neck. Said, shuddering like a horse tormented by flies: "This thing over in Star Lake, baby. It's ugly."

Star Lake. Pitman's old hometown. He had family there he kept his distance from. There'd been a murder/suicide in a cabin above Star Lake, detectives from the sheriff's office were investigating. Not from Pitman but from other sources I knew that a Star Lake man had strangled his wife and killed himself with some kind of firearm. I had not heard that any Pitmans were involved and was hoping this was so. Pitman had many blood relatives with names not known to me, including some living on the Tuscarora Indian Reservation.

I had learned not to press Pitman on certain matters having to do with his job or any of his personal life, in fact. He'd promised he would always tell me what I was required to know. He would not upset me with the things he saw that upset him or things a woman would not wish to know. Law

enforcement officers have this way about them: they don't answer questions; they ask. If you ask, you see a steely light come
into their eyes warning you to back off.

Pitman was asking did I know what a garrot was, and I
rightaway said no, no I did not know what a garrot was, though
in fact I did, but I knew that Pitman would not wish his
eighteen-year-old wife who had only graduated from high
school a few months before to know such a thing. Pitman
raised himself above me on his elbows, peering into my face.
He had horse eyes that seemed just a little too large for his
face, beautiful dark-staring eyes showing a rim of white above
the iris. They were eyes to express mirth, wonderment, rage.
They were not eyes to make you feel comfortable. Pitman
said, "A garrot is a thing used to strangle. It's two things. It's a
thing like a cord or a scarf you wrap around somebody's throat,
and it's a thing like a stick or a rod you twist that with. So you
don't have to touch the throat with your actual hands."

Pitman was touching my throat with his hands, though.
His hands that were strong, and big. Circling my throat with
his fingers and thumbs and squeezing. Not hard but hard
enough.

I laughed and pushed at him. I wasn't going to be frightened by Pitman-teasing.

I asked if that was how the woman at Star Lake was
strangled, and Pitman ignored my question as if it had not
been asked. He was leaning above me, staring at me. I remembered how at the wedding ceremony he'd been watching me
sidelong, and when he caught my eye he winked. Just between the two of us, a flame-flash of understanding. Like Pitman was thinking of that first secret between us, how he'd
handcuffed me in the police cruiser on Hunter Road.

How reckless Pitman had been! Risking all hell playing such a trick on a fourteen-year-old girl. Misusing his authority. *Sexual harassment* it would have been called if given a name. Except we'd been fated to meet, Pitman believed. That day or some other, in a town small as Au Sable Forks, we'd have met and fallen in love.

Of course I'd never told my parents. It was the great secret of my girlhood as it marked the end of my girlhood. Never told anyone except my cousin Andrea but by that time I was seventeen, a senior in high school, confounding my parents and teachers by deciding not to apply for college as I'd been planning and everyone was expecting of me.

(Secretly) engaged to Pitman by then. (Secretly) making love with Pitman every chance I had.

He was saying now, stumbling out the words as they came to him: "A garrot takes time. A garrot takes planning. Anybody who garrots his victim, it's premeditated. There's a sick purpose to it, Lucretia. You wouldn't know."

Damn right I wouldn't know! I was trying not to panic, pushing at Pitman's hands, easing them from my throat. His big thumbs I grasped in both my hands as a child might. It wasn't the first time Pitman had put his hands on me in a way to frighten me, but it was the first time when we hadn't been making love, the first time it hadn't seemed like an accident.

Pitman said, "See, if you garrot somebody you can strangle her till she passes out, then you can revive her. You can strangle her till she passes out again, then you can revive her. You don't exert any pressure with your own hands. Your own hands are spared. It's a cruel method but effective. It's the way Spaniards used to execute condemned prisoners. It's rare in the United States."

This was a long speech for Pitman. He was drunker than he'd seemed at first, and very tired. I knew not to let on any uneasiness I felt, for that would offend Pitman who deemed himself my protector. I only laughed now, pulling his hands more firmly away from my throat, and leaned up awkwardly to kiss him.

"Mmmm, Pitman, come to bed. We both need to sleep."

I helped Pitman pull off more of his clothes. He was big and floppy like a fish. By the time I leaned over to switch out the lamp, Pitman was asleep and snoring.

It was that night the thought came to me for the first time: *It's a garrot I am in.*

2.

"Such an ugly story! Those people."

My mother spoke with repugnance, disdain. "Those people" referred to people who got themselves killed, written up in local papers. People of a kind the Rayburns didn't know.

I was in my mother's kitchen reading the *Au Sable Weekly.* For some reason our paper hadn't been delivered. On the front page was an article about the murder/suicide in Star Lake, fifteen miles to the east. The name was Burdock not Pitman. I resolved that I would not make inquiries whether the two might be related. It was my reasoning that mountain towns like Star Lake are so small and remote, inhabitants are likely to be related to one another more frequently than they are elsewhere. If Pitman was related to the wife murderer/suicide Amos Burdock, it wouldn't be helpful for me to know.

"I didn't actually finish reading it." Mom sat across from

me, pushing a plate of something in my direction. It is a mother's destiny always to seduce with home-baked cookies evocative of someone's lost childhood, but I would not eat; I would save my appetite for my own mealtimes with Pitman. "I suppose Pitman knows all about it. Is he investigating?"

No mention of a garrot in the article. Only just the coroner ruled death of the female victim, the wife, by strangulation. The garrot was secret information, evidently. Known to only a few individuals.

"Pitman isn't a detective, Mom. You know that. So, no."

Strangle, revive. Strangle, revive. The way Pitman had teased me on the Hunter Road. Scaring me, then seeming to relent. Then scaring me again. Really scaring me. And then relenting.

Best keep it a secret between us, Lucretia.

Daddy's favorite music is opera. His favorite opera, *Don Giovanni*, which I came to know by heart, listening to it all my life. Daddy also took us to any production of any Shakespeare play within a fifty-mile radius and each summer for years to the Shakespeare Festival over in Stratford, Ontario.

For Daddy, *Don Giovanni* and Shakespeare were rewards for the time he spent in the world "out there." Dealing with men, customers and employees. Dealing with building materials. Making money. Pitman seemed to think a lot of money. *Your old man's a millionaire, baby. Why you're so stuck up. Hell, you got a right.*

When I'd wanted to rile Daddy up I would say the world isn't Mozart and Shakespeare, the world is country-and-western music. The world is cable TV, Wal-Mart, *People* magazine. I knew that I was right; Daddy's face would redden.

I was the bright schoolgirl, Daddy's little girl also something of a smart aleck, like Daddy himself. He's a handsome man for an old guy in his fifties with a high, hard little belly looks like a soccer ball under his shirt that's usually a white starched cotton shirt. Prematurely white hair, trimmed by a barber every third Friday. Daddy would no more miss a Friday in the barber's chair than he would miss his daily morning shower.

I knew that I was right but Daddy never gave in.

"Not so, Lucretia. The world is *Don Giovanni*, and the world is Shakespeare. Minus the beauty."

Not so, Daddy. The world is plenty beautiful. If you're lucky in love.

For a long time, I believed this. I think I did.

Soon as I married Lucas Pitman, I had to know the man was *vigilant*.

Through the day he'd call on his cell phone. Mostly from the cruiser. In his lowered sexy voice saying, "My little princess is never off my radar." Asking where was I, what was I doing. What was I wearing. What was I thinking. Was I touching myself? Where?

Pitman was proud of his little blond princess-wife. A rich man's spoiled daughter he'd seduced, slept with while she was in high school, and married soon as she turned eighteen, thumbing her nose at her old man. Pitman was proud of how she adored him, but he didn't like other guys staring at her. Well, he did, sure he did, but not too obviously. It had to be a subtle thing. It could not be crude. Pitman had a temper; his own friends backed off from him when he'd been drinking.

Weekends Pitman'd take me dancing in these country places, in the mountains where he was known. For a while after we were married, we'd go out as we'd done before we were married, and Pitman would dance like some stoned MTV kid, long legs, arms, feet as fast as my own, grabbing me and leaning me back in my high-heeled shoes, little T-shirt, and jeans tight so that the crease pinched me between the legs and Pitman could run his fingers along that crease, quick and sly, not minding who might be watching. Pitman the law enforcement officer out of uniform, wild to have a good time. Desperate to have a good time. He had a few cop friends, younger guys like himself. I was too young to realize that Pitman and his friends were not likely to be promoted very far up police ranks; I was too adoring of Pitman to guess that his superiors—if I even realized that Pitman had "superiors"—might not admire his brashness the way I did. His scorn was for desk work, computers, "investigating teams" that depended upon forensics lab reports and not action. He liked being in uniform, in the cruiser, and in perpetual motion. He liked the .45-caliber police service revolver visibly gleaming on his hip.

Pitman was an Adirondack boy; he'd grown up with guns. In our honeymoon bungalow he kept his "arsenal": two rifles, a Springfield double-barreled twelve-gauge shotgun, several handguns. He'd wanted to teach me to shoot so that we could go hunting (white-tailed deer, pheasant) together, but I refused—"Why'd I want to kill some beautiful blameless creature?" Pitman winked, "Well hell, baby, somebody's got to." I had to love how Pitman took boyish pride in his Smith & Wesson .45-caliber revolver with "zebra wood" gun grip, he'd acquired in a poker game. He took pride in his Winchester .30-caliber deer rifle with its long sleek blue-black barrel and maplewood handle he was obsessive about keeping polished the way, at our house, my mom kept the good silverware polished; this was the firearm Pitman kept loaded and ready at all times, in case of intruders, break-ins. He'd showed me where the rifle was positioned on the closet shelf, how I was to take it up and hold it, how I was to shift the safety off in any time of danger, but I was nervous, backing off, laughing, and fluttering my hands. No, no! Anybody was going to protect me, it had to be my husband.

At our kitchen table while I prepared a sizzling frying-pan meal, Pitman would drink Coors and listen to Neil Young, sometimes Dee Dee Ramone, turned up high, as he dismantled, cleaned, and oiled his long-barreled police service revolver with the tenderness you'd hope to see in a man bathing an infant. Pitman interpreted my fear of firearms as respect for him, and he liked that. Of all things, Pitman required respect. The Pitmans and their numerous kin were not generally respected. They were feared and scorned in about equal measure. Pitman wished to be feared and respected in equal measure. Sure, he liked to laugh and have a good time, but respect was more important. He knew of my father's disdain for fishing, hunting, guns of any kind, and had a way of alluding to "your esteemed father, Mr. Everett, who pays other guys to do his shooting for him" that was startling to me, like for an instant Pitman's brain was sliced open and you could see the shrewdness inside, the class hatred, the anger. The next instant it was gone. Pitman liked to tease-taunt me in a way that was like sex, the prelude to sex. Telling me of the times he'd had to use his weapon. Drew his gun and aimed it as he'd been trained and called out a warning—"Put your hands where I can see them! Put your hands where I can

see them! Come forward slowly! Come forward slowly!" —
but he'd had no choice except to fire. Since being sworn in
as a deputy sheriff he'd had to shoot and kill two men, and
he'd wounded others. Not always alone but with his partner,
or others. It was rare for a law enforcement officer to use his
weapon alone. Did he have any regrets? Hell no. He'd never
been reprimanded for excessive force. The shootings had
been investigated and cleared. On one occasion, Pitman was
credited with saving the life of another deputy. He'd received
citations. He never dreamed about these actual shootings, but
he dreamed about shooting. A lot.

Pitman smiled his slow easy smile, telling me this. I felt
my breath come short.

It was a requirement of the St. Lawrence County sheriff
that deputies were required to fire no less than two bullets at
their target if they fired one.

"Why is that? What if you change your mind?"

"You don't."

"But, if you've made a mistake . . ."

"You don't make a mistake."

"A deputy never makes a mistake?"

Pitman laughed at me. Those days, I never knew if I was
pretending to be shocked by him or truly was shocked. I saw
that steely light come into his eyes. He leaned over and drew
the revolver barrel along the side of my thigh, slowly. In a way
that made me know he was quoting somebody he revered, he
said: "A forty-five is not an equal opportunity employer."

The last time Pitman took me dancing.

This hillbilly tavern out on Hammer Lake. We'd been
married about three years. We'd go out with other couples, the

guys were friends of Pitman's. (My old high school friends, I
rarely saw. They were away at college. When they came home
to visit, I made excuses not to see them.) Still I was Pitman's
blond princess he loved to show off. Still I was in love with Pitman, in terror of what it might mean if I was not. Old disco
music blared on the jukebox. Music to make you laugh it's so
awful, yet there's the beat, the tawdry-glamor beat, raw-sex
beat, gets you on your feet dancing like the floor beneath you
is burning hot; you can't stop. I felt Pitman's strong arms
against my ribs and smelled his breath and oiled hair and it
came over me like a sickness how I missed Daddy, I missed my
mom and the house on Algonquin Avenue so bad.

Sharp-eyed Pitman knew my every shift in mood.

"Where's your mind, baby? You look spaced-out."

I was drunk. A few quick drinks made me drunk. And "I
Will Survive" pounding on the jukebox.

I laughed and hid my face against Pitman's chest. Slid my
arms around him and pressed so close against Pitman I heard
his big heart beating like it was my own.

It was after Pitman's partner and close friend, Reed Loomis,
died, Pitman began to drink mornings.

This was early in April. Not long before the anonymous
calls began.

Was there some connection? Yes, I guess there must have
been. I tried not to think what it was.

Oh, I'd liked Reed Loomis! Everybody did. The friend-
liest man, a blunt porky face and buzz-cut hair, more re-
sembled a high school sports coach than a sheriff's deputy.
Loomis was six years older than Pitman and even bigger; he'd

asked Pitman to be his son's godfather and Pitman was deeply moved by the request. "Only time anybody's going to hear 'god' and 'Pitman' in the same breath."

Pitman wasn't the one to tell me, he could not utter these words, but Loomis had died of a fast-spreading pancreatic cancer. Pitman was stunned and distracted. Pitman looked like a man staring into a blinding light unable to shield his eyes. Muttering, "Can't believe it. Reed is gone." He'd been noticing how lately he was doing most of the driving in the cruiser because Loomis had a headache, trouble with his eyes, was feeling "weird"; one day Loomis's legs give out in the parking lot and his white blood cell count is crazy, there's a diagnosis, and a few weeks later Loomis is dead.

Abruptly one day Pitman ceased speaking of Loomis. If I brought up the subject, he chilled me out.

Sometimes he tried to hide the morning drinking from me. Sometimes not.

"It won't bring Reed back, honey. What you're doing to yourself."

(Did I say these words? These are words you say, believe me.)

Pitman sneered like he was just discovering he'd married a mental defective. "This ain't for Reed, baby. This is for me."

Sometimes hearing just the intake of my breath, Pitman reacted quick as an animal defending itself. Shoving me aside, hard.

"Get away! Don't touch."

And he's out the door, and gone.

It was a cold season; I wore long sleeves to hide the bruises.

Scarves tied around my neck. Makeup layered on my thin pale face and lipstick so cheery you'd expect me to burst into song.

Never said a word to Andrea. Certainly not to Mom.

Nor to Daddy who it seemed was watching me, waiting.

By this time, four years into the marriage and still living in the four-room bungalow off the Hunter Road, I understood that Daddy had forgiven me. Daddy had not a thing to say about my marriage. So much time had passed, maybe he was impressed I had not once asked him for money. In fact, Daddy had offered Pitman and me money at Christmas to buy a new car replacing the '88 Chevy Malibu, but Pitman had his pride just as Daddy did, I knew to say, "Oh thanks, Daddy! But no."

During the day Mom frequently called. A ringing phone and RAYBURN E. on caller ID meant my mother. Sometimes I picked up eager as a lonely child. Sometimes I backed off, sneering.

Oh Mom was cheerful! Though cautious. An intelligent woman aware of mother-in-law jokes. She knew not to press too far with her questions. Asking how is Pitman and I told her Pitman is fine, you know Pitman. And I'm fine, Mom. What about you and Daddy.

Like a tick beneath the skin the idiot word *fine* had snagged in my vocabulary. Itchy as hell, hard to dislodge. There was always a beat, a moment when I might have told Mom more. And maybe Mom knew more. Probably yes she knew more. Au Sable Forks is a small town; word travels fast.

Mornings, afternoons! The slow slide into evening.

It was, as Pitman said, a shitty spring. Pelting rain, so much mud that people laid down planks to walk on.

Cloudbursts, and a leaking roof. Like an animated cartoon figure I set out pots, pans, baking trays, to catch the drips. Then the sky opened, there came blinding sunbursts. Truly, your brain is sliced open. In rubber boots I went tramping along Hunter Road, along farmers' lanes and into fields. I hiked beside Au Sable Creek where the mud-colored water rushed like a speeding vehicle. This is a part of New York State where the sky draws your attention. Not the mountains, which are mostly covered in trees, but the sky forces your eyes to lift. Always there is the anticipation of seeing something in the sky you can't name except to know you won't see it anywhere else.

This was the season I sent away for catalogs from Cornell, St. Lawrence University, McGill University in Montreal. Hiding them in the closet beneath towels and bed linens where Pitman would never look.

Cornell was where I'd been planning on going. Before I fell in love with Pitman.

Except maybe this wasn't so. Maybe I'd fallen in love with him that day on the Hunter Road. The rest was just waiting.

You never think you will get old. Or even your face.

The happiest time of your life. Oh, Lucretia . . .

Mom was weepy, nagging. My senior year at Au Sable Forks High.

That year I'd quit most of my "activities." Cut classes. A blur in my memory as if I'd been riding in a drunken speeding vehicle. The landscape is beautiful but moving too swiftly past to be seen.

Think what you are giving up. For that man.

It's your body, Lucretia. Wanting to have babies.

I hit her then. I hit my mother. I saw my hand shoot out, I saw my mother wince, I never told anyone, not even Pitman.

Didn't want Pitman to know the meanness in my heart. His blond princess.

Daddy had ceased interfering. Daddy kept his distance, a gentlemanly distance, those final months. While I was still his daughter, living at home. Could not trust himself to speak to me.

Goddamn I'd vowed I would not cry. Neither of my parents could make me cry. I wasn't their virgin daughter; I was Pitman's girl. I would be Pitman's wife. You want to know if he fucks me? Yes, he fucks me. I fuck him, the way he's taught me. I don't cry for you now; I cry for Pitman. Of all the world only Pitman has that power.

The one thing Mom did, with Pitman in agreement, was arrange for a church wedding. An actual church wedding. Very small, and hurriedly arranged. Daddy threatened to stay away but was finally the gentleman. Of course he came, though stony-faced, force-smiling. Having to see how at the very altar Luke Pitman nudged his daughter in her silken-white side and cast her a sidelong winking bad-boy grin.

I was repainting the bathroom, a better quality paint this time.

Smiling. I think I was smiling. Having to concede, when you're in high school you can't wait to get out, it's like a prison you have come to hate, then when you're out you look back, remembering.

I didn't drop out of school, finally. Attended my graduation with the others. My last term was the worst in all my school years, not a single A. If I hadn't broken his heart marrying a man my father considered low-life Adirondack trailer trash, I'd have broken his heart getting such rotten grades.

Painting the bathroom ivory. Not hearing the phone ring.

The anonymous calls came in the evening or middle of the night when Pitman was out. Whoever it was knew Pitman's schedule. Or knew from the driveway that Pitman's car was gone.

Or it was Pitman. One of his games.

Sometimes I drifted to the phone waiting for it to ring. And it rang. And I saw UNAVAILABLE on caller ID and I smiled thinking, *You can't. You have no power over me. I am not afraid of you.*

I never answered. I erased the answering tape without listening.

Well, maybe I listened. Maybe once, twice. The voice was as I'd remembered it: husky, Canadian-sounding. I had to wonder if it belonged to one of Pitman's fellow deputies. One of Pitman's relatives. Someone Pitman had made an enemy of. Gotten under the skin of. It was no one from my life, I knew.

"Hey I know you're there, baby! Know you're listening. Whyn't you pick up, baby? Afraid?"

Pause. Breathing wetly into the mouthpiece.

"'Lady of the house Ms. Pitman.' *Pig*man? Standin' there all alone."

Another pause. (He's trying not to laugh?)

"Maybe not alone enough, eh? Baby?"

It wasn't Pitman's way of speech, I thought. The broad Canadian vowels, the quirky *eh*? Still, this might be a trick. Pitman might be there beside the caller, listening.

After the calls, when Pitman came home there was a strangeness between us. I think this was so. I don't think I was imagining it. Pitman was waiting for me to mention the calls. (Was he?) But it was too late now. There had been too many. And if the calls were made by someone else, Pitman would be uncontrollable. So furious, I had to acknowledge, he might blame me.

I'd had boyfriends, a few. In school. But only just boys. And nothing sexual. Pitman knew this but possibly he'd forgotten. He was likely to be jealous. Suspicious. Why hadn't I told him after the first call? I could not tell him, *But maybe it was you.*

He'd snag on a word, sometimes. A word would snag on him. I wondered was this a thing that happened to drinkers.

Face, for instance.

Baby-face he'd call me. Angel-face.

Or, "Just don't get in my face, Lucretia."

Or, "Want me to break your fucking face?"

Burdock had been a relative, in fact. He'd garroted his estranged wife, blew himself away with a shotgun. Not from Pitman did I learn this, of course. Pitman never spoke of any of his relatives. His mother was still living, I think. He had an older half brother in Attica serving a sentence of thirty years to life.

Like shrapnel working its way outward through tissue, Pitman's fury was surfacing. *Pitman! Crazy guy.* That admiring way men have of speaking of a friend who's cracking up. Bringing Pitman home falling-down drunk and the Chevy Malibu left behind as far away as Tupper Lake, in the morning I'd have to drive Pitman back to retrieve it. In June, Pitman pursued a drunk driver west out of Malvern on Route 3 resulting in the young man (twenty, from the Tuscarora reservation) crashing his vehicle into a bridge and shearing off part of his skull. The St. Lawrence County sheriff defended his deputy (publicly) but reprimanded him (privately). Pitman spoke of quitting his job. He spoke of reenlisting in the navy. He seemed, in his indignation, unaware that he'd become a man in his thirties and was no longer a brash young kid of eighteen. A ring of flesh around his waist, his tar-colored hair streaking with gray and thinning. No longer could Pitman stay up much of the night drinking and rely upon three or four hours' sleep to restore his strength, his clarity of mind, and his willingness to face the next day.

From the cruiser Pitman would call on his cell: "Hey baby, this is a fucking long morning. It ain't even noon?"

You could get addicted to it. The anger. The taste of it on his mouth like hot acid. I never believed that Pitman was crazy. He was too shrewd and methodical. Just this fury in him. It was more than Reed Loomis dying. Those little mountain towns dying. Pitman himself dying. He'd sweat through the bedclothes, groaning and grinding his teeth. After the boy died on Route 3, Pitman insisted he had done nothing wrong. He had followed procedure. He'd used his siren, his lights. The kid had outstanding warrants which was why probably he'd accelerated his speed to almost eighty miles an hour on that sharp-curving highway in the mountains, narrowing to a single-lane bridge. Drunk kid, thumbing his nose at the law. Pitman said fuck, he had no regrets, wasn't going to lose sleep over this one.

One Sunday afternoon lying with me on our bed gripping me in his arms as if we were drowning together. Not releasing me for forty-five minutes and only then when I begged him, insisting I had to pee, did he want me to wet the bed?

"You would not ever betray me, Lucretia. Would you?"

In the cruiser calling on his cell. These were not UNAVAILABLE but WIRELESS CALLER, so I could pick up if I wished. Calling me baby, saying he loved me he did not ever mean to hurt me, I was the only thing he loved in this shitty life, he hoped to Christ I knew that, he'd make it up to me. Saying it was a hard time for him right now he was begging to be forgiven. Saying I was his princess, I was never off his radar.

Phone rings. Impulsively my hand lifts the receiver.

"Yes? Hello?"

It's like striking a match. That quick. UNAVAILABLE isn't prepared for a living voice. I hear him draw breath. I've surprised him. Maybe I've shocked him. It takes him a moment to adjust.

That low gravelly mock-courteous voice, "The lady of the house, Ms. Pitman?" and I hear myself say, "Who's this?" and he pauses not expecting this, either; doesn't expect a female voice that isn't intimidated.

"Your friend, Lucretia. This is your friend."

There's excitement here. The way he pronounces *Lu-cre-tia*.

It's no way I have heard Pitman pronounce my name. These past few months Pitman has not called me by my name at all only *baby*. Or *you*.

This is the first time I've heard my caller's living voice since that pelting-rain night in April. And it's late August now. And Pitman is away. I've been watching TV news, surfing the

channels. It's nearing midnight. Old movies, *Law & Order* re-
runs. I am lying on the jangly brass bed. The handmade quilt,
fraying soft from many washings, is neatly folded at the foot of
the bed. I'm in a silky champagne-colored nightgown Pitman
bought me when we were married. Naked beneath the nightgown of course. Still warm, flushed-feeling from my bath. And
still with some makeup on my face. Pitman doesn't care for
washed-out female faces, I know from remarks he's made. I try
to look good for Pitman; it's a habit. Whether he sees or not.
Whether he's here or not. In my hand a juice-sized glass of
Parrot Bay Puerto Rican rum I stole out of Daddy's teakwood
cabinet last time I visited the house on Algonquin Avenue. It's
the type of liquor Daddy never drinks, the near-full bottle had
been pushed to the back of the cabinet.

I'm not drinking to get drunk. Only to make the sharp
edges of things softer.

Saying, in my scratchy voice, "My friend who? Who's my
friend? I want a friend, friend. I'm needful of a friend."

My heart is pumping. My toes are twisty, twitchy. Wish I
could see this guy's face, the surprise in it like someone has
grabbed him between the legs.

Now it begins. Now, like Ping-Pong. He's asking me why
I need a friend and I'm saying 'cause I'm lonely, that's why.
He's asking what am I wearing, and I say this outfit with just
one button, a single button I got for my birthday. So funny,
I'm laughing to make the brass headboard jiggle. I'm laughing, the plummy-dark rum near about spills on my belly. My
caller, my friend he calls himself, is laughing, too. Saying he
wishes he could see that birthday suit. I say, actually I just got
out of the bath. I'm all alone here just out of the bath. And he

says, D'you need help drying, and I say, Noooo. Maybe. And he says, First things first: your titties. Start with your titties, baby. Your nipples. And I'm feeling my breath come short. And I'm laughing so it hurts, like a knife blade in my side. He's saying more words, I can't hear for laughing. Throwing your life away, oh Lucretia, my mother had wept. It's my life to throw away, Goddamn my life. It's my life not yours—leave me alone. And I'm thinking, *This is Pitman; he is testing me. He will murder me.*

Might've said, Pitman! I know it's you. Damn you, Pitman, come home I'm lonely.

Instead, I slam down the receiver. I've been staring at my toes. Narrow waxy-white feet. Haven't polished my toenails in years. Last time, Pitman failed to notice. In fact, my feet look like some withered old-woman feet, not a young girl's any longer.

So help me God is a way of speaking. You might laugh at such desperate speech before it becomes your own.

It was to keep him from hurting me. It was to keep him at a distance. Just to frighten him off. I believed that I deserved to be hurt by Pitman but I was terrified of the actual hurt. A man's fingers closing around my throat. He would thump my head against the wall, Thump—slam!—my head against the wall. I seemed to be remembering this, it had already happened. Unless it was the brass headboard he shoved me against, jangling and creaking.

You would not ever betray me, Lucretia. Would you?

Fumbling in Pitman's gun closet. Overhead the lightbulb swings on its chain. This closet I have avoided, disliking and fearing Pitman's weapons. Repugnance for Pitman's weapons.

Now I need the rifle. Haven't seen Pitman's deer rifle in years but I recognize it: the long sleek blue-black barrel, polished wooden handle Pitman so admires. *Loaded and ready.*

Safety lock *off.*

You have been so reckless. You have made a mistake. Drunk reckless mistake. Others can forgive, but not Pitman.

The rifle is heavier than I expect. Clumsier. You think of a rifle as a graceful weapon unlike a shotgun, but this rifle is awkward in my arms, and so heavy. I don't believe that I am drunk any longer, I believe that I am starkly sober as a creature that has been skinned alive. My heart is beating like a crazed thing inside my rib cage. My breath comes so fast and ragged, I'm having trouble focusing my eyes.

Trying to see where the trigger is. How my fingers should fit.

He'd wanted to teach me. He'd taunted me, I was my daddy's little princess, content to have others do my shooting for me.

Pitman arrives home early; this is a bad sign. Lately he's been staying away until the taverns close at 2 A.M., won't be home before 2:30, but tonight his headlights swing into the driveway at just 1 A.M.

I am waiting for him, hiding. I am in a state of terror not knowing what I will do.

Useless to run away: I am Pitman's wife. Nowhere for Pitman's wife to hide. If I ran to my parents, he would find me. He would punish them, too.

Pitman enters the house through the back door, into the kitchen. Making no effort to be quiet. Stumbling, cursing. In the bedroom where I am crouched behind the bureau, amid a smell of spilled rum, animal panic, perfumy steam from the bathroom, the TV is on, muted. The phone receiver is off the hook. Only the bedside lamp is burning. At the foot of the brass bed, the quilt of lavender and purple squares has been neatly folded. Often in the night Pitman kicks the quilt off; in the morning I haul it up, spread it back over the bed neatly. Pitman has acknowledged, yes the quilt is "nice." Like other things I've brought into the house. If "nice" things matter.

The heavy deer rifle I've laid across the bureau top, aimed toward the doorway. I think it must be a child's desperate strategy. A hope that magic will intervene. I don't know how to shoot a firearm except to aim, shut my eyes, and pull the trigger. It might be a Pitman trick; the rifle isn't loaded.

"Hey, baby. What the fuck."

Pitman stands swaying in the doorway. His face is dark and glowering, but bemused. His jaws are stubbled; he hasn't shaved since six the previous morning. His eyes are Pitman-eyes, horsey eyes, glassy but alert. There's a relief in this. I'm thinking that I will never again have to smell another woman on him. I will never have to smell the fury leaking through his pores. A slow smile breaks over Pitman's face. You'd say it was a mean taunting smile but mostly it's teasing.

"Baby, you better take careful aim with that fucker. You got one shot before I'm on you."

3.

"What we will do, Lucretia, is . . ."

He's my daddy, come in the night to help me. Ashen-faced and shaken, but taking charge. He's in clothes he threw on

hurriedly over his pajamas. Saying, licking his lips and repeat-
ing as if he's having difficulty articulating such words, "What
you will say, Lucretia, is . . ."

I called home at 1:14 A.M. Not 911. Phone records will
show.

How soon after I called, Daddy has arrived I don't know.
I was on the floor in the darkened living room where he found
me. Through this roaring in my ears I am not able to hear
everything Daddy says; he must grip my shoulders, shake me
gently. This drawn, sickly white face is not exactly Daddy's
handsome face, but of course this is Everett Rayburn. I can't
recall when his hair has become so thin. He has led me into
the bathroom to wash my face. Comb out my matted hair. I
rinsed my mouth, that plummy rum taste. I could not reenter
the bedroom; Daddy went inside to bring clothes for me. A
pair of sandals, I laughed to see sandals! I have not looked into
the bedroom since Daddy arrived. When he first came and
went immediately to see Pitman where he'd fallen, I'd been
frantic crying, "Is he dead, Daddy? He's dead, isn't he?"

Dial 911. Daddy dials 911. Daddy dials the (memorized)
number of his lawyer who lives in Canton.

"Yes, honey. He's dead."

The rifle that was too heavy for me to lift in my arms and
aim is on the floor of the bedroom, where it fell. Daddy has
seen but not touched the rifle. Daddy has crouched over the
man's body, seen but not touched.

Two bullets. For the first was not enough to stop him.

In the distance, a siren. It's rare to hear a siren in the night
in the country. In my skinned-alive state that seems to me a
pure and spiritual state I am sitting on the living-room sofa in

the way my parents wished their daughter to sit at mealtimes. Perfect posture. Head back. Take pride, don't slump shoulders. Not ever.

Now we're alone in this house Daddy has never visited, Daddy seems clumsy, confused. He's breathing so quickly. Gripping my hands in his. Before he became a builder and a rich man Daddy was a cabinetmaker, still works with his hands sometimes and his hands are strong and callused. I like the feel of Daddy's hands, though the fingers are not warm as I remember. Hands so much larger than my own.

Daddy is swallowing hard and trying to control his breathing, hearing the siren approach saying again that I must tell the truth exactly as it happened, why I had to fire that rifle to save my life.

And all that led to it. All.

"Just tell the truth, Lucretia."

Which is what I will do, so help me God.

The Banshee

On Hedge Island, in Nantucket Sound, a twenty-minute ferry ride from Yarmouth Harbor, Massachusetts. On the promontory above the wide raked beach, the Hedge Island Yacht and Sailing Club. On another matching spit of land to the east, the Hendricks' "cottage"—stately weathered-gray Victorian clapboard, three stories, numerous tall narrow windows, a tower and a widow's walk, steep shingleboard roofs, and a wraparound veranda with a floor so shiny gray it appeared lacquered. On the veranda, wicker furniture with bright chintz cushions. On the choppy waters of the Sound, sailboats looking like white paper cutouts.

Cries of gulls. Mixed with the wind. And that flap-flapping sound overhead! Each time she glanced up, fearful she would see giant birds flapping their wings as they swooped down upon her, but it turned out to be just the flag whipping in the wind at the top of the gunmetal pole.

The flag was Daddy's flag. But this summer Daddy was gone.

In her new coral-pink tank top and wraparound denim skirt with the big patch pocket in the shape of a kitten from

Gap Kids, she wandered among the guests seeking Mummy. So many strangers! Mummy had so many friends. On the flagstone terrace, and around the swimming pool, and on the grassy lawn where the bar had been set up, even on the tennis courts. Bloody Marys and long-stemmed glasses of white wine, mushrooms stuffed with crabmeat, Russian caviar smeared on dark bread like jelly, smoked salmon and thin-sliced cucumbers on Swedish crackers. Music booming so loud, you almost couldn't hear it. Women like Mummy in sleek swimsuit tops, silk slacks with pencil-thin legs. Bronze-skinned men in white trousers, sports shirts open to midchest. Men like Gerard, Mummy's new friend with a wide white smile that glistened. Oh, here's a pretty girl! Here's the princess! Face like a flower! The strangers marveled but were soon bored with her. The Irish girl had brought Baby to Mummy, who'd showed Baby to her friends; for a while Baby had stirred interest, but babies are even more boring than six-year-olds and soon the Irish girl was sent back up to the house, for it was time for Baby's diaper change, Baby's bottle, and Baby's nap.

Oh, there was Mummy: that waterfall of straw-colored hair spilling on bronze-tanned bare shoulders. Laughter like glass breaking.

Mum-*my*? Plucking at Mummy's hand. Which Mummy did not like, not at such times. Mummy with Gerard in his dark glasses and windblown hair bleached from the sun, Gerard in white-dazzling sailing clothes and Mummy was wearing her "funky" top that was just a black silk scarf tied about her narrow chest and her wraparound silk skirt the color of neon strawberries. Bare-legged Mummy in high-heeled sandals that made her teeter. Mummy's fingernails were neon strawberry, too, and perfect like plastic. Mummy slap-slapped at her as you'd brush away a pesky fly meaning, Go away! Go back to the house! Isn't that Irish girl supposed to be watching you!, even as Mummy was laughing at Gerard telling one of his comical stories.

When she'd been a little girl, Mummy had curled up to nap with her sometimes. It had not been that long ago on Hedge Island in the summer. In the big old iron bed in Mummy's and Daddy's room with the goose feather pillows. Cuddled together in midafternoon, which was a special time. Whispering and laughing and suddenly sleepy on the bed facing the window so you could see (through your eyelashes) the sky, and a little of the Sound. You could imagine sailing in the sky, in thin floating clouds. Now she was no longer little but six years old and soon to start first grade in the city and a new baby had come. She was given to know *there can be only one baby*. She had believed always that she was this baby, but now Baby had come and so she could not be Baby. And yet when Mummy and Gerard went sailing they refused to take her with them: she was *too little*.

Too little, and it was dangerous. Gerard's route eastward between Monomoy Island and Nantucket Island and into the open Atlantic, doubling back then westward and circling all of Hedge Island to return in triumph to the Hendricks' dock.

She was running back to the house. Pushing through the legs. Oh she hated Mummy's friends, even Gerard smiling at her pretending she was special!

She hated Daddy, for going away. For leaving Hedge Island. This is the safe place, Daddy used to say. Why'd Daddy say that if it wasn't true! And anyway it wasn't true: on Hedge

Island there were summer squalls, there were hurricanes some-times and howling winds, and the dock had been torn up by ice (over the winter) and had had to be repaired. Daddy lived in the city now, but it was a different city. She'd been looking for Daddy hiding among the guests at the party, for it was that kind of party—neighbors dropped by, summer guests and vis-itors to Hedge Island, the Yacht and Sailing Club people—so maybe Daddy had slipped among them. He'd changed how he looked; last time she'd seen Daddy he'd had scratchy black whiskers and a vertical line between his eyebrows she'd rubbed at with her fingers wanting to erase. Oh Dad-*dy*.

Daddy was not Baby's daddy (that was strange, but Mummy said), but Daddy was still her daddy (yes, Mummy said that was so) and that was why he might be at the party ex-cept—how could they find each other in such a crowd?

If!—if she stood on the veranda!—on the wicker sofa on the veranda!—in her pretty new summer outfit from Gap Kids maybe Daddy would see her? But there were too many people on the veranda, too.

Inside the house the walls were blinding white, there was a mirror over a chintz sofa that reflected more light that made your eyes hurt. She rubbed at her eyes. She was not crying! Panting like a little dog that has been kicked, but she was not crying.

There was Baby in his downstairs crib. Upstairs in the nursery Baby had another crib. Both cribs were white.

Baby was a *little boy*. As she was a *little girl*. Mummy said, oh she loved both! Mummy said she had not wished to stop with just one, and that one a *little girl*.

Mummy said when you're a mother you become supersti-

tious you think, What if? What if something happens to—?
Oh it's the worst thought, it's the unthinkable thought, so you
start obsessing about more than one, a kind of disaster insurance; maybe it's just primitive instinct, but we are primitive
aren't we.

The Irish girl was laughing with the dark-tanned boy
wearing a Red Sox cap. He was the son of one of Mummy's
friends; he lived a few houses down on the beach. He'd
brought a "special cigarette" for the Irish girl and himself to
smoke; they were laughing together as Baby lay in his crib by
the French doors opening onto the veranda and the breezy
salt air. Baby's eyelids fluttered as her shadow passed over his
face.

Ba-*by*?

She knew to lilt her voice like Mummy's voice. Carefully
she lifted Baby in her arms. Her little brother!—that is what
he was. She was fascinated by Baby's eyes that were so small
and blue and bright with moisture and always moving, trying
to focus on her face. She liked to touch the smooth skin like
a doll's rubber skin. And there was the small perfect mouth.
Yet Baby had a temper: you could not believe the sounds that
issued from that mouth. In the night, the Irish girl had to tend
Baby if he woke and would not sleep and made his fierce
choking noises. For sometimes Mummy was away. And sometimes Mummy was home and with Gerard in the big bedroom, and at such times she did not appreciate being wakened
by the screams of a banshee.

What is a *banshee*, Mummy? she asked, but Mummy
seemed not to know, and was annoyed at her for asking. Gerard always knew what a word meant, saying a banshee is some

kind of Southwest Indian like Apache. But the Irish girl, who kept to herself mostly and rarely said anything to Mummy except "yes, ma'am," "no, ma'am," "thank, you ma'am," now said in a thrilled voice, "Oh ma'am, a banshee is a wild spirit sounding like the wind. It screams in the night in a household where someone is soon to die."

Mummy laughed. Like glass being broken. So you knew that Mummy was displeased. The Irish girl's pale freckled face reddened, and she said, "Oh ma'am! I am sorry."

Sometimes in the night this summer on Hedge Island, which was a lonely summer, she would slip from her bed in the room close by the nursery and tiptoe barefoot and breathless into the nursery to peer into Baby's crib that was so white it seemed to float in the shadows like a little boat in the water. When there was a moon, especially. When the moon was shining like a milky eye. When the Irish girl was snoring in her sleep. Like a ghost she would come to stand beside Baby's crib. She had overheard Mummy saying it had been her crib once upon a time and it was so strange to think that a long time ago she had been Baby, but now Baby was someone not-her who she could look at as he slept. Baby slept so very hard; his small body quivered with the heat of his mysterious dreams. Oh, what was Baby dreaming? He was so small, he had not yet learned to speak. And so his baby-dreams were lost when he wakened.

It was so thrilling, she was holding Baby in her arms! And no one knew and could scold.

She was holding Baby as the Irish girl held Baby, snug in the crook of her left arm when she gave him his bottle. And her elbow lifted a little to support the nape of Baby's neck for they said that an infant's neck is not yet strong enough to support his head. Baby was not asleep and not awake. This was a good time for Baby, for he was not likely to cry just now. How warm Baby was! Hedge Island was always cooled by sea breezes, but Baby's body was hot from such hard sleeping. She liked it that Baby was trying to smile at her, his little snail mouth wet with spittle. For Baby knew her and trusted her.

She had no trouble carrying Baby. Baby didn't weigh much more than the big ceramic antique doll that Grandma had given her. Past the doorway opening out onto the veranda and the noisy guests she carried Baby, and past the doorway leading to the pantry where the Irish girl and the boy in the Red Sox cap were standing very close together. Up the creaking stairs to the second floor. Along the corridor. Past doors opening upon sunlit rooms. Past the nursery and past the bedroom that had been Daddy's and Mummy's but was now Mummy's and Gerard's. And there was her own room with her little bed snug in a corner, her bedspread was snowy white ducks and kittens on a blue background like the sea. Her curtains matched the bedspread. On a little rocking chair, the big ceramic Victorian doll in what's called a pinafore. She carried Baby to the window seat where they could rest. She showed Baby the people below. The tennis courts, and the grassy lawn, and the terrace. Amid so many strangers she could not see Mummy, and she could not see Daddy. It was difficult to know if Baby was seeing what she pointed out to him. Baby gurgled and wheezed and made his little cooing noises and squirmed, and one of his pudgy baby-hands touched her cheek. As if in gentle rebuke, *We can't stop here; we are not high enough for them to see us.*

The tower! The widow's walk! She would carry Baby there.

It came to her so fast: like switching on TV with the remote.

But on the stairs to the third floor, that were so much narrower than the other stairs, and where the carpeting was worn almost through, she had to stop more than once, to lean Baby against the railing. Suddenly Baby was heavier, and warmer. A sweetish-sour smell from Baby's diaper. She was panting again, and her left arm was aching. Clumsily she shifted Baby to the crook of her right arm. Baby did not feel comfortable there for she had never before held Baby in the crook of her right arm and she had not seen the Irish girl hold Baby that way, and she did not think she'd seen Mummy hold Baby that way.

But it was all right—Baby surprised her by laughing!

Only once that summer had Mummy climbed with her to the tower, but Baby had not been with them. The higher we can climb, the clearer our perspective, Mummy said. If we could fly to the moon and look back to earth we would see ourselves better. We would laugh at our so-called tragedies. From the widow's walk you could see farther inland, sand dunes and sand fences and wild rose briars twined about the fences. You could see out into Nantucket Sound where the waves were always choppy and dark blue, leaden blue, greeny blue, depending upon the sky. The gulls look free, see the gulls! Mummy said, shading her eyes. But gulls are creatures driven by hunger, every waking minute of their lives is a matter of hunger. If Mummy wanted her to feel sorry for the gulls or to think that the gulls were silly, she could not know.

It was harder for her to remember the summer before when Daddy had taken her up into the tower. She tried very hard to remember Daddy climbing the third-floor stairs with her and hand-in-hand with Daddy the almost unbearable excitement of stepping through the door onto the roof where there was a platform protected by a railing: this was the widow's walk. She'd been frightened at first, but Daddy held her hand saying it was absolutely safe. Yes they were high up and there was no roof here, but they were not in any danger of falling. Many times she'd blinked her eyes, startled at the bright blinding air that was so much windier up here than on the ground. The widow's walk was so exciting! Like flying in the eight-passenger plane to Hedge Island, from the Boston airport. Much more exciting than the ferry ride from Yarmouth Harbor that was so boring since you stayed inside your car and could hardly see the water.

She had to lean Baby against the wall, fumbling to open the door. She was panting hard now, her skin prickled with heat. It was hard to believe, Baby was so *heavy*. And Baby was beginning to fret as if impatient with her, wanting to get outside in the bright air and kicking his plump little legs in the way of a cat you've picked up to hug but the cat struggles and squirms trying to get away.

Baby, *no*.

Baby, see where we *are*!

Oh they were outside now, in the open air. Suddenly there was just the sky overhead. Blinding-bright windy air whipping her hair and clothes and making the flag, which was close by and only a little higher than the roof of the house, flap like it was a live thing, desperate to loosen itself from the gunmetal pole and fly off into the sky. Oh baby, *see*!

By standing on her toes and leaning over the railing, she could see some of the people on the ground below. But it was disappointing: she could not see them very well, and they could not see her. The railing was high as an adult's waist, and she was so much smaller. So she could not see anything very exciting except the sky, where a small propeller plane was passing by, droning its motor like a hornet, and she could not be seen. And Baby could not be seen. Nobody below was noticing!

She would have to crawl through the railing out onto the roof and bring Baby with her. She could do this, she thought. Last summer a crew of dark-skinned men had torn out old shingleboards and nailed new shingleboards onto the roof. Five or six men with hammers walking about the roof, hunched over, sometimes squatting on their haunches, slip-sliding, crawling, then again walking straight up on the different sections of the roof. For there were steeper sections than others and the section beyond the widow's walk was not one of the steep ones.

So she laid Baby down on the floor of the widow's walk and pushed her head through the railing and squeezed the rest of her through like a cat. Now she was outside the railing, on the roof!—one leg on either side of the peak to balance herself. This was more daring than a cat—this was a monkey! She was able to turn herself around saying aloud, "Don't look down!" for this was what Mummy said in the rattly little plane as it circled to land at the Hedge Island airport with its single dirt runway fading out into a field of sand dunes and wild rose briars. Don't look down! she told herself sternly. Baby, don't look! as she reached through the railing for Baby who was oblivious of her command, lying on his back flailing his arms and legs like a silly beetle, beginning to go red in the face with

that look of baby vexation that made you want to laugh sometimes it was so comical, other times you wanted to shake Baby
quick, to prevent the banshee wail. Baby, *no*.

Because Baby was kicking it was difficult to pull him
through the railing. The rungs were far enough apart, but
Baby was not cooperating. Oh, she was becoming impatient
with Baby! For what if Daddy was here waiting to see them—
what if Daddy was below at the edge of the noisy party, Daddy
was about to glance up at the roof to see her and Baby—and
there was no one visible, to be seen? And Daddy lost interest
and went away? And Mummy didn't see, either?

When Baby was new, and very little, she'd been jealous,
maybe. The Irish girl had said, Oh don't be jealous! You are
the pretty one; you will always be the princess. And so she
knew, what she was feeling was *jealous*. She'd been sulky and
sullen and cried easily and was mean to her doll and hated
Mummy. She'd cried for Mummy to take Baby back where
she'd gotten him. (Why was that silly? Mommy was a shopper!
Big packages tied with ribbon. Heavy glossy-paper bags with
plastic handles. Sometimes Mummy returned what she'd
bought in the stores; why couldn't she take Baby back, too?)
But Baby had not been taken back. Baby had stayed, and
everyone adored Baby. And after a while she hadn't minded
Baby so much, hadn't minded being told he was her *little
brother*. She had wanted a puppy but instead she had a *little
brother*. Every time she peeked at him, there were Baby's moist
blue eyes fixed on her face. Oh, she had to laugh at Baby! Except sometimes she became confused and her thoughts hurt
her head: she was Baby, and Baby was her? Was that how it
was meant to be? Or had Baby come to take her place?

She had tried to ask Daddy this. If Baby was her, and had taken her place, where was *she*?

Daddy laughed as if she'd meant to be funny. Daddy kissed and hugged her, but his whiskers scratched her.

She was on the roof, and Baby was with her. When Daddy saw he would be impressed. My little monkey! Daddy would tease.

This section of the roof was not so steep, or so high. There was another, higher, roof with a steeper pitch where the brick chimney pushed through. If she could get to that roof! Yes! She could get there by sliding along this roof—as long as she straddled the peak she would not lose her balance and as long as she didn't look down. She was grunting, carrying Baby in this new way. Bump-bumping Baby along. Baby did not like the bump-bumping and began to fret. His head was rolling back because the crook of her arm wasn't right. She could see how it wasn't right, but she could not correct it. And the sun was so strong, blinding. And the wind from inland, from the west, miles away at the far end of the island where there was an enormous garbage dump and a frenzy of gulls and other scavenger birds and the wind blew these smells to the inhabitants of East Beach as it was called. And there were gulls here, too. Swift-darting shadows on the roof. The panicky thought came to her, *They will peck out our eyes.* She would have to protect her eyes from the gulls, yet she could not drop Baby!

Now she could hear the strangers' voices below, more clearly. Laughter and loud thumping music like a heartbeat.

The gulls circled near as if curious, only just screamed at her and Baby and spun away on the wind. And Baby blinked at them gaping, and his little snail mouth was wet with spittle, preparing to scream back at them, but they were gone.

Oh, her bottom! Beneath her denim skirt she was wearing pink cotton panties. The shingleboards were rough and scratchy. Her bottom was tender and beginning to hurt.

Like a swift hard slap from Mummy. From Gerard, too. Only what she deserved they said. A spoiled little girl always sulking!

Her arm was hurting, too. Where Baby flailed and kicked like a crazed cat, her arm was *so* tired.

Hush, Baby! Hushaby, Ba-*by*!

By slow inches she was pushing her bottom along the peak of the roof. This wasn't so much fun as she had thought it would be. It was more like work, having to clean up something she'd spilled, or crawl beneath her bed to retrieve something she'd kicked there. No one had seen her yet. It was taking so long! Possibly she wasn't fully in sight yet and had to go farther. Her head felt strange. Like sharp-edged insects were inside buzzing to escape. *Don't look down,* she told herself in Mummy's stern voice, which was a voice to be obeyed, but in the corners of her eyes she was beginning to see, she could not help herself. There was shouted laughter below, a blond blur that was (maybe) Mummy's hair, and so she looked, and gave a little scream of fear she was so high! She and Baby were so high above the ground! She was dizzy suddenly and dry-mouthed, paralyzed staring at the people below who had not yet seen her and Baby. Oh and Baby was kicking and fretting at such a bad time, so heavy in the crook of her arm, her heartbeat hard in her rib cage she could not seem to catch her breath as if she'd been running, biting her lip to keep from crying, Oh how many more minutes before one of them glanced up to see her and Baby and all their eyes flew open?

Doll:
A Romance of the Mississippi

What happened between Ira Early and his (step)daughter Doll is a secret between them of long standing. What has happened to x number of men as a result of this secret is more public.

Is Doll your actual name? (Doll is frequently asked.)

Doll is trained to say, Yes.

Yes, but you may call me anything you wish. If calling me by another girl's name is what you wish. (Doll giggles. Doll nibbles at the end of one of her pigtails, winningly positioned over her slender shoulder.)

In fact: Doll is not her name but what she is called. Doll has difficulty remembering her baptismal name as she has difficulty remembering the years before she turned eleven. Now Doll has been eleven for so long it's like trying to remember an old TV movie you hadn't paid much attention to when you saw it. You can remember, but only in patches. And why?

———

Doll is not a worrier. Doll leaves worrying to her (step)father, Ira Early.

And Mr. Early is a worrier. Complaining how first there were individual gray hairs in his thick dark hair that proudly swooped from his brow like a rooster's comb, then swaths of gray, a kind of ugly tarnished gray, now this kind of piss-tinged white, and a bald spot at the crown of his head big as a grapefruit, as a result of Doll's unpredictable behavior. When Doll swerves from the script and gets down-dirty *mean*.

Mr. Early sighs, shudders. Runs a hand through his thinning hair, strokes his bristly beard. Plays the role of the addle-brained old coot, granddaddy or bachelor uncle, in a TV family sit-com of the 1950s. As if he, a reasonable man, a man another man can trust, can't control his daughter in these down-dirty *mean* moods.

(Is Doll in such a mood tonight? Mr. Early worries. It has been how many weeks since Doll's last mean mood? He's counting on his fingers, one, two, three . . . and a half? Not a good sign.)

In the cushioned interior of the stately old LaSalle luxury sedan, Mr. Early, awaiting Doll's return, pours himself a much-needed drink from his chilled thermos. A martini prepared exactly to Mr. Early's taste, very dry. Tiny cocktail onions bob in the liquid; he scoops them out deftly in the crook of his little finger. Doll sneers at her (step)daddy for exhibiting what Doll believes to be incipient alcoholism, some notion Doll has picked up from afternoon TV, but Mr. Early knows better.

Mr. Early drinks, nods. Ah yes. Much needed.

A fierce December wind rocks the stately old relic of an automobile. A battalion of storm clouds like clotted intestines are being blown high overhead, in and out of the moon's ghastly light. Mr. Early shivers. What city is this? East or west of the Mississippi?

(Doll has some childish notion, doesn't like to stray too far from the great American river. Ask why, she'll pucker her snippy little face and say, Who wants to know? *You?* Which is an answer Doll has begun to give often, when she doesn't like Mr. Early questioning her.)

(Who are you to judge *us?* What right do you have to believe yourself superior to *us?* So Ira Early fantasizes defending himself, in some public place. Blinding lights in his eyes, possibly he's handcuffed, legs shackled.)

Doll appears! Doll has been with [a Mr. X, prepaid] and has subsequently fetched late supper for her daddy and herself. In knee-high white leather boots that grip her slender legs like pythons, in stiletto heels that add several inches to her diminutive height, Doll makes her way with childish carelessness across patches of icy pavement. Her plaited pigtailed milkweed hair bobs winningly about her small head. Mr. Early calls out the window: Doll, damn! Don't slip and fall.

For Doll is a beautiful little girl, but breakable.

Yessir, we have money saved from our travels. It has been years now. Two or three days in a city, then move on. Sometimes, just possibly this will be one of those times, I will behave badly and we'll have to move swiftly on, not even staying the night and getting a little rest. Mostly we straddle the Mississippi River. You'd have to ask Daddy what his investments are.

At first Doll can hardly see her (step)daddy in the back of the La Salle where he's waiting in the shadows. That ample belly, a fat old spider. Oh Dad-*dy*! Surprise.

Doll is bringing Mr. Early his seafood sushi (ugh!) and carrying her (yummy) taco burger with home fries, coleslaw, giant Pepsi in a waxed container. Oh Daddy, open the damn door. Expect me to do goddamn *everything*?

Of course, Mr. Early has the door open, quick.

This child just enjoys being bossy. (Like her late mother.)

Mr. Early sure doesn't approve of Doll's eating habits. Bad as a taco burger is, and deep-fried fries, Doll can devour even worse food. Her nervous metabolism burns calories away. At the present time, she's just a child, but what about later? Years to come? Mr. Early's face crinkles in worry envisioning a fattish Doll. The nougat-creamy skin puffed and bloated and certain to attract a less-discerning, less-well-bred category of admirer.

A wild windy river-smelling wind. A weekday night in Anonymous Metropolis, USA.

Yes, we are on the Web. Daddy hooked on; it's been a long time now. Like shrewd financial investments. Daddy looks like a dear old cuddly-cozy fat thing, but Daddy is *wired*.

There's a pleasure in food when you're hungry as there's a pleasure in drink when you're thirsty. Ira Early and his (step)daughter Doll devour their takeout suppers, sip and swallow their precious drinks, even as, less than two miles away in room 22 of the E-Z Economy Motel, the next [friend, prepaid] stares at himself in a scummy mirror. He's faded-red-haired, with a maggoty pale skin even his doting (now deceased) mother dismayed over. He's a man of conscience, or wants to think so. Staring at his reflection murmuring, Sicko! Now we know.

The phone on the burn-scarred bedside table rings.

Ira Early watches Doll's rapid fingers, pointy bloody-red manicured nails, as she punches numbers in the cell phone, an absurdly small gizmo (to Mr. Early's bifocaled eye, most new electronic gadgets are gizmos you halfway expect to explode in your face) that never ceases to surprise him, it actually works. Like a regular phone.

Doll laughs at Daddy. Of course it works like a regular phone, silly. It *is* a regular phone.

(But isn't a cell phone actually a radio? Some kind of miniature radio? Ira Early knows better than to argue with a moody daughter.)

Mr. Early takes the gizmo from Doll after she has dialed the number he's told her. (His fingers are too big for the task.) Clears his throat, assumes his formal frown, elocution.

Hel-lo! Sir, this is—

Doll doesn't pay much attention as her (step)daddy confirms with Mr. X—place, time, duration. Doll has heard it all before, numberless times. (Hundreds?) Already in this old midwestern city on the river they've had good luck, and you have the feeling there's more to come. Yesterday, today, now this evening. Mr. Early has planned a third day of appointments before moving on. Doll yawns into her hand that smells of taco burger.

No. Doll isn't yawning, Doll is wiping her greasy mouth. That barracuda-flash in Doll's glassy dilated eyes. Mr. Early, fumbling to turn off the phone, happens to see. Or thinks he sees.

Doll? You're going to be good tonight, yes?

Pouty Doll shrugs. Wriggles that little Doll-shiver that can mean yes for sure, or just the reverse.

Mr. Early fumbles now with the remains of his sushi. Doll jeers at him for using chopsticks. Chopsticks! Damn, Dad, we're *Americans*. Raw tuna glop and crumbling rice that looks to Doll like dried-out brown ants drops into his crotch. Doll tosses him a soiled paper napkin with a snort of derision.

Ira Early is a worrier because he's a perfectionist. He's a perfectionist because he's scared as hell of things going wrong. He's scared as hell of things going wrong because he has long witnessed, and witnesses almost daily, things going wrong for other people. Sometimes seriously wrong. (Mr. Early can't know how wrong things will go for Mr. X in room 22 of the E-Z Economy Motel except, having caught a glimpse of Doll's barracuda eyes, he has an uneasy premonition.)

Still, there's the solace of the Do Not Touch Policy. This, implemented by Ira Early from the start of his and Doll's travels, is a shrewd piece of strategy. Do Not Touch (DNT on the Web) guarantees a discerning class of admirers. Also the age — eleven: young, prepubescent, but not too young. Doll attracts a higher class of (male) individuals of varied ages but tend-ing to the educated middle-to-upper-middle-income levels. Rarely less than college degrees, predominantly liberal arts. DNT among such individuals is an enticement, a novelty, and a relief.

Doll, you navigate. We'd best be on our way.

Doll whines, Oh Dad-dy! I'm not finished with my supper. You know I can't eat fast as you.

Read off the directions, dear. We have only fifteen minutes. He'll wait. Geez!

It's nearly 11 P.M. The moon has shifted conspicuously in the sky, like a protracted wink.

Driving south, or what seems to Mr. Early south, into the hive of the inner city. Maze of exit-only lanes, exit ramps, cloverleafs, glaring lights. He hates expressways but has no choice. Beside him Doll balances her giant Pepsi between her knees and reads off directions from a sheet of paper. For a girl so clever and canny as Doll she has difficulty with words of more than a single syllable or containing unfamiliar consonants.

"Kway top of the ramp. Exit right."

What's that?

"Kway—"

"'Key' you mean. Q-U-A-Y pronounced *key*."

Doll turns sullen. How the hell would I know that, home-schooled like I am?

Unknown to old-fart Daddy I have my neat little razor hidden in my boot. Wrapped in aluminum foil, for safety. Maybe yes maybe no is what I'm thinking.

Since St. Louis it's been a long time on the road.

Saying to Daddy, Know what? I want ostrich boots for Christmas. I want some sun in New Orleans.

At the E-Z Economy Motel he washes face, forearms, under-arms, and hands. Though he isn't (swears he isn't!) going to touch the girl. His maggoty skin inflamed as if peppered with acne. Thirty-seven years old, not seventeen, still has pimples; something must be wrong with his basal metabolism.

Now he's out, on parole, should check this out.

When Mr. Early and his (step)daughter Doll, known then as Margaret Ann, were living at what authorities called a Fixed Address, up to two years ago, in fact in Mr. Early's late-wife's family home in a dignified old historic district in Minneapo-lis, there were problems in their domestic life which going on the road have largely solved.

Hated to take this bright questing child out of school. My solace is, she's scrupulously homeschooled. Hardly a day passes we don't visit natural history museums, butterfly houses, pioneer villages. Planetariums.

Ira Early, long ago a student of Latin, mathematics, and world history at the Cincinnati Academy for Boys, is one to prowl secondhand bookstores and flea markets. The trunk of the La Salle is crammed with random volumes of the *Ency-clopaedia Britannica,* Readers Digest Condensed Books, and even *Webster's Unabridged Dictionary.* Doll has, or used to have, a photographic memory and can still entertain enrap-tured Mr. Xs by reciting in a breathless schoolgirl voice the American presidents and their little-known vice-presidents, summaries of economic theories (Kondratieff long wave cycle, econometrics, monetarism, neo-Keynesianism), major wars of Europe from the One Hundred Years to World War II. Also, major cranial nerves and arteries.

What's my favorite? The carotid.

We tried! We did. But domestic life on Mount Curve Avenue was not for us.

Doll's mummy departed this world when Doll was, let's see, two or three years old. At least it's believed that Mrs. Early departed this world; in fact her remains have never been found. Doll has said indignantly that she *does not* believe "allegations" that her daddy murdered his wife/her mother, dismembered her corpse, and scattered the pieces along forty miles of the Mississippi south of Minneapolis, weighed down with rocks and never to surface, no Doll *does not*.

Doll says, It was a long-ago time before cable TV and cell phones. I know my daddy's heart and he would never harm a hair on anyone's head who did not deserve it.

When one of Them asked me, Does your father mistreat you, showing me silly naked rubber dolls, I said, No no no! I hummed loudly to myself and rocked from side to side.

I love my daddy. (It's true, Ira Early is Doll's biological father. Not her (step)father as they tell associates and Mr. Xs. Even among Mr. Early's widespread contacts there exists the principle of drawing the line at certain forms of behavior, and this principle, if you're in business for yourself, it's wise to respect.)

———

(The long-ago time? Some say it was in the early 1970s, and some say it was 1953, but still others argue that Ira Early and his (step)daughter Doll began their travels in 1930, after the crash. Doll is perplexed by this notion; she's been eleven years old for more than seventy years?)

How old are you, Doll, Mr. X will surely inquire if Mr. X in room 22 of the E-Z Economy Motel is any kin to Mr. X of the other motels scattered along the Mississippi. That question I've been hearing all my life, getting so it seriously pisses me off.

Daddy says, Humor 'em. They are a priceless (because inexhaustible) commodity.

Daddy says, Play the script. See, they'd recoil from *ten*. They don't want to hear *twelve*, either. Still less *thirteen*. There's a kind of consensus.

DNT has worked out really well. Or almost.

On Mount Curve we tried. There was even a Grandma with a withered-cherry face and Jell-O eyes, Mummy's mother, Doll tried hard to love but failed. Sniffing in the old woman's arms, holding her breath as long as she could, then gagging and pushing free. And Daddy, who was a youngish widower bearing his grief stoically, one day tugged at his then-dark goatee and said, Margaret Ann, you're my daughter, aren't you! And nothing of hers. My genes are your destiny, darling. Gravely shaken Daddy was, he'd not realized father-love until that instant.

Still we tried for (how many?) years to lead "normal," "average," "approved-of," lives. Even went to Mummy's old church, sometimes.

For all the good it did us.

———

Always motels or cabins. (Yes, there are still motor cabins in the rural American Midwest.) Never hotels with lobbies. (Though Mr. Early and Doll sometimes check into Marriotts on the expressways, father-and-daughter traveling under a variety of names and guises.) If Mr. X, Mr. Y, Mr. Z, journeys to meet them in an Anonymous Metropolis, if he wishes to stay at a good hotel, he will have to take a room at a motel, too, like the E-Z Economy. Best for Doll not to appear in any populous brightly lit lobby in her high-heeled white leather stiletto boots, purple suede jacket, plaited pigtailed milkweed hair bobbing about her exquisite Doll-head.

Parentless eleven-year-old with painted eyes, luscious peachy lips, and blusher on her cheeks. Oh, no.

They fled Minneapolis for a good reason. Hounded out, you could say. Persecuted. That terrible day the public health inspector arrived uninvited, unexpected, at the house. An officer with the fascist power to report Ira Early to the authorities and to threaten him with arrest for parental negligence.

Well, possibly there'd been warnings. Registered letters from Margaret Ann's school addressed to Ira Early, importunate telephone calls from the principal of Mount Curve Elementary he failed to take seriously. *Margaret Ann Early* who is enrolled in sixth grade, where is she? Why is she so frequently absent from classes? Why, when she's in school, does she fall asleep at her desk? Why are her grades so poor, her deportment so rebellious?

Examined for Signs of Abuse. There were none.

In room 22 of the E-Z Economy Motel the man known variously as Mr. X and (as mischievous Doll is shortly to call him)

Mr. Radish gazes at himself in a scummy bathroom mirror. Runs his hands through his thinning faded-red hair, observes liquidy despair and mad, exulting desire in his otherwise ordinary, mildly bloodshot eyes. Thinking it isn't too late, he could call this off. Could just walk out.

He's a decent guy, really. He's made mistakes he will never make again. (He believes.)

His groin is throbbing, a pleasurable sensation that fills him with disgust. Do. Not. Touch.

He flushes the toilet to make sure it's flushed and reenters the other room, smooths the soiled rust-colored corduroy bedspread with both his hands. It's 11 P.M., maybe the child won't be delivered?

It's 11 P.M., true. But Ira Early can't be coerced into speeding even by his own wish. In fact, he has an exasperating habit of driving ten miles below the speed limit. In the restored 1953 relic he drives with the fussy demeanor of an elder who disdains contemporary life. It's part of Mr. Early's gentlemanly style. It's part of why you trust him. In his suits with vests, neckties from another era, rimless bifocals riding the bridge of his slightly pudgy nose. His white hair and whiskers give him an appealing Santa Claus look, or maybe it's that kooky genius Albert Einstein you're made to think of. Ira Early's cold shrewd eyes sparkling behind the bifocals like a schoolteacher's and that vague smile, lips tight over big chunky carnivore teeth. Bartenders, motel managers, the majority of Mr. Early's colleagues and associates, persist in the error: *This old fart is no threat.*

After Quay, what?

Looks like — City Center? Exit left.

This Anonymous Metropolis is a maze of ugly streets that should be familiar to Ira Early: he's been here before, and Doll has been here before, who knows when. You will have noticed that the Inner City is the same city through the Midwest. Endlessly repeated Decaying Inner City of a Once-Thriving Metropolis. It's like a suction tube, drawing them in. Like bloody water swirling gaily down a drain just-slightly-clogged-with-hairs.

(Why is Doll thinking such a wicked thought? Snaky little pink tongue wetting her crimson lips.)

Exit *left*, I said. Dad-dy! You're headed right.

You said left. I mean, you said right.

I said fucking *left*, Dad-dy.

Just watch that mouth, miss.

And I'm hungry, too, Doll says loudly. After this I want some ice cream. Fucking fudge ripple.

I said, miss — watch that mouth.

Watch your own mouth, Dad-dy. You're the wicked ol' pre-vert.

(Doll is slipping into a mean mood. The taco was mostly cheese. She's thinking possibly she won't go for just the carotid, that's too easy. That was St. Louis. It's been eight months at least since she did the other, that's more challenging. And brought back a certain rubbery goody for Dad-dy.)

(Who pretends to be horrified, sickened. But for sure Mr. Early keeps these Mementos of Adventure like any honest pre-vert.)

"Front Street." See it, Daddy?

Of course. I'm not blind.

———

In the E-Z parking lot Doll repairs her makeup. For an impatient, spoiled girl, she's surprisingly deft at painting her face, the eyes especially. As Mr. Radish nervously strokes his flushed face, turns his head from side to side, staring at himself in the mirror.

But is that me? Or some sicko who has dragged me here?

Mr. Early escorts Doll to room 22 (which is lighted within, shades drawn). But Mr. Early discreetly steps back into the shadows of a Dumpster when Doll knocks and the door swings open.

Silently mouthing the words, God be with you, dear.

And your daddy close by, standing watch.

(Should he have forced his moody prepubescent daughter to show him the contents of her handbag? Her jacket pockets? Her sexy leather boots? Damn, he'd meant to, but forgot.)

The door is opened warily. Doll is invited inside. Biting her lower lip to stifle a nervous giggle. Why, Doll isn't fearful of this individual she has never glimpsed before—is she?

Not Ira Early's (step)daughter. Not Doll.

This guy reminds Doll of an upright radish. Mr. Radish!

He's nervous of her, too. He's excited. He's just standing there. Fingers twitching, and a sickly oily glow to his face. Like he has never seen anything like Doll before. Like he's trying to decide what to make of her. But he has enough presence of mind to shut, lock, double-lock, the door.

Trying to smile. Licking his wormy lips.

"D-Doll." That's your—actual name?

Doll shrugs. Maybe yes maybe no.

And you're — (Mr. Radish has a stammer?) — elev-elev-ven years old?

Doll shrugs and mumbles what might be yessir. She's a fascinating mix of mute, shy, sly, naughty-girl, fluttery eyelashes and something sullen beneath, like the beat of hard rock. Mr. Radish is enraptured, gaping and smiling and flexing his long fingers.

Saying, stumbling with the words, You l-look older than eleven I guess — but you're v-very beautiful, Doll. Whoever you are.

Doll mumbles, Um, thanks mister. Shrugs off her purple leather jacket, lets it fall onto the bed like this is the most natural gesture in the world. Flicks back her bristly plaited pigtails, seeing in the corner of her eye how ol' Mr. Radish stares.

Long as the policy is Do Not Touch, what's it matter?

Oh he's feeling morose, melancholy.

Maybe this isn't the right life, sometimes you wonder. The moon so vivid, like the eye of God. Seeing all, and forgiving? Maybe not.

Ira Early has emptied the thermos of its contents, decides to drop by the Kismet Lounge he'd noticed a block from the E-Z on Front Street. Doll won't know: be gone just a few minutes, sweetheart.

This Mr. X, junior high school teacher, Mr. Early has been assured wouldn't hurt, wouldn't so much as touch, a flea.

Where's the TV remote? Doll's eye scans the grungy room.

Mr. Radish just wants to talk. Well, fine. Except, Doll can't be expected to answer his meandering questions, or even to listen. She's done her part, she's wound up like a mechanical doll, one-two-three-four, the usual. But it sure looks spontaneous! Facial movements, fluttering eyelashes, more of the smile, variants of the smile, sweet lowered gaze, snaky pink tongue moistening her lips, simulation of a blush, if Doll could blush. She's a little pissed at this guy, saying she looks older than eleven—fuck that!—obviously she looks older than eleven, but not that much older! Doll's thinking she has been insulted, she'll slash this asshole's carotid artery, watch him bleed out like the last one. Except this time, for sure, Doll won't get blood splatters. Bad enough on your clothes, but in your pigtailed hair it's a bummer.

Bum night, sort of sad-making says the graying balding ponytailed bartender like he's wanting to converse with Ira Early, the joint is so dead. Mr. Early runs his fingers through his white hair and beard like the rakings of conscience. Yes, says Mr. Early, with biblical intonation, it is sad indeed. Mankind's lot.

The ponytailed bartender, you can imagine was a flower child in the previous century, says eagerly, Tragic, d'you think?

Mr. Early gazes into his drink. Frank truth resides there.

Well, maybe just sad, my friend. "Tragic" is big-league.

Mr. Radish manages a coughing sort of laugh. Bad as clearing his throat. Saying, like an upright corpse flirting, Doll you say you're c-called "Doll"—meaning your name is something else?

Doll bounces on the bed, stinky old corduroy cover, softly squealing, giggling, in the manner of a six-year-old, since this is expected. Mr. Radish is an ideal audience, gaping and gazing with mouth slightly ajar as if he has fallen asleep on his feet.

Doll shrugs. Maybe yes maybe no.

You can tell me, Doll. Your name.

Doll has located the TV remote, half hidden beneath *USA Today* on the bedside table. Graceful as a child ballerina she leaps from the bed to snatch it up.

My n-name is—

Doll isn't listening. Doll sees this guy is no threat. Homely as a broken-down shoe, faded-red hair like an old brush, those blinking doggy eyes. Almost you'd feel sorry for this creep. (Almost.) He's no age Doll could judge, but then Doll is no judge of adult ages: anyone not a kid is old—"old bag," "old fart." Mr. Radish, she sees, is wearing a white shirt, sleeves rolled up to reveal hairy forearms, but hairy in patches, like he has the mange. Trousers that look like he's been sleeping in them. Ugly old lace-up shoes. Mr. Radish is flabby-muscled, slope-shouldered, otherwise he'd be tall as Ira Early. But lacking what you'd call dignity, stature. And Mr. Radish smells.

Ugh. That boring odor of an excited male. Plus anxiety, and shame. An odor Doll has been smelling in rooms like this for a long, long time since leaving Mount Curve Avenue.

It's TV time. But Mr. Radish keeps pacing in nervous half circles around Doll, making asshole small talk in this hoarse crackling voice like something you'd want to mash beneath your stiletto heel.

Saying, D-Doll? Who are your people?

Ummm. Dunno.

Is that man who—that man who spoke with me on the phone—really your stepfather?

Doll drawls, Stepdaddy.

Why, that's terrible!

Doll switches on the TV. Doll drawls some answer that sounds right.

Your own stepfather? Has done this to you?

(Fudge ripple is what Doll wants. Damn, she deserves it.)

(This guy. Not worth his throat cut; he's just a sad jerk. Or the thing between his legs, assuming he has one, sawn off. Not tonight.)

But, dear—how has this—your life—happened?

Doll drawls, Dunno, sir. Just happened.

Do you go to school, Doll? I mean—are you being educated?

Mr. Radish with his fidgety hands shoved deep into his trouser pockets stands staring at Doll on the bed and breathing like something wounded.

Doll says, a little sniff of pride, I'm homeschooled.

Homeschooled! Mr. Radish laughs like someone has grabbed him and squeezed between the legs.

In the mostly deserted dark of the Kismet Lounge, Mr. Early is nursing a second martini. Down-in-the-dumps he'd better be careful he isn't losing track of time, he'd meant to return to the E-Z after a ten-minute break but more minutes have passed.

Frankly, Ira Early has been hurt: his own (step)daughter he adores called him a wicked ol' pre-vert. That's unfair.

Wicked ol' pre-vert, she'd said. And laughed.

Well, maybe there is something to this: those mementos Doll has given Mr. Early, consequences of Doll's mean mood in one or another E-Z motel, he has not discarded in haste like you'd expect. For some reason, he can't. These goodies as Doll calls them are signs. Symbols. Hard to say what they mean. But they do mean something.

See, Dad-dy? What you made me do.

Better them than me, girl.

An old-fart nervous-type would dispose of such evidence in case of police intervention, but Ira Early is a unique personality. More unique, you might say, than the legendary Doll.

Chronicles of midwestern crime will never plumb the depths of Ira Early. Even those who'd met Ira Early and his (step)daughter Doll will not know how to speak of them.

These mementos, Mr. Early stores in jug bottles, in formaldehyde. He has five, six . . . seven? . . . scattered in rental lockers as far north as Mille Lacs, Minnesota, and as far south as Greenville, Mississippi. Under various names not a one of them Early. Some kind of sentimental record maybe he'll look back on one day when Doll is finally too mature to be Doll. Beforehand, Mr. Early is feeling maudlin.

Refresh your drink, mister? inquires the ponytailed bartender.

Mr. Early shakes his Santa Claus head no, better not. Hears himself say, Well. If you insist.

Doll, sprawled provocatively on the bed, hasn't removed the sexy white knee-high boots, her black satin miniskirt rides up her lovely thighs. Her spaghetti-strap top is crushed-velvet gold and there's a teasing suggestion of little-girl breasts, or padding, at her bosom. Those bristly pigtails sprout from her small head with a look like, if you touched them, they'd give you a shock. (Mr. Radish's wickedest dream come true. Maybe he should rape, murder, or murder, rape, this exquisite child, get it over with in a burst of passion, and then murder himself? But how, practically speaking, is a man like Mr. Radish going to murder himself? He's not made for heroics.)

Doll is watching a game show. Looks like *Millionaire*. Squeals and applause and that sappy MC who bears a resemblance to Ira Early, in fact. Bored, Doll switches to another channel. She's gotten too restless, these months and years of traveling with her (step)daddy, to watch any TV program more than three or four minutes, likes to surf the channels from one to ninety-nine, back again, like a merry-go-round. If Mr. Early is present he'll take the remote from Doll's fingers firmly no matter how she protests; TV is just plain bad for the brain, Mr. Early believes. But Mr. Early is not here, only just Mr. Radish who seems to adore her and will not touch her. Staring as Doll aims the remote at the TV like a wand.

Doll hates commercials but she's staring at this one, for PMS. That is, for the prevention of. "Premenstrual syndrome." Doll whispers these mysterious words aloud. Her daddy has assured her this will never happen to her. He gives her pills daily, and there are other ways of keeping Doll from that ugly phenomenon called *pubescence*.

Switches the channel to *Funniest Animal Videos*. There's a mournful-looking basset hound and a bald, oblong-headed baby sharing an orange Popsicle as family members look on howling, tears running down their cheeks. Doll laughs, too, but in disgust. Yuck! Everyone knows dogs' mouths are cesspools of germs.

Mr. Radish has tugged his shirt open, revealing a patchily red-haired pimply chest Doll doesn't wish to see. Mr. Radish is still chattering excitedly, maybe he's drunk or high on painkillers. Doll seems to recall Mr. Early mentioning that this Mr. X at the E-Z is something like a junior high teacher, an educator and an idealist.

Saying, swallowing hard, D-Doll, are you listening? I'm real ashamed of myself, for this. You're a beautiful child. I just know you have a b-beautiful soul. It's shitty what your own stepfather has done to you. You deserve a whole lot better than—this.

Doll shrugs. Un-hmm?

Frozen-faced Doll ignores this bullshit. Staring fiercely at the TV screen as she clicks through the channels rapid as a lizard scaling a wall. Her Cleopatra eyes have the glassy-hungry TV look of a child rushing through the channels certain that something special is waiting. In a cold fury she's thinking maybe she'll not only saw open Mr. Radish's bulgy carotid artery, she'll gouge out one of his bulgy eyes. That time she surprised Mr. Early with a coin-sized slab of flesh containing the belly button of some crude Ozark trucker, the old humbug had been truly amazed. Doll: this goes beyond my DNA, I swear.

Wish I could, Mr. Radish says, oh God wish I could save you. Beautiful little girl like you.

Mister thanks, but I'm *saved*.

(Doll checks the time: Oh God, not even 11:30 P.M.)

I could p-pray for us. The power of prayer is awesome.

Mister thanks, it's okay.

A man like that stepfather of yours, Mr. Radish is panting, should be cast down in fire and brimstone forever. Should be turned in to the police, at least.

Doll pretends she hasn't heard this. Though she has heard it.

Well. Let Mr. Radish say what he wishes, that's part of the fee, and he can do what he wishes, to himself exclusively; Doll won't so much as glance around at him. If this creep strangles in his own spit, if his face turns the color of boils, she won't glance at him.

But she might say, if the urge comes upon her, Oh mister, is it time for Doll's bath?

Or, smiling the naughty-little-girl smile, batting her eyelashes like butterfly's wings, Doll wants her bath. It's time!

In the Kismet Lounge, Mr. Early sees suddenly to his horror it's 11:46 P.M. He's been in this place far longer than he'd planned, and he's had more to drink than he'd planned. Shame! What if, back at the E-Z, his little girl is crying piteously for him?

Nothing like that has happened yet, exactly. Not since an unfortunate night in El Dorado, Arkansas, when Ira Early and his (step)daughter Doll were new and naive in their adventures.

Are you nek-ked, mister? Don't peek.

From inside the steamy bathroom Mr. Radish croaks out *Yes*.

Doll, naked too, biting her lower lip to keep from giggling, pushes open the door. Looks like, Mr. Radish has done as she requested.

The last twenty minutes of Mr. Radish are going to be a game.

Mr. Radish has been told it is a Bath. Doll has another game in mind.

(Seems that, that morning, I'd done the bad thing. Prepared a fresh razor blade on a ballpoint pen from one of the motels, fixed with that Krazy Glue that can't ever be pried off, as my daddy had forbidden, after St. Louis. Oh, this blade is *sharp*.)

Doll is slender and small-boned as an actual doll might be, of some long-ago time. Doll has tiny breasts with warm brown flowerlet nipples and no more hairs at the fork of her legs than the down on the back of her neck. Her legs are long, like they could spring into action and run her out of your reach, just make the wrong move. In the humid bathroom air, Doll's creamy nougat skin is slightly flushed and her big eyes shine with anticipation. Doll's bristly pigtails are pinned up neatly onto her head and covered with a cheap plastic shower cap provided by the E-Z Motel. Must be in one of her mean moods, as Mr. Early would say, but in fact Doll is laughing.

Like an actual eleven-year-old might cry, breathless, Is that bathwater nice and hot?

It's hot, Doll. It—is.

Mr. Radish, obeying the rules of the Game not to peek, splashes the water with his cupped hands. Doll sees a wedge of sickly pale chest and a swath of faded-red hair. It isn't too hot, mister, is it?

No! It's just right.

I don't want to be burned, see. But I like a hot bath.

D-Doll, it's just right. You can stick a t-toe in . . .

Is there some nice soap, mister? I want lots and lots of suds.

There's a real nice soap here. Big as the palm of my hand, see?

Don't peek! I can see.

It smells real nice, too. Ivory.

Doll says, chiding, as if Mr. Radish had naughtily begun to peek over his shoulder at her, Mister! Turn your head and shut your eyes, too.

I am, Doll. I am.

Poor Mr. Radish quivering and shivering in the bathwater in that grimy tub, and the tattered shower curtain like a stage curtain pulled back to reveal him to jeering eyes. Doll summons forth her Doll-rage. Doll is holding the razor-on-the-stick just behind her right buttock, along the smooth curve of her warm flesh. Seeing naked hairy knees drawn up to a collapsed-looking chest reminds her of Ira Early and that look of a man who, in his clothes, looks solid, but without his clothes is flaccid and lumpy and you just want to slash-slash-slash.

Doll's eyes are revealed, a sharp glassy-green, like reflectors.

Mister? Pro-mise? Don't look till I'm in the tub?

Back in the bedroom the TV is turned up loud but not too loud. The E-Z is that kind of reliable motel; people mind their own damned business. The time, Doll has shrewdly noted, is 11:48 P.M. A practical time. If her weak-willed daddy has drifted down the street for a drink or two, by this time he's back. Mr. Radish croaks out a final reply, yes he p-promises not to l-look, and Doll tiptoes to the tub to where the naked man awaits her trembling in anticipation and she strikes unerringly with the razor — one! two! three! — in the sawing technique she has perfected, and a four! and five! for good measure with such deadly force (city homicide detectives will marvel) that the victim's head is nearly severed from his body.

Softly Doll murmurs, See?

———

Oh, God—it's after midnight. Mr. Early pulls into the parking lot panting and repentant. Where is Doll? Hasn't Doll left the motel room yet? He'd had a premonition something bad might happen; he'll never forgive himself if it's his own daughter it happened to.

The moon has slid halfway down the sky behind the E-Z Economy Motel and when he glances up, shreds of cloud like broken cobweb are dragging across its surface.

Dad-dy. I'm not mad at *you.*

Departing this city south on I-55, thirty-six hours earlier than Ira Early planned. He's speechless in indignation and worry and Doll just laughs at him, tossing a small wad of bills onto his lap when she climbed into the car, no credit cards. Ira Early never swipes credit cards; that's how you get caught. Doll is humming to herself, unplaiting her pigtails. Oh, her scalp hurts, the roots of her hairs hurt and every hair. And she's hungry.

Across the state line in Missouri they stop at a 24-hour diner. Sliding into a corner booth, not wanting to be noticed, Mr. Early is wearing a coal miner's cap meant to hide his hair, but there isn't much he can do about the Santa Claus whiskers. Orders a beer; he's damned thirsty. But too upset to eat. Doll shamelessly devours a fudge-ripple sundae. Wiping her prim little mouth to say finally, knowing how Mr. Early has been frantic to hear, Well, Dad-dy. Could be I have something for you.

Oh, Doll. No.

A good-*y.* For Dad-*dy.*

Giggling, passing to him beneath the table the aluminum-wrapped thing out of her purple leather jacket. Mr. Early would shove it back onto her knees in disgust, except his fingers grasp it instead, groping. He wonders what it might be, something soft and fleshy, still warm inside its wrapper? You ol' pre-vert, Doll giggles. All for you.

It's our reputation I'm worried about, Doll. Our livelihood.

Oh hell. Nothing can stop *us*.

Maybe it's true. Ira Early wants to think so.

Before they leave the diner Mr. Early takes out the AAA map, much wrinkled from their travels, and smooths it open on the tabletop. It's their custom to allow Doll to choose, mostly. Though sometimes in the interests of business pragmatism, Mr. Early intervenes. Doll's pointy red-painted nail hovers over the map. Where next?

Madison at Guignol

It was said of her that she was shallow, vain. It was said of her that though she trailed the most seductive of scents, L'Heure bleue, she had no charm. It was said of her, the rich man's wife, cruelly it was whispered and laughed in her wake, that she had no soul. *But it's my soul I seek continuously! Where I can, and however.*

On Madison Avenue she sought her soul. Elusive, teasing as a wraith it hid from her. In Prada, in Gucci, in Nautica, in Armani. In Baccarat, in Yves Saint Laurent. Her anxious eyes hidden behind oversized dark lenses. Her tense mouth, disguised by midnight-plum lipstick, glossy as plastic. Searching amid the reflections of store windows on this sunny October Saturday, Dior, Ralph Lauren, Calvin Klein, Rikki, there came Mrs. G. in oyster-beige silk, slender legs encased in silky pale hose, her feet in pale kidskin pumps with a glamorous three-inch heel, a dazzling flamey-orange silk scarf tied loosely about her neck. In the broad display windows of Shanghai Tang her reflection moved uncertainly, the figure slight as a child's, though Mrs. G. was no child, thirty-seven years old, or was she forty-two, as some whispered? In Steuben's display window she saw the reflection without recognizing it as her own, or as herself. She'd had her champagne-blond hair restyled the previous afternoon at Jubjub, Madison and Seventy-first, severely scissor-cut, chic, swinging about her perfect cosmetic-mask-face and framing it like a grasping hand. *Is that meant to be me? Am I meant to know her?*

It was unfair, unjust. No one had mercy on her.

She knew, they laughed behind their hands. Thousands of dollars yearly on the most fashionable clothes, shoes, accessories, beauty care, and yet it was said of her she had *no instinct for fashion.* It was said of her by Mr. G's incensed relatives that she, the rich man's second (or was it third?) wife, had *no instinct for family life.* The dusky-skinned women who cleaned, cooked, served for her and Mr. G., flashing adoring smiles at her, never failing to call her Mrs. G. as if naming royalty, yet shouted with laughter behind her back, claiming the bitch was stingy as hell, cruel, crazy, she adored you one day, was disgusted and furious with you the next, she screamed, spat, wept, apologized, and screamed again. Stumbled in her high heels and you had to catch her beneath her arms, rot-smelling armpits no matter how much perfume she sprayed on herself; she'd collapse at the kitchen table panting like a dog and rubbing at her eyes with the palms of her hands as if hoping to erase whatever vision she'd seen. *Where is it? Is it lost? How can it be lost? Give it back!* You'd want to comfort her but—no! Mrs. G's the one who runs the household. Mrs. G's the dictator who hires and fires. Writes out checks in a trembling hand, misspelling your name, goddamn, or puts down the wrong date, wrong month, or wrong year. Tears up checks, throwing the pieces down onto her Aztec-tile kitchen floor. *No one manipulates me! Never!* If the rich bitch loses that gold watch, that diamond ring, that platinum-and-pearl earring that's a gift from Mr. G., beware! If a drunken dinner guest screams her handbag's been rifled, cash has been taken, beware! You did it. You took it. You're a thief. You, or the other Maria who's the laundress. Or your black boyfriend Mrs. G. is convinced she's seen (no matter you don't have a boyfriend or any man daring to visit you in the rich man's apartment building guarded by doormen and security cops like a fortress), accusing you of letting him in through the delivery entrance, screaming what's to stop him from returning some night to slash everybody's throat?

White motherfuckers. Throats deserve to be slashed.

Mrs. G. hears this, for Mrs. G. reads minds. Those pig eyes shining in horror and her lips, wormy-thin lips except for the lipstick, quivering.

Something I've lost, what is it? Where? Did you take it, Maria?

Sometimes, it's Maria who half carries Mrs. G. into the master bedroom for her late-afternoon stuporous nap.

A dozen times a day, breathless, Mrs. G. calls Mr. G. On the phone in the penthouse apartment, on her trim little cellular phone in a dressing room at Armani or in the Café at the Plaza or from an escalator at the Museum of Modern Art or in the jolting rear of a bright yellow taxi being driven from one crucial address to another. *Hello, hello? Darling, hello? I decided to skip the matinee, I've been having such a—sort of frustrating—* But Mr. G., a rich man, a busy man, a man of mystery, seems never to be in his office to take his wife's call; of course Mrs. G. can leave a message with one of Mr. G's assistants if she wishes, but she breaks the connection with a pout and a curse. *Damn you, I hate you. Think I don't know what's going on? You'll regret this one day I swear.*

Already, women of Mrs. G's youthful age are dying. Rich men's wives who could afford the very best medical treatment are not immune to breast cancer, cancer of the cervix, leukemia—that'd seemed almost fashionable last summer: Mrs. K. stricken in East Hampton and Mrs. C. on the Vineyard. And Mrs. D., the glamorous ex-model, in her *Times* obituary her age given as thirty-six, practically the same as Mrs. G.'s official age. (After this shock, Mrs. G. ceased reading the *Times* obituaries.) Not that Mrs. G. is morbid-minded. Nor neurotic. She belongs to a Midtown health club, if only she had time to drop by. She belongs to the First Unitarian Church of Manhattan, if only she had time to drop by. For three weeks last winter she had a personal trainer come to the penthouse and you could see Mrs. G.'s just perceptibly flabby muscle tone improving, and she'd gotten to the point where she actually, sort of, enjoyed the aerobics and leg raises. The other, push-ups, goddamn she just couldn't do. No upper-body strength, just puffing and panting and finally collapsing back on the mat, tears streaking her mascara, and the sleek-muscled personal trainer with eleven little gold rings glittering in her ear made a sneezing sound, trying to keep from laughing aloud at her rich-bitch client.

Mrs. G. terminated the personal trainer. Called and left a terse message on the woman's answering service.

Please don't return, I never want to see you again. Send me your bill. DO NOT CALL.

———

Morning shopping can be exhausting. Beyond Madison Avenue to Fifth Avenue, beyond the exquisite small shops to Bergdorf Goodman, Saks, Trump Tower. Mrs. G. is fiercely driven, seeking the perfect belt to match her Garibaldi chino pants; the perfect frock to wear to Mr. G.'s youngest niece's wedding in Rye, Connecticut; the perfect shoes to wear with her new Amalfi black silk for the Friends of the New York Public Library fund-raising ball. Mrs. G. compares notes with her friends with whom she has brunch, lunch, tea, cocktails. Morning shopping whets the appetite, so often she meets women as much like herself, you'd think seeing them across the room in one or another stardust-spangled flattering tinted mirror, they were sisters. Champagne scissor-cut hair, glittering rings like miniature suns, glossy smiling lips, and sudden squeals of laughter. If not friends exactly, these women are friendly acquaintances, you might say, wives of Mr. G.'s friends or colleagues, or women she's met through her charities, Friends of the New York Public Library, for instance; Friends of the Museum of Modern Art; Friends of Literacy. Women like Mrs. G.: rich men's wives with adolescent-monster stepchildren; breast implants; shadowy feuds with husbands' relatives; collagen-injected, cosmetic-mask skin; beguiling French perfume; doctors' prescriptions for Xanax, Prozac, Serentil; tales of treacherous live-in help, the interchangeable Marias; and ninety-nine-pound emaciated bodies, taut as bows. And death's-head grins startled up in zinc-framed mirrors in such chic dining spots as Le Bernadin, Chanterelle, Le Cirque, Jean-Georges. These opulent interiors hushed and reverent as chapels. Mrs. G., who struggles with her weight, Mrs. G., who is a perfect size six and in terror of gaining, is a penitent, cruelly restricting herself to grilled vegetables, green salads sparsely dabbed with lemon juice, soup du jour if it's vegetarian and non-cream-based. Like her companions who so resemble her, quivering eyelids, shaky hands, that restless searching of the eye — *for what? what invisible figure or object?* Mrs. G. drinks solely sparkling water, maybe a tiny glass of tomato juice, or, if the others are, a single glass of very dry white wine. (Just one! The women giggle together, vowing.) The meals are spare but require beyond ninety minutes. There are ceremonies not to be hurried. There are trips to the restroom. Moderate-to-generous tips are left for the help. Mrs. G. is adored; look at the welcoming smiles. Maître d's, waiters, busboys. Eyes on Mrs. G.'s tight, polished mask-face, Mrs. G.'s Gucci handbag, Cartier wristwatch, Shanghai Tang raw-silk suit. Louis at La Grille all but bowing and sometimes does bow: Hello Mrs. G.! hello ladies! What a beautiful day isn't it? for beau-ti-ful ladies? Greedy eyes, pursed lips, and clenched teeth. Envy, resentment, loathing. Mrs. G. wants to press the palms of her hands over her eyes and not see, wants to press the palms of her hands over her ears and not hear, but bravely she marches forward. How can she retreat? Where? Though knowing as in her most hideous nightmare how at Nikki's on Gramercy Park there was an AIDS-infected kitchen worker who deliberately pierced his skin with a knife to dribble blood into the pureed lentil-and-eggplant soup that was the soup du jour devoured with such rapture by Mrs. G. and her companions, oh she knows! And she knows how in the main dining room of The Pierre, the maître d' sneers behind her back, how in Lutèce the Italian boy-waiters who hover about her table with such feline attentiveness wink at one another in bemused

contempt, how in Le Traub, Kutina, Regency, and the Four
Seasons, waiters routinely spit into her food or stick their
thumbs into her white wine hoping to infect her with E. coli
from their bacteria-teeming intestines.

Sniffing after her like she's a bitch in heat, L'Heure bleue
in her wake, the crude Latinos sneer, mouthing the words
white cunt and laughing together. Still Mrs. G., like her companions, leaves moderate-to-generous tips. What alternative?

She can't stay home. In the floating penthouse rooms,
barely a hum of traffic from the streets, the erratic screams of
jackhammers, helicopters and airplanes overhead—oh she'd
go crazy! she knows. *Where is it, what have I lost, who has
taken it from me?* They mistook her for a predator, she who
was prey. They mistook her for a selfish rich man's wife, she
who thought of everyone—oh, anyone!—before she thought
of herself. (Her fourteen-year-old daughter Meredith for instance. Stepdaughter, actually. Living with the former Mrs. G.
on Central Park South and, seeing Mrs. G., mimes nausea,
sends her looks of loathing with those lovely washed-blue eyes.
The cruelty of adolescents!) They mistook her for bold, brash,
brazen, pushy, querulous, and complaining when in fact she
was shy—yes, *she was shy!* She was shy and had simply had to
learn to assert herself. Fearful of the exquisite expensive shops
of Madison Avenue and of the four-star restaurants and hotels,
dreading the museums where a malaise as of the tomb awaited
her sensitive nostrils in the larger wings, and in the smaller ex-
hibits, photography, for instance, at the Guggenheim and at
MOMA, claustrophobia. *I hate this, I don't want to be here—
Why am I here? What am I seeking?* Never could she use a
public restroom, or, in fact, a bathroom in a private home not

her own, without first laying wads of tissue on the toilet seat and afterward lathering her hands with soap, soap, soap and drying them thoroughly. *And yet, am I safe? How can I protect myself?* Never could she relax as a passenger in any vehicle driven by a stranger, taxi or livery driver, and yet she was dependent upon such transportation every day of her life. Some days, exhausted by her adventures, she returned staggering to the penthouse apartment for a long soaking bath and a delirium-nap to follow, with tightly drawn venetian blinds and a cool-wetted cloth over her aching eyes. Other days, all her strength was required just to kick off her shoes and sink onto her bed, entering at once the delirium-nap like a corpse, exquisitely attired, sinking dreamily to the bottom of the ocean.

This Saturday in mid-October, sunlight blazing as if overhead there's an immense fiery eye opening wider, wider, wider. *What I've been seeking, today I will find. I know!* Mrs. G. is one of many shoppers on Madison Avenue this afternoon, most of them women, women of all ages, though predominantly Mrs. G.'s age, and here and there are quite young girls, Meredith's age, all of them walking purposefully, their faces glowing with hope. Dior, Ralph Lauren, Calvin Klein, Rikki, Shanghai Tang, Krill. Glittering display windows, subdued interiors, mannequins posed for contemplation like iconic statues at which shoppers stare. Mrs. G. pauses, staring. Into Prada, into Kizia, into Frou Frou. Sometimes she isn't certain if it's her own reflection she sees, or an actual mannequin, a stranger. She's searching still for the perfect frock for Mr. G.'s youngest niece's wedding, unless it's the perfect black silk suit for Mr. G.'s eldest brother's funeral? And she's looking, too, with girlish anticipation, for the perfect gift for Meredith, her step-daughter who will be fifteen on November 8. (Where do beautiful Meredith and her girlfriends shop? Not Madison Avenue like their mothers but miles away downtown in gritty SoHo in shops with matte black walls and hammered-tin ceilings out of which hard rock blares and the salesgirls speak a dialect Mrs. G. would not recognize.) Mr. G. is away on business this weekend in Australia, unless it's Saudi Arabia or Taiwan. The twelve-room penthouse is deserted except for the Marias chattering away in their bird speech Mrs. G. can't comprehend, can't trust. *Talking about me, laughing at me. I know!* On Madison Avenue, in this familiar territory, Mrs. G. can breathe. Lights up a cigarette with trembling fingers—smoking on the street isn't (yet!) forbidden, is it? She's a happy woman again, an eager woman, a woman-with-a-mission. The scissor-cut hair gives her a certain confidence, as do the beautiful raw-silk suit and new vanilla-leather three-inch-heel sandals. *Why do they say I have no sense of fashion, the bastards!* Working her way down from 86th Street, like a pilgrim except not on her knees, Mrs. G. is thinking suddenly that she will not telephone Mr. G. this weekend. Let Mr. G. telephone *her.*

Staring at the oyster-beige wraith in Prada's tinted display window, a figure that resembles Mrs. G., or is it, in fact, Mrs. G., her ghostly reflection? Posed with her head tilted to one side, an arm uncertainly raised, eyes blurred as if unfocused. A casual row of stylishly costumed mannequins with blank-moon faces, silvery blind eyes and parted lips, and, oddly, no hair. When Mrs. G. moves, nervously smoking her cigarette, the wraith moves, too, so she realizes it's herself, and laughs.

I'm a live woman, still.

Entering the elegantly spare interior of Prada, where like sleek predator fish the salespersons await their rich customers, gliding forward soundlessly, Mrs. G. who's spent so many transfixed hours in this store explains in an urgent voice what she's seeking today, a belt, a perfect belt for a beautiful girl about to be fifteen years old, or another accessory perhaps, or a special item of clothing but it must be very special, except— what's wrong? Mrs. G.'s cigarette fouling the air, no smoking allowed, madame, *sorry.* Mrs. G. laughs in embarrassment and annoyance, forgetting she'd lit up. Halfway she's thinking someone in Prada slipped the cigarette into her fingers as a prank— *Where'd this nasty thing come from?* Winks at the salesperson, one of those chic emaciated boy-women, but the joke is lost; anyway the cigarette is taken from her and dis- creetly disposed of. The crucial issue is a belt, a perfect belt, for a tiny waist, smaller even than Mrs. G.'s waist (of which she's proud, it measures twenty-three inches when she sucks in her stomach). Mrs. G. is shown belts. But none of the costly Prada belts is quite right. Mrs. G. takes a long time consider- ing them as the salesperson waits patiently, then suddenly she's shaking her head hurt, disappointed. *Nothing here. Good-bye!* As if she's been personally insulted, Mrs. G. exits Prada leaving the salesperson and the store manager staring after her. Impulsively then crossing the avenue to drop into Brass, a boutique for younger shoppers she believes Meredith would like, where soft-rock–Bach Muzak is piped seductively into dressing rooms, and the salespersons are emaciated and androgynous with close-cropped hair, but again, looking at belts, at handbags, jackets, trousers, T-shirts, bulky sweaters, all in dark muted hues, gunpowder-gray, bruise-black, mud-iridescent-gray-green, Mrs. G. is disappointed. *Ugh! I hate these ugly things.* As in a dream in which she speaks her innermost thoughts with impunity, as others stare, silent and abashed, Mrs. G. laughs at the sales staff's faces and exits Brass, vowing she'll never return.

Next, Pal Zileri.

Next, Rikki.

Next, Shanghai Tang.

Next, Zallerne. Where amid giant ferns, glaring hardwood floors, and chrome-and-glass fixtures, Mrs. G. feels a surge of desperate hope, for the salespersons here know and respect her, she's spent thousands of dollars in Zallerne, the smiling manager calls her by name: Welcome Mrs. G.! On this beau-ti-ful October day! But it's only briefly that Mrs. G. feels relieved, for soon she's being shown the newest fall arrivals, direct from Milan, and there's nothing here that pleases her eye, no belts, no trousers, no jackets, nothing for a hard-to-impress teenaged daughter. *Oh, is this all? Just—this?* Mrs. G.'s expression of hurt, bafflement, dismay, disgust. Not just for Zallerne but for the previous stores, disappointment, betrayal of her hopes, she's feeling this is a personal insult. The collagen injections have left hard little grimacing worms bracketing her mouth, just beneath the skin, and at the corners of her eyes are faint red lines like burst capillaries. Mrs. G.'s face is turning to a sort of chemical-dried hide in the effort not to rot. *Think I'm a fool? Like your other silly customers?* In a mirror there's a gaunt pale pouting face and disheveled champagne-blond hair and a stick figure in expensive silk, is that Mrs. G.? Except—what has become of her beautiful scarf? Her flamey-orange scarf from Yves Saint Laurent that had cost, the previous spring, $648? But Madame, no, Madame we have no knowledge of . . . , as Mrs. G. stares at their faces, their lying mouths and eyes, but no one in Zallerne will admit to having seen Mrs. G.'s scarf, let alone having taken it; in fact, the store manager is suggesting that Mrs. G. hadn't been wearing it when she came into the store, for surely someone would have noticed an Yves Saint Laurent scarf, and Mrs. G. says, *How dare you! That's an insult.* She turns on her heel and stalks out of the store vowing *never, never* to return.

One by one she tours the stores of Madison Avenue like side chapels in a magnificent cathedral to which, she vows, she will never return, *never!*

At Seventy-seventh and Madison there's Roma, a jewel of a boutique specializing in the finest leather goods; Mrs. G. once purchased a thousand-dollar attaché case for Mr. G., who'd lost it (or so claimed) on a trip, and in this fragrant interior Mrs. G. asks to see belts — belts suitable for a beautiful fifteen-year-old girl, her daughter. Mrs. G. tells the salesperson (one of those lean sexy Italian boy types who smile dreamily even as they're sneering at you, one of those who inhale your scent even as they're gagging at the smell of you) about her daughter as he shows her an array of belts, but Mrs. G. is almost immediately disappointed in Roma's goods; Mrs. G. is frowning and shaking her head. *No no no no. Nothing here for me.*

Quickly then descending the avenue. The sun has shifted in the sky. It's late afternoon, muggy and tumescent. It's early evening and Mrs. G. has not found what she's been seeking. Mrs. G. is hurt, angry, almost despairing. In Nicole Farhi, in

Rafaella, in I. Nostrom, she's been treated rudely, she believes. It's as if the Madison Avenue shops are now anticipating her arrival, determined to disappoint her. Overpriced shoddy goods! Such ugly things! In Casa Noir, in Mandrake, in Elizabeth Arden, where Mrs. G. has facials, purchases expensive beauty-care medicines and cosmetics, she sees in reflective surfaces her gliding-wraith figure like a heraldic figure on an ancient wall or urn, an Egyptian goddess, or a virgin sacrifice, Greek, Aztec ... At Mirabel she's turned away; to her shock the manager says it's closing time, no more customers, though Mrs. G. can see favored customers still inside, and salespersons attending them like handmaidens. At Klaus, at Perdito, at Sabine on Seventy-sixth Street, Mrs. G. raps urgently on the locked glass door, crying, *Let me in, please! You know me.* The Sabine manager, a woman of about thirty named Tikki, comes reluctantly to unlock the door; she's dressed in black, rapier thin, frosted lips and eyelids, and talon nails, pretending at first not to recognize Mrs. G., the rich man's wife, one of Sabine's faithful customers. Mrs. G. is allowed entry, and the door locked behind her. There's a hush in the store except for piped-in music like distant rumbling thunder. Mrs. G. explains her quest to Tikki, as several salespersons appear, like gaunt black-feathered predator-birds in their Sabine costumes — skintight black trousers and tunic tops. Mrs. G. hears herself say impetuously, *Oh I know you have more to sell than you're showing me. Don't you think I can afford it?* There's a moment's clumsy silence. An exchange of glances among the Sabine sales staff — guarded, guilty? — that Mrs. G. can't decode. Tikki tells Mrs. G. please to come back another time, Madame, our store is really closed for the day, but Mrs. G. says curtly, *Don't humor me; I know better.* After a display of reluctance, the elegantly black-clad Tikki leads her customer into an alcove of the store where individual items of clothing hang like works of art. These are new imports, Tikki confesses, silk-brocaded kimono jackets in rich colors—crimson, apricot, lime, royal purple—with slightly padded shoulders and pearl buttons. Mrs. G. stares. Her lips shape *Beautiful!* She seizes one of the crimson jackets to try on even as Tikki discreetly takes it from her and leads her into a mirrored dressing room at the rear: Madame, you will have more privacy here: take your time. Mrs. G. has tried on clothes numerous times in dressing rooms at Sabine; the rooms are comfortably large, not cramped as in some other stores. She feels at home here, removing her clothes with impatient fingers, trying on the crimson jacket, but when she turns to regard herself in the mirror she sees to her dismay that the rich crimson hue has faded, soured, like a rotting orchid, and her hopeful face has become drawn and sallow as a hag's. *How is this possible?* Mrs. G. is a very attractive woman, her face is a flawless cosmetic mask. *Is it the lighting in this dressing room? Is the jacket damaged goods of some kind?* Tikki has knocked lightly on the door to ask how Mrs. G. finds the jacket, and may she enter, nudging the door open as Mrs. G. in a sudden childish sulk roughly removes the offending jacket and tosses it to the floor. One of the pearl buttons rolls at her feet. *It's ugly. I hate it. Something's wrong with it.* Tears of fury sting Mrs. G.'s eyes. *Why do you all cheat me? Why do you hate me—I'm your most faithful customer!* Tikki has picked up the offending jacket and asks Mrs. G. if she would like to see another, in a more subdued shade, but Mrs. G. in her fit of frustration has pounded her fists on the mirror, and, strangely, the mirror clicks open as if it's a door . . .

Madame, Tikki says quickly, in a lowered, urgent voice, do not enter, please!

Is this a door? But where does it lead? Mrs. G. might have forgotten that she's only partly clothed, in a lacy ivory brassiere, half-slip and panties, hose and three-inch high-heeled shoes; she's bold, you might say reckless, opening the mirror door and stepping inside into a storage room of a kind, quite large, dimly lit, smelling of something dark, rich, earthy like blood pudding. Tikki hisses, Come back, Madame, please!—but Mrs. G. isn't a woman to be restrained. Hadn't she pursued Mr. G. with just such determination? Isn't it the way of the predatory female? *What is this?* Mrs. G. cries. *What are you hiding from your customers? I demand to know.* She throws off Tikki's chill talon-fingers on her wrist and steps forward, blinking and staring. The storage space is filled primarily with mannequins. Naked mannequins, female figures, some of them mere torsos, headless, and others with hairless heads, yet not smoothly bald but—bloodied? As if their hair has been yanked out in clumps? Mrs. G. looks about, in a paralysis of wonderment and growing horror. The mannequins resemble Sabine's usual highly stylized show-window mannequins, yet these are curiously twisted, disfigured, in arrested poses of agony, their pale bodies covered in welts and bloody patches. Some of the mannequins are fallen, in untidy heaps, with bare jutting legs and feet, and some, so strangely, are hanging upside down from—can it be meat hooks? Like Titian's nightmare vision, *The Flaying of Marsyas,* a painting from which Mrs. G. once shielded her sensitive eyes, recoiling in disgust from the spectacle of a naked humanoid figure hanging upside down from a tree, being skinned alive. *Oh! oh! oh.* Mrs. G. turns aside now from the hanging mannequins, and sees, propped against a wall, a soiled, battered mannequin with mutilated breasts and gouged-out eyes — Mrs. D.? Is this Mrs. D., who'd once been so glamorous, the most envied of the rich men's wives? And, close by, on her back, legs crudely spread, and an immense gaping wound between her thighs, encrusted with blood drops like tiny jewels, is the very woman — champagne-blond like herself, but a decade older, with a sulky drooping jawline and embittered eyes — who'd preceded Mrs. G. as Mr. G.'s wife.

Mrs. G. draws breath to scream, but her throat constricts in a paroxysm of horror and no sound emerges.

"Madame, know this: we are in your service."

In freshly laundered and quite stylish white butcher aprons the Sabine sales force, led by the now-energetic Tikki, encircle Mrs. G. and restrain her. The trembling woman's few remaining clothes are cut from her with knife blades so sharp, they leave a filigree of thinly bleeding wounds in her flesh; her expensive shoes are wrenched off her feet, and her hose peeled away. How vulnerable she is suddenly! Naked and exposed, shrinking from harsh overhead lights as her cruel, smiling tormentors pinch, pull, claw, stab at her flesh. A female body no longer young, emaciated by dieting except for the swollen-looking little potbelly, her breasts are flaccid, though shrunken, and her pale thighs and buttocks are striated with myriad creases and fault lines, invisible in flattering light but rudely exposed, even magnified, here. That patch of fair brown pubic hair that doesn't match the hair on Mrs. G.'s head. Those thin legs and ankles, but the deformed-looking, rather long and narrow white feet. "Be assured, Madame, as the others: our service to you is what you seek." Swift and assured, the dazzling-white-garbed Sabine staff binds Mrs. G., tying her wrists behind her, knocking her to the stained earthy floor; now she's beginning to scream, panting for breath, and what some might call the cruelest part of the ceremony occurs: Mrs. G.'s words are torn from her. Tikki pries open her jaws and seizes her tongue and cuts it out at the roots, tossing the bloody piece of flesh away even as Mrs. G.'s language, her very name, or what her fading memory can retain of her name, is tossed away. "*Voilà*, Madame! It is done."

The three-inch heel of the exquisitely fashioned kidskin sandal is thrust repeatedly into the groaning woman's vagina; in fistfuls, her champagne-blond hair is torn from her head and scattered to the air; her fingernails that were manicured and polished only the previous day at Elizabeth Arden are torn one by one from her fingers, her breasts razor-slashed, and the nipples removed with unsentimental surgical precision. Bleeding from her mouth, from the countless wounds and lacerations of her body, the woman who was once Mrs. G. stares down upon herself with eyes maddened in pain and terror even as with rough skilled hands she's hoisted up, bound by her ankles to a meat hook, and her still-smooth, or nearly smooth, throat slashed with a scimitarlike blade. Within a few minutes the ceremony is completed: the woman's life bleeds out into a trough as the Sabine staff watches with excited yet respectful eyes.

Not one for Sabine's much-revered show window of

course. The mannequin is bloodied and battered and, most importantly, it's a woman-no-longer-a-girl.

Contemplating the corpse with a practiced eye, yet not without a measure of sympathy, Tikki says, "Madame, you see, you are at peace now, yes? In our private collection."

The Haunting

There's nothing! You hear nothing. It's the wind. It's your dream. You know how you dream. Go back to sleep. I want to love you, stop crying, let go of me, let me sleep for sweet Jesus' sake I'm somebody too not just your mommy don't make me hate you.

In this new place Mommy has brought us to. Where nobody will know us Mommy says.

In this new place in the night when the rabbits' cries wake us. In the night my bed pushed against a wall and through the wall I can hear the rabbits crying in the cellar in their cages begging to be freed. In the night there is the wind. In this new place at the edge of a river Mommy says is an Indian name — *Cuy-a—hoga.* In the night when we hear Mommy's voice muffled and laughing. Mommy's voice like she is speaking on a phone. Mommy's voice like she is speaking, laughing to herself. Or singing.

Calvin says it might not be Mommy's voice. It's a ghost voice of the house Mommy brought us to, now Mommy is a widow.

I ask Calvin is it Daddy? Is it Daddy wanting to come back?

Calvin looks at me like he'd like to hit me. For saying some wrong dumb thing like I am always doing. Then he laughs.

"Daddy ain't coming back, dummy. Daddy is dead."

Daddy is dead. Dead Daddy. Daddy-dead.
Daddydeaddead. Deaaaaaddaddy.

If you say it enough times faster and faster you start giggling. Calvin shows me.

In this new place a thousand miles, Mommy says, from the old place where we have come to make a *new start*. Already Mommy has a job, in sales she says. Not much, but only temporary. Some nights she has to work; Calvin can watch me. Calvin is ten: old enough to watch his little sister, Mommy says. Now that Daddy is gone.

Now that Daddy is gone we never speak of him. Calvin and me, never when Mommy might hear.

At first I was worried: how would Daddy know where we were if he wanted to come back to us?

Calvin flailed his fists like windmills he'd like to hit me with. Told and told and told you—Daddy is D-E-A-D.

Mommy said, "Where Randy Malvern has gone is his own choice. He has gone to dwell with his own cruel kin." I asked where, and Mommy said scornfully, "He has gone to hell to be with his own cruel kin."

Except for the rabbits in the cellar, nobody knows me here.

In their ugly rusted old cages in the cellar where Mommy

says we must not go. There is nothing in the cellar Mommy
says. Stay out of that filthy place. But in the night through the
wall I can hear the rabbits' cries. It starts as whimpering at first,
like the cooing and fretting of pigeons, then it gets louder. If I
put my pillow over my head, still I hear them. I am meant to
hear them. My heart beats hard so that it hurts. In their cages
the rabbits are pleading, *Help us! Let us out! We don't want
to die.*

In the morning before school Mommy brushes my hair,
laughs, and kisses the tip of my nose. In the morning there is
a Mommy who loves me again. But when I ask Mommy about
the rabbits in the cellar, Mommy's face changes.

Mommy says she told me! The cellar is empty. There are
no rabbits in the cellar; she has shown me, hasn't she?

I try to tell Mommy the rabbits are real: I can hear them
in the wall in the night, but Mommy is exasperated, brushing
my hair—always there are snarls in my curly hair, especially
at the back of my neck; Mommy has to use the steel comb that
makes me whimper with pain, saying, "No. It's only a silly
dream, Marybeth. And I'm warning you both: no more
dreams."

Now that Daddy is gone we are learning to be cautious of
Mommy.

Always it was Daddy to look out for. Daddy driving home
and the sound of the pickup motor running off. And the door
slamming. And Daddy might be rough lifting us to the ceiling
in his strong arms, but it was all right because Daddy laughed
and tickled with his mustache and Daddy brought us presents
and took us for fast swerving drives in the pickup, playing his
CDs loud so the music thrummed and walloped through us

like we were rag dolls. But other times Daddy was gone for days and when Daddy came back Mommy tried to block him from us and he'd grab her hair saying, What? What the fuck you looking at me like that? Those fucking kids are *mine*. He'd bump into a chair and curse and kick it and if Mommy made a move to set the chair straight he'd shove her away. If the phone began to ring, he'd yank it out of the wall socket. Daddy's eyes were glassy and had red cobwebs in them and his fingers kept bunching into fists and his fists kept striking out like he couldn't help himself. Especially Calvin. Poor Calvin if Daddy saw him holding back or trying to hide. Little shit! Daddy shouted. What the fuck you think you're doing, putting something over on your fucking Dad-*dy*? And Mommy ran to protect us then and hid us.

But now Daddy is gone, it's Mommy whose eyes are like a cat's eyes jumping at us. It's Mommy whose fingers twitch like they want to be fists.

You know I want to love you, honey. You and your brother. But you're making it so hard . . .

Our house is a "row house" Mommy says. At the end of a block of row houses. Brick houses you think, but up close you see it's asphalt siding meant to look like brick. Dull-red brick with streaks running down like tears.

This is a city we live in now. A big city, Mommy says, far away from where we used to live. Nobody will follow us here, and nobody will know us here.

Mommy says.

Don't talk to neighbors. Ever.

Don't talk to anybody at school. Any more than you need to talk.

Mommy says, smiling at us, hard.

Mommy's eyes shining, she's so happy.

Nothing was ever proved against Mommy.

Mommy says, Know why? Because there was nothing to be proved.

When Daddy drove away the last time in the pickup we saw from the front window. Red taillights disappearing into the night. We were meant to be sleeping, but we never slept; the voices through the floorboards kept us awake.

Later, Mommy ran outside where a car was waiting. Whoever it was in the car came to take her with him, we didn't know. We would not know. The man drove away with Mommy and later I would come to think that I had dreamed it because Mommy said she had not left the house, not for five minutes, she swore *she had not.* When they asked me, I shook my head, shut my eyes not-knowing. Calvin told them Mommy was with us all that night. Calvin told them Mommy slept with us and held us.

I was only five then. I cried a lot. Now I'm six and in first grade. Calvin is in fourth, he had to be kept back a year for *learning disability.* This is a joke, Mommy says: Calvin is the smartest of us all; he is only pretending. Mommy laughs and tickles Calvin. He is her favorite. Calvin says it's a good thing, being kept back. In this new school he's one of the big boys now—nobody better pick on *him.*

Whoever came to question Calvin and me, if it was the social services lady, bringing us oatmeal cookies she'd baked herself, or the man from the sheriff's office, calling us Calvin, Marybeth, like a trick to make us think he knew us,

Calvin would say the same thing. *Mommy held us all that night long.*

The cellar. That is forbidden to Calvin and me.

Mommy says nothing is down there. No rabbits! For Christ's sake will you stop, both of you. *There are no rabbits in the cellar.*

The cages are still in the cellar, though. There are some cages outside in the backyard almost hidden by weeds, but there are more in the cellar—rabbit hutches, Calvin calls them. Mommy has made phone calls about the cages in the cellar and the smell in the cellar and the cellar walls that ooze oily muck when it rains and the roof that's rotted and leaking, and Mommy starts to cry over the phone, but the man hasn't come yet to make things right.

The cellar! Wish I didn't think about it so much. In the night when the rabbits cry for help, it's because they are trapped in the cages and it's like they know I can hear them; I am the only one to hear them. *Help us! Help us we don't want to die!*

In our other house built on a concrete slab there was no cellar. Then Daddy moved into a mobile home, as he called it, that was on just wheels. Here the cellar is like a big square dug in the ground. The first time Mommy went away and we were alone in the house, we went into the cellar giggling and scared. Calvin turned on the light—it was just one lightbulb overhead. The steps were wood, and wobbly. The furnace was down there, and a smell of oil and pipes. In a corner were the rabbit hutches. Ugly old rusted wire cages stacked together almost to the ceiling. We counted eight of them. The cellar smelled bad, especially the cages smelled. You could see bits of soft gray fur stuck in the wires. On the concrete floor were dried little black pellets: Calvin said they were rabbit turds. Oily dark stains on the concrete and stains Calvin teased me about, saying they were blood.

A smell down here of old musty things. Muck oozing through the walls after a heavy rain. Calvin said Mommy would kill us if she knew we were down here. He scolded me when I reached inside one of the cages, where the door was open, saying, "Hey! If you cut yourself on that, if you get tet'nus, Mommy will give me hell."

I asked Calvin what *tet'nus* is.

In a sneering voice, like he was so smart because he was in fourth grade and I was only in first, Calvin said, "Death."

I was afraid Calvin would see I had scratched my arm on the cage door. Not a deep cut, but like a cat scratch, only bleeding a little. I would tell Mommy that I'd scratched my arm on the screen door.

Oh! Calvin.

Something was moving in one of the cages. Away back in the corner. I could see it was a small furry shape. I could see the gleaming eyes. I grabbed at Calvin and he shook off my arm.

Calvin made a scornful noise he'd got from Daddy. When Daddy would say *Bull-shit* drawing out the word like a yawn.

I told Calvin that you could see a rabbit there, almost. You could see the other rabbits in their cages. Look!

But Calvin wouldn't look. Calvin called me a damn dumb dopey girl. Yanking at my arm to make me come back upstairs.

Lots of times now Calvin calls me worse things. Nasty things rhyming my name Marybeth to make me cry. Words I don't know the meaning of except they're meant to hurt like words Daddy called Mommy in those last days Daddy was living with us.

Saying now, "If she finds out we were down there I'm gonna break your ass. Anything she does to me, I'm gonna do to you, cunt."

Calvin makes me cry, but I know he doesn't mean it.

Calvin is my brother; he loves me. At school, where we don't know anybody and people look at us strange, Calvin stays close to me. Only just, words fly out of his mouth sometimes like stinging wasps. Like with Daddy, and Daddy's fists.

Not meaning to hurt. It just happens.

Now Daddy is gone, Mommy plays his old music.

Daddy's music she'd used to hate! Daddy's CDs. Rockabilly and heavy metal mostly, Calvin calls it. Like steel-toed boots kicking kicking kicking a door that won't budge. Low and mean like thunder.

Now Daddy is gone, Mommy brings home bottles like Daddy used to bring home. The label is a mean-looking wild boar head with tusks and staring eyes. Calvin says there's an actual hog living in a swamp a few miles away and his favorite food is little girls eaten *alive and kicking*.

Not to scare me, Calvin is just teasing.

Now Daddy is gone and not coming back, Mommy has taken up his old guitar that none of us could touch, not ever. Mommy picking at the strings and trying to strum chords like

Daddy did. Except her fingers aren't strong like Daddy's. Except Mommy is happy; Mommy is drinking from the wild-boar bottle and Mommy is singing *On the banks of the O-hi-o* and *Yonder stands Little Maggie, suitcase in her hand.* Mommy says this shit gets into your blood—it's cool. One of the strings on Daddy's guitar breaks, but Mommy doesn't care. Calvin and me are rapt with listening to Mommy; she's got a way to her, like radio voices you find you are listening to. Like Mommy says, it gets into your blood.

Some nights, Mommy is in the kitchen straddling the guitar across her legs, strumming it hard and quick and moving her head around so her long hair (that's the color of beets now, and shiny) ripples to her waist. Oh, Mommy is pretty! Singing songs she doesn't know all the words to, making up for what she doesn't know. *Yonder stands Little Maggie, thirty-eight in her hand, Little Mag-gie was made for lovin', cheatin' another man.*

I asked Calvin what is a thirty-eight and Calvin says a thirty-eight is to blow your head off, *boomboom!*

A lady in the next-door row house says to me, Your mommy is looking good these days now her face is mostly mended and her hair grown out real pretty like a girl's. But don't tell her I said so. She'd think I was nosy.

So I didn't tell. Anything to make Mommy upset, I don't tell.

"Marybeth? If there's anything you wish to confide . . ."

In school my eyes keep shutting. It's like some flashlight beam is inside my head then switches off, my head falls forward onto my arms on my desktop and there's a lady asking is something wrong, my teacher leaning over me.

The lady's name, I don't remember. She smells like blackboard dust, not like Mommy who smells so sweet and sharp now when she goes out.

". . . can tell me, dear. If there's anything wrong at home . . ."

I shut my eyes and rub them. It's like there is woodsmoke in my eyes, they burn and sting. I feel myself freeze like a scared rabbit.

". . . wrong at home? Every morning in class, Marybeth, you . . ."

When Daddy went away, and we were told he would not be coming back, you could see in people's eyes how they didn't know what words to use. They could not bring themselves to say *Your father is dead*. They could not say like Calvin, *Daddy is dead. Dead-daddy*. My teacher can't bring herself to say *Every morning you look so haunted*, for this is not anything you would say to a little girl whose father has gone to hell to dwell with his own cruel kin.

". . . look so hollow-eyed, dear. Don't you sleep well at night?"

I shake my head the way Calvin does. Tears spill from my eyes. I'm not crying, though.

In what's called the infirmary, the school nurse tugs off my sneakers with the frayed laces and pulls a blanket up over me so that I can sleep. I'm shivering and my teeth are chattering I'm so cold. I hold myself tight against sleep like one of the rabbits hunched in his cage, knowing he must stay awake, but it's like the lightbulb in the cellar when it's switched off: everything goes dark and empty like nobody's there. And after a while somebody else comes into the infirmary. Her voice and the nurse's voice I can hear low and almost quarreling on the other side of the gauze curtain pulled around my cot. One voice saying, "This isn't the place for a child to sleep. Not at school. She is missing her schoolwork . . ."

The other voice is the nurse. Saying quietly like there is a secret between them, "She's the Malvern girl. You know."

"Her! The one whose—"

"Must be. I've checked the name."

"'Malvern.' My God. The boy Calvin is in fourth grade; he's fidgety and distracted and falling asleep, too."

"You think they know? How their father died?"

"God help us, I hope not."

Nasty things were said about Mommy. Like she'd been arrested by the sheriff's deputies. That was not true. Mommy was never arrested. Calvin ran hitting and kicking at kids who said that, jeering at us. Mommy was taken away for questioning. But Mommy was released and was not ever arrested. *Because there was not one shred of evidence against her.*

During that time when Mommy was away a day and a night and part of a day, we stayed with Aunt Estelle. Mommy's older sister—half-sister. Mommy spoke of her with a hurt twist of her mouth. We didn't have to go to school. We were told not to play with other children. Not to wander from the house. We watched videos, not TV, and when the TV was on, it was after we went to bed. In that house there was no talk of Daddy. The name Malvern was not heard. Later we would learn that there had been a funeral, Calvin and I had been kept away.

Aunt Estelle smoked cigarettes and was on the phone a lot and said to us your mother will be back soon, you'll be back home soon. And that was so.

I hugged Auntie Estelle hard when we left. But afterward Mommy and Aunt Estelle quarreled and when Mommy drove us a thousand miles away in the pickup with the U-Haul behind she never said good-bye to Aunt Estelle. That bitch, Mommy called her.

When Mommy first came home from what they called *questioning*, her face was still raw and swollen and her eyes tired. But in this new place, Mommy got young again. It did not happen overnight, but it did happen. Mommy's hair changed color and grew out to shimmer and ripple over her shoulders. There was a way Mommy had of brushing her hair out of her eyes in a sweeping gesture that looked like a drowning swimmer suddenly shooting to the surface of the water. *Ah-ah-ah*, Mommy filled her lungs with air.

With a lipstick pencil Mommy drew a luscious red-cherry mouth on her pale twisty lips. Mommy drew on black-rimmed eyes we had not seen before.

Mommy strummed her guitar. It was her guitar now that she'd had the broken string mended. Saying, "It was his own choice. When one of their own comes to dwell with them there is rejoicing through hell."

By Christmastime in this new place Mommy has quit her job at the discount shoe store and works now at a café on the river. Most nights she's a cocktail waitress but some nights she plays her guitar and sings. With her face bright and made up and her hair so glimmering, you don't notice the cracks in Mommy's skin: in the drifting smoky light of the café, they are invisible. Mommy's fingers have grown more practiced. Her nails are filed short and polished. Her voice is low and throaty with a little burr in it that makes you shiver. In the café, men offer her money which she sometimes accepts, saying quietly, Thank you. I will take this as a gift for my music. I will take this because my children have no father; I am a single mother and must support two small children. But I will not accept it if you expect anything more from me than this: my music, and my thanks.

At the River's Edge, Mommy calls herself Little Maggie. In time she will be known and admired as Little Maggie. She's like a little girl telling us of the applause. Little Maggie taking up her guitar that's polished now and gleaming like the smooth inside of a chestnut after you break off the spiky rind. Strumming chords and letting her long beet-colored hair slide over her shoulders, Mommy says when she starts to sing everybody in the café goes silent.

In the winter the rabbits' cries grow more pleading and piteous. Calvin hears them, too. But Calvin pretends he doesn't. I press my pillow over my head not wanting to hear. *We don't want to die. We don't want to die.* One night when Mommy is at the café, I slip from my bed barefoot and go downstairs into the cellar that smells of oozing muck and rot and animal misery and there in the dim light cast by the single lightbulb are the rabbits.

Rabbits in each of the cages! Some of them have grown too large for the cramped space; their hindquarters are pressed against the wire and their soft ears are bent back against their heads. Their eyes shine in apprehension and hope seeing me. A sick feeling comes over me; each of the cages has a rabbit trapped inside. Though this is only logical, as I will discover through my life: *In each cage, a captive.* For why would adults who own the world manufacture cages not to be used. I ask the rabbits, Who has locked you in these cages? But the rabbits can only stare at me, blinking and twitching their noses. One of them is a beautiful pale powder-gray, a young rabbit and not so sick and defeated as the others. I stroke his head through the cage wire. He's trembling beneath my touch; I can feel his heartbeat. Most of the rabbits are mangy and matted. Their fur is dull gray. There is a single black rabbit, heavy and misshapen from his cage, with watery eyes. The doors of the cages are latched and locked with small padlocks. Both the cages and the padlocks are rusted. I find an old pair of shears in the cellar and holding the shears awkwardly in both hands I manage to cut through the wires of all the cages. I hurt my fingers peeling away openings for the rabbits to hop through, but they hesitate, distrustful of me. Even the young rabbit only pokes his head through the opening, blinking and sniffing nervously, unmoving.

Then I see in the cellar wall a door leading to the outside. A heavy wooden door covered in cobwebs and the husks of dead insects. It hasn't been opened in years, but I am able to tug it open, a few inches at first, then a little wider. On the other side are concrete steps leading up to the surface of the ground. Fresh cold air smelling of snow touches my face. "Go on! Go out of here! You're free."

The rabbits don't move. I will have to go back upstairs and

leave them in darkness before they will escape from their cages.

"Marybeth! Wake up."

Mommy shakes me, scolding; I've been sleeping so hard.

It's morning. The rabbit cries have ceased. Close by, running behind our backyard, is the Cuyahoga & Erie train with its noisy wheels; I almost don't hear the whistle any longer. In my bed pushed against the wall.

When I go downstairs into the cellar to investigate, I see that the cages are gone.

The rabbit cages are gone! You can see where they've been, though—there's empty space. The concrete floor isn't so dirty as it is other places in the cellar.

The door to the outside is shut tight. Shut and covered in cobwebs like before.

Outside, where cages were dumped in the weeds, they've been taken away, too. You can see the outlines in the snow.

Calvin is looking, too. But Calvin doesn't say anything.

Mommy says, lighting a match in a way Daddy used to, against her thumb, and raising it to the cigarette dipping from her mouth, "At last those damn stinking cages have been hauled away. It only took five months for that bastard to move his ass."

Burned alive were words that were used by strangers, but we were not allowed to hear. *Burned alive in his bed*, it was said of our father on TV and elsewhere, but we were shielded from such words.

Unless Calvin heard. And Calvin repeated to me.

Burned alive drunk in his bed. Gasoline sprinkled around the trailer and a match tossed. But Randy Malvern was a man with enemies; in his lifetime that was thirty-two years, he'd accumulated numerous enemies and not a one of these would be linked to the fire and not a one of these was ever arrested in the arson death though all were questioned by the sheriff and eventually released and some moved away and were gone.

Now the cages are gone. And now I hear the rabbits' cries in the wind, in the pelting rain, in the train whistle that glides through my sleep. Miles from home I hear them; through my life I will hear them. Cries of trapped creatures who have suffered, who have died, who await us in hell, our kin.

Hunger

1.

That moment. That insight. Flaring like pain. When Kristine will think, *I've made the worst mistake of my life.* When she will feel like a many-legged beetle whose nerve center has been cut—the paralysis is multiplied, with so many legs.

The worst mistake, O God help me to make things right.

2.

It's at a distance she first sees him. Not knowing him then.

Yet seeming to recognize him. Shading her eyes as the chill Atlantic surf froths and foams over her bare feet. He's a silhouette crouched amid rocks and sand at the ragged edge of the surf; he seems to be washing his hands, his forearms, splashing water up onto his face. Then he stands, stretches, takes up a backpack, which he slings over his shoulder, and turns to move in her direction. Yet oblivious of her, she thinks.

Striding along the beach like a pent-up, now released, young animal. Striding along the private beach as if he owns it. It's a sheltered rocky cove where "cottages" have been built high atop the crest of a hill overlooking the ocean, most of them with meticulously kept picket fences surrounding their property. At this hour of the morning the beach is virtually deserted. Kristine and her five-year-old daughter, Ceci; an older white-haired man walking his dog; and now this young man in khaki trousers damp from the spray, a white shirt flapping over his bare torso, thick dark shoulder-length hair whipping in the wind like flames. A stranger? A neighbor? Kristine notices that the young man seems to be limping, just slightly favoring his left leg.

He's tall, very thin. He has a childlike eager look. A hungry look. His ribs are prominent against his taut, pale torso, which is narrow and covered in fine dark curly hairs. Kristine has an impression of a young unlined face, a face of delicate-boned male beauty—but she doesn't want to stare. *I know him. Do I know him?* The young man appears foreign, exotic: Turkish, Russian? Portuguese? In Rocky Harbor, just south of Provincetown, Massachusetts, on Cape Cod, where Kristine and her daughter are spending two weeks in August, there are numerous summer workers of foreign extraction, young men and women from Boston, Providence, New Bedford, on the staffs of the resort hotels and restaurants. Kristine guesses that this young man is one of these. Unless maybe he's an artist. (She doesn't want to think he might be a drifter, and dangerous.) It isn't likely that he lives in Rocky Harbor, where oceanside property has become grotesquely expensive, and yet he might be, like Kristine, someone's houseguest.

Kristine thinks, *He's a dancer. A wounded dancer like so many.*

It's one of those swift unexamined thoughts that sometimes fly into Kristine's head when she's in a heightened mood—not alone and not lonely yet alone in her mind—a childish wish (and in this case a lethal wish) that others for whom she feels a mysterious tug of kinship are persons like herself, sharing a secret unspoken bond.

A wounded dancer, an ex-dancer like me.

3.

"Ceci, honey! Take care."

But Ceci, running and squealing at the edge of the splashing surf, about twenty feet ahead of her mother, doesn't hear.

Ceci's energy! Long ago as a girl only a few years older than Ceci, Kristine was in training to be a dancer, obsessed with being a dancer, capable of sustaining hours of physical exertion and emotional strain; now she's thirty-four and out of breath trying to keep up with a five-year-old.

How exposed Kristine feels. At this early hour, not yet 7:30 A.M., she isn't wearing makeup, not even lipstick; her hair is windblown. Her white sailcloth trousers, her long-sleeved shirt tied at the midriff over a T-shirt, are being blown by the wind tight against her breasts, belly, thighs.

I won't look at him. I won't see his eyes. If he's looking at me, or if he isn't.

The limping young man. Kristine isn't staring at him yet seems to note how, as he approaches Ceci and her, he's trying to walk normally. She can imagine him steeling himself against pain. A torn tendon, an injured knee. Her own dance injuries were minor but cumulative. She feels a rush of warmth for him. Male vanity! And the limping young man so strong a presence ... Ceci, running headlong in that careless way of young children, even shy children, eyes shut against the stinging spray, seems to be unaware of the young man approaching her. Though Kristine has warned her countless times, she isn't watching where she's going, oblivious of the hard-packed wet sand underfoot, the snaky hieroglyphics of seaweed, driftwood, Styrofoam litter, clamshells, and shards of glass. Kristine flinches as Ceci stumbles against a jutting rock, teeters, and would fall—except, reacting instantaneously, the young man breaks into a run, limps to her, stoops, and catches her beneath the arms.

This moment Kristine will see many times repeated in her memory, through her life.

The long-haired limping stranger out of nowhere. Out of the stinging spray. The fiery opalescent morning sky, banked with cloud. A stranger's surprisingly strong-muscled legs, and his strong arms scooping Ceci up before she can fall. Dangling in his arms for a brief moment, like a child dancer, Ceci blinks and gapes, too surprised to burst into tears or even to react with her usual abashed shyness in the presence of strangers.

Kristine, the grateful young mother, cries, "Oh, thank you! Thank you so much."

She takes Ceci from him. The transfer of the child's weight from one adult to the other feels natural, companionable. Kristine is herself feeling stricken with shyness. She has an impression of dark, deep-set eyes, beautiful bloodshot eyes. Heavy dark eyebrows nearly meeting over the bridge of an aquiline nose. Jaws lightly stubbled, needing a shave. The young man says, "She's a beautiful little girl; you must love her so much."

His speech is lightly accented. Italian? French?

Kristine can't think of any reply except a stammering, "Oh, yes."

The young man walks on, making an effort not to limp.

Kristine, with Ceci firmly in hand, fondly scolding the child, decides to return to her aunt's and uncle's house above the beach. Twenty-six steps to climb. Her heart is beating painfully by the time she's at the top. She's conscious of—or imagines she is or should be—the young man turning to look after her. Of course, Kristine doesn't look back.

4.

Yet we would have met in some other way. Obviously.

Kristine and Ceci are guests of Kristine's aunt and uncle at their elegant "cottage" on the Cape: a twenty-room saltbox of faux-weathered wood with floor-to-ceiling glass panels over-looking the rippled dunes, tall rushes, and wild rose, the rocky beach and white-capped waves, the astonishing sweep of the Atlantic, and a horizon shimmering in the distance—the fabled oceanside view at Rocky Harbor, an exclusive enclave of less than a dozen large custom-built houses. Kristine has visited her mother's elder sister, Betsey, and her investment banker husband, Douglas Robbins, several times in the past, often without her busy, distracted husband, Parker Culver, the CEO of a prosperous computer software company in Boston; Parker has promised to take a shuttle flight out to the Cape for at least one weekend but hasn't yet. Kristine and Ceci telephone him each evening at seven; sometimes they call him in the late morning. "Daddy, I miss you!" Ceci says. "Daddy, we want you here." Kristine speaks more calmly, knowing it's not a good idea to beg her husband for anything, especially not to beg him to do something for his own well-being. Kristine and Parker have been married for nearly eight years; Ceci will be their only child.

(Parker, sixteen years older than Kristine, was hesitant to have this child. He has an emotionally disturbed thirteen-year-old son from a previous marriage, living with his former wife in New Hampshire. Lucky for Kristine, and for Ceci, that Parker relented and "allowed" his new young wife to become pregnant.)

In Rocky Harbor, Kristine has noted her aunt's searching gaze, the not-quite-articulated query, *Is something wrong between you and Parker?* She has noted her uncle's kindly but unwanted solicitude. *If there's anything you'd like to tell us, Kristine?* Kristine wonders if something shows in her face of which she's unaware. These sunny seaside days. A wave of vertigo washes over her, she's so lonely. Hungry. But determined not to show it.

Determined to suggest to her aunt and uncle by her buoyant tone of voice, her resolute smile and cheerful public manner, as well as the fact (of which surely they're aware) that she telephones Parker so often, that things are fine in her marriage. She says, entertaining anyone who listens, charmed by the very pretty ash-blond young mother with the delightful five-year-old daughter, "My husband is a workaholic type-A. *Vacation* is a word he despises. It sounds too much like *vacant—vagrant.* And really"—Kristine always adds this, with a sympathetic frown—"he is enormously busy." And productive, and prosperous in his competitive field. But is the intimate state of her marriage anyone's business except hers and Parker's?

Marriage, a mystery. Why we love, and what we do to define and contain our love. To protect it. As if love is a flame that can be blown out . . .

Yet Parker Culver is solid, hardly flamelike. He's a broad-shouldered handsome man with thick white hair and bristling eyebrows: from a short distance he looks like a distinguished elder; close up you see that he's a man of youthful middle age, no more than fifty. His handshake is pulverizing, his embraces and hugs are rib cracking, his kisses wet, doggy, possessive. He's a good-hearted man whom everyone adores. He's a good sport, rarely holds a grudge. (Why would Parker Culver hold a grudge? He's been a winner all his life.) When Kristine and Parker are together, often they're mistaken for daughter and father: amusing to Parker, annoying and embarrassing to Kristine. "What does that make Ceci, your granddaughter? Offspring of an incestuous union?" Kristine asks. But Parker can't be riled, not by so trivial an issue.

When Kristine shows Jean-Claude a snapshot of her husband, the young man will stare at it, deeply moved; he'll wipe at his eyes and say in a whisper, "This man! So like my father . . . My father I lost when I was a little boy and whose grave somewhere in Bretagne I have never seen."

5.

I won't look at him. I didn't look. His eyes . . .

Jean-Claude, he calls himself.

Jean-Claude Rivere? Ranier? Raneau? At the home of the Pearsons of Rocky Harbor, he's introduced to a group of guests, of whom Kristine Culver is one, as "Jean-Claude" with a murmured last name, a "Parisian-born American" brought to the party by a friend of a friend of the Pearsons'. At the home of the Feldmans of Provincetown, he's introduced as "Jean-Claude" with a murmured last name, an actor, poet, ex-dancer, a friend of the companion of the artistic director of the Provincetown Theater. At the home of the Sterns of Wellfleet he's "Jean-Claude" with a murmured last name, "actor, choreographer, poet." At the Robbinses' home, where Kristine is staying, Jean-Claude is introduced as a "fascinating new acquaintance" of Betsey's, who met him just the previous week at a neighbor's dinner party and was "utterly charmed" by him. Here Kristine learns that the young man, Jean-Claude with his murmured last name, is not only a photographer, an actor, a former dancer, a choreographer, and a poet, he's also a "gifted translator." Proudly Aunt Betsey shows Kristine a copy of a slender novel, *The Vice-Consul*, by Marguerite Duras, translated by "Jean-Claude Ranier." The inscription on the title page reads, in a sweeping hand, *Pour la belle Madame Robbins! avec admiration, Jean-Claude.* On the back cover there's a small photo and a brief biography of the French novelist, but only a brief photoless biography of the translator, Jean-Claude Ranier. Of this individual it's said that he was born in Brest, France, in 1965; studied French and English literature at the Sorbonne; has translated a number of twentieth-century French novels into English; and divides his time between Paris, London, and New York City.

Is it possible? Kristine looks across the room at this Jean-Claude Ranier, being introduced to guests by her uncle. Born in 1965, he'd be thirty-six. An astonishingly youthful thirty-six. Kristine would have estimated the young man's age as twenty-six, if not younger.

She says skeptically, "He seems . . . very young. In his person."

Mrs. Robbins, a woman in her midsixties given to community and cultural enthusiasms, says, "Exactly what we need in Rocky Harbor."

"But he isn't a resident here, is he?"

"He's spending the summer with . . . A friend of . . . Someone in Provincetown, I think. Or Wellfleet."

Kristine tells her aunt that she's already met Jean-Claude. She doesn't tell her aunt that they'd met on the beach the other morning, near the Robbinses' private cove.

And when Kristine and Jean-Claude again meet, shaking hands and smiling, Kristine feels that unmistakable tug of kinship between them. That rapport. *Here we are! And here are these others.*

Jean-Claude is the youngest man in the room, as well as the tallest and the most striking in appearance. His skin is unnaturally pale for late summer on the Cape. He's very thin; an upright flame, Kristine thinks. His smile bares small slightly misshapen stained teeth, and when he isn't smiling, he appears brooding, restless, uneasy. His mass of hair, heavy as dreadlocks, is tied at the nape of his neck with a piece of hemp; he looks both boyish and savage. Amid this gathering of mostly middle-aged and older men and women he certainly stands out, like a lead dancer, Kristine thinks, amused. How strange this is! "Jean-Claude Ranier." She likes it that that probably isn't his name. No one knows any more about him than she does. She likes it that he's wearing a stylish white silk shirt (borrowed? a gift?) and white cord trousers; he has shaved for the Robbinses' party, but hastily, so that his jaws are tender, chafed. He gives off a briny odor mixed with cologne: expensive cologne, Kristine recognizes the scent. This, too, he has probably borrowed from one of his Provincetown friends.

Kristine has seen that, in this gathering, Jean-Claude is polite, reserved, quick to smile but taciturn. Despite the hair and the briny sexual aura, he's an ideal young man: subordinate to his elders. She's touched by the way the young man tries to disguise, or minimize, his limp. He doesn't want sympathy or unwelcome questions. Much of the time he stands with his weight on his right leg; when he has to walk a short distance, he stiffens his left leg and tries to move normally. But it's an effort. Kristine can sense pain in his knee. His jaw stiffens. His eyes cloud. But he won't show pain; that's his secret. Kristine has noted, too, that he's hungry. Whenever he has the opportunity, even as eager middle-aged women hover about him, smiling and chattering, he devours appetizers as quickly and efficiently as possible.

A wild creature, temporarily tamed.

Pretending to be tamed.

Jean-Claude asks after *la belle jeune fille* and Kristine tells him that Ceci has gone to bed early. She's touched that the young man should remember Ceci; that he should ask after her, with a look of tenderness. "The ocean fascinates and exhausts Ceci. She can't get enough of it. *She* exhausts me." Kristine hasn't meant to say this; it's a kind of boast. But she's smiling so radiantly, half consciously brushing her shiny, bobbed ash-blond hair from her face, it's evident that she isn't exhausted now.

Jean-Claude has been watching her closely but hasn't said much. He's strangely reticent, shy. Kristine wants to ask if he's truly the translator of Marguerite Duras—"Jean-Claude Ranier." Or does he simply share that name? Or has he simply appropriated the name? She's certain, from the way he moves, that he's a former dancer. Yet she hesitates to ask for this would suggest intimacy; it would suggest that Kristine has taken note of his physical infirmity, which he tries so valiantly to disguise. To speak of it would be like touching him intimately. Slipping her hands inside his silk shirt, stroking his slender chest . . .

"Jean-Claude, are you hungry? For a meal? I'll take you to dinner." Kristine laughs recklessly. "*I'll* pay."

Kristine can't believe she has uttered these astonishing words. She isn't a woman to speak so aggressively to anyone she has just met, male or female; even before marrying, she wouldn't have spoken like this to a man she scarcely knows.

If Jean-Claude is startled, he gives no sign. He draws closer to Kristine, saying, with a shy smile, "Mrs. Culver, I would like that very much. But, I'm sorry"—with a swing of his head of the kind an adolescent boy might make, bemused, trapped, determined-to-be-stoic, he indicates a stylishly dressed middle-aged woman at the far end of the Robbinses' living room—"Mrs. Bernhardt has already invited me."

6.

How to explain. Such appalling behavior. Hoping to God no one heard, overheard. As if another woman took Kristine's place. Summoned by the long-haired young man. Like a dancer, summoned by music she can't resist.

7.

Kristine stares uneasily. Yet with some fascination.

"Kitty-kitty-*kitty*!" Eerily, in unison, the older women croon as if calling their lovers.

Kristine and Ceci are watching stray cats being fed by a "delightfully eccentric" bushy-haired woman in her eighties, on the beach below the woman's house in Rocky Harbor; watching as Kristine's aunt Betsey assists the old woman, squatting to shake cat food out of cans and onto pie tins for the pack of cats to devour.

It's a daily ritual. Quite a scene. Famished cats come running from all directions.

Ceci claps her hands and cries, "Mommy, look! Lookit the kitties!"

Black cats, tortoiseshells, orange tigers, speckled white and gray, smoky gray—so many! Most of them are painfully thin, with bitten ears and suspicious yellow eyes like warning lights; a few are softer bodied, with a look of daze and hurt in their eyes, obviously abandoned pets. Kristine should help the older women, she supposes. But she doesn't want Ceci to get too near the cats. Some look diseased and others look dangerous.

It's late morning of a cloudy, gusty August day. The morning following the cocktail party. After a night of disturbed sleep, Kristine has accompanied her aunt Betsey into the village, where sometimes Betsey goes at this hour expressly to help Mrs. Vandeventer, a multimillionaire's widow who lives alone, year-round, in the "oldest private dwelling" on the Cape, feed an unruly pack of homeless cats.

Ceci is almost too excited. She tries to count the cats but becomes confused, for the animals keep shifting positions, eel-like, ill-tempered, nudging one another out of the way, baring teeth, hissing, and growling deep in their throats, swatting with their claws. Ceci is accustomed to house cats, friendly pets who brush against a little girl's legs and look up expecting to be petted and fussed over, but these cats ignore their human benefactors, shrink away and hiss with bared teeth even if Mrs. Vandeventer, their special friend, gets too near. Most are scrawny specimens, shorthairs, with mangy fur, looking as if they've been wild all their lives; one or two are high-bred cats—there's even a rail-thin Siamese . . . How cruel people are, Kristine thinks with a shudder.

Hunger. So raw. Ugly.

Ceci begs, "Mommy, can I help feed the kitties? *Please?*"

"Maybe next time, honey." Kristine is annoyed at her aunt—and at herself—for having brought Ceci to see this sorry spectacle. It's like exposing Ceci to videos that are too mature for her, having taken the advice of other parents. After any upsetting interlude, Ceci will ply her mother with questions for days.

Yet there's something comical about this scene, too. The crooning older women, of a moneyed class, squatting on the beach setting out food for homeless cats that betray not

the slightest sign of gratitude or even awareness of their benefactors. Domesticated animals at least make a display of gratitude, however hypocritical; these are as lacking in sentiment
as sharks. Jean-Claude would laugh, Kristine thinks. What
foolish women! As soon as the cats finish one mound of food
they seek out another, rudely nudging their comrades aside,
clawing, snarling, hissing.

When they eat their fill they simply turn and trot away
without a backward glance.

Ceci wants to pet one of the softer-looking young cats and
has to be restrained by Kristine. "Honey, *no*! Don't pet that
kitty. He isn't a pet—he's a wild cat."

Ceci is shocked when the cat, a striking orange tiger with
a white nose, hisses and claws at her. Fortunately, Kristine
pulls Ceci out of range.

"Mommy, why doesn't the kitty like me?" Ceci asks, hurt.

"I told you, honey: he isn't a pet; he's a wild cat."

"A wild cat?" Ceci is of an age to be fascinated by nomen-
clature, precise terms and distinctions. "Why are the cats wild,
Mommy?"

"Because—" Kristine stops to think. She doesn't want
Ceci to know that pet owners sometimes abandon their pets,
this will upset her. Ceci's favorite book-characters are cats with
human names and attributes. Kristine says, "Well, they're wild
to begin with. Some of them. And they have kittens, and the
kittens grow up wild."

Ceci looks puzzled. "But why, Mommy?"

Kristine hasn't answered her daughter's original question,
she knows. But she has no idea how to answer it. "Kitties
began as wild animals, Ceci. A hundred million years ago.

Over time they became tamed. Some of them. But the rest were never tamed. They're called 'feral.' Wild."

"'Fer-al.' 'Wi-ld.'" Ceci enunciates these words with care. She looks pleased. It's enough of a lesson for her, for today.

Kristine is relieved when the last of the cats finish their food and trot obliviously away even as the older women croon after them — "Kitty-kitty! Good-bye." Both Mrs. Vandeventer and Mrs. Robbins are flush-faced as girls, suffused with pleasure and a sense of their own generosity. Next morning the cats will be back, timed to the minute, for another unsentimental feeding frenzy. Kristine shakes her head, disapproving. But the wild creatures are hungry; perhaps nothing matters more than that their hunger be fed.

Kristine says to the older women, with a smile, "You're such good people, so generous . . ." even as she feels a wave of pity and revulsion.

Never. I will never. I vow. Not me!

8.

Alarming news on the Cape.

The murder victim is no one Kristine has met, no one whose name she believes she has heard. DiParma, Austin. Sixty-one years old. A Boston art dealer. A longtime summer resident whose partly decomposed body has been found in his oceanside house a mile north of Rocky Harbor. Said by his neighbors to have been "increasingly eccentric" — "difficult" — "self-destructive." Since his breakup with a younger companion, DiParma had become a virtual recluse, living alone and refusing to see friends and neighbors. According to the county medical examiner, DiParma died of a severe beating and strangulation, sometime in the early morning of August 11; his body wasn't found until the afternoon of August 14. DiParma had also been robbed of cash, credit cards, a wristwatch, and other personal effects. The murderer or murderers turned up the air-conditioning in DiParma's bedroom to retard decomposition . . . "What a terrible, terrible thing!" Betsey Robbins shudders, speaking on the phone with a Rocky Harbor neighbor. "Yet, God forgive me, it isn't so surprising, somehow. Poor man!"

The Robbinses' telephone rings repeatedly. Friends and neighbors drop by. Betsey and Douglas receive, and provide, scandalized news. Without wishing to, Kristine learns that DiParma, that "poor, tragic man," was also an alcoholic; a lover of gourmet food and wine; under treatment for "chronic depression"; a onetime tournament bridge fanatic; a onetime art historian with an international reputation; a multimillionaire; a near-bankrupt; a "booster" of young artists, especially young men; an "exploiter" of young artists, especially young men. He was a man with "many friends—too many"; a man with "no friends, any longer"; a man with "scattered, secret enemies." His former companion, a younger man of about forty, a sculptor, is recalled as "strange"—"childlike"—"capable of sitting in silence for an entire evening"—"sweet"—"hostile"—"susceptible to extreme mood swings." In Rocky Harbor it seems to be generally assumed that this former companion is responsible for DiParma's death, as it's assumed that the robbery motive is secondary to the murder. There was no evidence of a forcible break-in at the victim's house. Whoever killed DiParma had a passionate, particular dislike of *him*.

Kristine's uncle Douglas says in a lowered voice, "I wouldn't be surprised if it turns out that Austin was killed by someone he picked up and brought home with him."

Kristine's aunt Betsey says, "Douglas, *no*. The fact is, Austin wasn't going out at all. When his own sister drove out to see him he only spoke to her through a screen door; he wouldn't let the poor woman *inside*. That was just a few days before he died."

"He wasn't going out in circles we know. But there are others."

Police are searching for the former companion whose name, Kristine learns, is Trim? Trimmer?—he hasn't been seen in Rocky Harbor in months. Police are also canvassing the northern Cape, asking for information about DiParma's private life; asking if anyone saw a "suspicious stranger or strangers" in the area, particularly on the morning of August 11.

Kristine tries to calculate: when had she first seen Jean-Claude? How many days ago? If today is August 15, and the cocktail party was August 13—or was the party August 12 . . . Like Ceci trying to count the pack of unruly cats, Kristine can't seem to concentrate. She shuts her eyes and sees again the young man in silhouette limping along the edge of the beach, pausing to squat in shallow water, vigorously washing hands, forearms, face; then rising, turning, and continuing on his way, striding in her direction, and by degrees, as he sees Kristine and Ceci, trying to disguise his limp. Was this on the morning of August 11? Around 7:30 A.M.? Kristine can't be certain. She doesn't think so. It was the previous morning . . .

She can't involve Jean-Claude in a murder investigation, any more than she could involve others she'd seen that morning on the beach, a white-haired old man walking his dog, a middle-aged couple in straw hats, carrying binoculars . . . She feels a thrill of foreboding.

He's capable of it. You know that.

No. I don't know. It's ridiculous to think of such a thing!

A Rocky Harbor detective visits with Betsey and Douglas Robbins, interviews them briefly, then speaks with Kristine; during Kristine's interview, Betsey takes Ceci down to the beach. "I don't want my little girl to be upset," Kristine tells the detective. Her voice is severe; her manner tense. "I'm trying to keep her from knowing anything about this . . . ugly incident." Kristine tells the detective that she's sorry to disappoint him; she has nothing to report. She didn't know Mr. DiParma: she's only visiting her aunt and uncle for two weeks. She'd seen no one "out of the ordinary." Yes, she walks quite early along the beach, she and Ceci, but she doesn't especially remember the morning of August 11, and she doesn't remember seeing any suspicious strangers. "Or anyone suspicious at all."

The detective, brisk and businesslike, is satisfied with Kristine's remarks. He rises to leave, and Kristine accompanies him. The lavish interior of the Robbinses' house, the sweep of sky, sea, sunshine . . . Kristine expects the detective to remark about the view, something polite, predictable and banal, but the man says nothing. The local residences of the privileged aren't unfamiliar to him. There's little romance in the lives of the rich when you come to know some of their most intimate "tragic" secrets. Kristine repeats that she's only a houseguest here on the Cape, as if this might make the detective trust her more.

It seems natural to ask, as Kristine does, whether the police have any suspects yet. The detective tells her what's been on TV and in the news is what they know. So far. Kristine asks if there are . . . fingerprints? At the crime scene? The detective smiles at her, amused. Kristine is an attractive young woman; her manner is both somber and flirtatious. In her loose-fitting T-shirt and shorts, she looks much younger than her age. "Sure, Mrs. Culver. Always." Kristine doesn't wish to register the rebuff as she follows the man outside. Impulsively she asks, "Footprints, too? There would be so many of them, in the sand. On the beach. Leading away from the house. And days went by before anyone noticed . . ." The detective doesn't reply; Kristine hasn't asked a question exactly. But he pauses, and waits. Kristine hears herself say, brushing her hair out of her face, "If there was something unusual about any of the footprints, you would notice, I guess."

The detective smiles quizzically at Kristine. He's a man of moderate height, prematurely white-haired like her husband, of about her husband's age. He seems to lack Parker's forcefulness, but this might be a misconception. His gaze drops to Kristine's feet, bare in sandals, and rises slowly to her face. "Why do you ask that question, Mrs. Culver?"

"I was just curious. No reason."

Kristine watches the detective drive away in an unmarked car. She's nervous, excited. She wonders if her voice quavered, if the detective noticed.

Yet by the man's tone she surmises that police found nothing to remark upon at the crime scene. At least, no unusual footprints on the beach. No sign of a limp. For a limp would show in the sand, wouldn't it? Even if the individual tried to disguise it, such an irregularity in footprints could be detected. A sharp-eyed forensics expert would discover it amid dozens of other prints . . .

She did the right thing, then, not to mention Jean-Claude to the detective. She knows he isn't capable of such a brutal act, really. Why involve him?

She supposes police will question him in any case. Or have already questioned him. As they've been questioning everyone in the area.

Unless he's gone. If he's guilty he will have gone.

If he's gone, I'll never see him again.

When Kristine joins Ceci on the beach, Ceci hugs her around the knees and squints up at her. "Mommy? Why are you so happy?"

Kristine laughs and kisses her daughter. Her heart is suffused with love, warmth, the joy of simply being alive. "Mommy's always happy, honey, with you. Haven't you noticed?"

9.

If he's gone. If, gone.

Never see him again . . .

Later that day at Provincetown Harbor as she's parking her car Kristine sees, in an alley close by, a shocking sight: a bare-chested, very thin and very pale young man rummaging in a Dumpster behind a seafood restaurant. The young man has wild matted hair to his shoulders, dull red. And he's only a boy. Still Kristine feels a stab of shock in the instant before she realizes, *It isn't him.*

10.

"This caviar! Isn't it heavenly."

The woman actually smacks her lips, which are greasy, fleshy, bright with juvenile lipstick that mocks her wrinkled, collapsed bag of a face. A diamond ring flashes on a liver-speckled hand, a square-cut emerald flashes. She's of no age Kristine can estimate except no longer young. Possibly Betsey Robbins's age. It's possible to see that she's a ruined beauty. Strawberry blond hair, scanty and elaborately puffed above her arched penciled-in eyebrows . . . She's one of dozens of guests at the South Wellfleet home of acquaintances of Kristine's aunt's and uncle's who've brought their niece to yet another cocktail party on a redwood deck above the beach where marbled clouds overhead are slowly darkening, deepening into dusk.

Caviar, this particular Russian brand, currently sells for more than sixty dollars an ounce. So Kristine, who doesn't much like caviar, seems to know.

The woman says, with lascivious enthusiasm, "Usually with such caviar like this, the servings are *parsimonious*. Of course! But look at the servings here, they're *lavish*. You never have enough caviar, always you have to stint—except not *tonight*. Oh God."

Kristine is standing foolishly with a caviar canapé on a napkin in her hand. She turns and sees Jean-Claude. His hungry narrowed eyes, the tightness in his jaw.

He's hating these people, too.

But not me! Not me.

They exchange looks. Subtle, secret smiles. No one seeing them would notice. They haven't seen each other for several days, yet it's as if they've only just been together. The intimacy passing between them.

The woman extolling caviar devours one of the canapés and pats her smeared mouth with a napkin. Seeing Jean-Claude, her eyes lift. Her lipsticked mouth smiles. She brings the silver platter of canapés to him and Kristine sees beforehand that, though very hungry, he will perversely decline. "No thank you, ma'am."

"'Ma'am'! Am I your mother, dear?"

Jean-Claude says coolly, "Ma'am, no. You are not my mother."

He's so beautiful. An upright flame. It won't mean more than that.

In an alcove off the living room, in a darkened corridor at the rear of the sprawling house, she steps uncertainly into the shadows and his hands await her.

In the near distance, out on the redwood deck, the others are talking, laughing. Braying.

He's kissing Kristine. Kisses rapid and light as fluttering moths. Questions he's putting to her. *Yes? Like this? Do you want this?*

Kristine's arms are around his neck. Helpless. Helpless to resist. She tells herself it won't mean anything to this nomadic young man, it's the impulse of the moment, he won't remember her name. One of the women of privilege. One of the younger women. The little girl's mother.

Kristine bites her lip to keep from crying out.

"Oh. God."

Swiftly flaring up, like a flame. Then dying out.

11.

The second time, it's premeditated.

Making love with Jean-Claude, sharing a joint with Jean-Claude . . . smoking marijuana for the first time in—can it be?—nine years; and gripping her fists in a man's thick hair, loving the feel of the hair that's slightly matted, oily. The feel of the man's ropy arm and shoulder muscles. His lean back. The thinness of his torso, the feel of his skeleton inside his skin. His swift sharp lovemaking that turns suddenly tender. And then swift, sharp, hard again. And again tender. Until she clutches at him, hands, arms, knees, thighs. Until she feels her facial mask contort, stretched to breaking.

Where is Jean-Claude staying that night? Somewhere along the beach—friends of friends . . . Very nice generous newly made friends. Yes, he's a nomad. Homeless and wants no home. He's been traveling about for months, years. Parents? None. Family? He laughs, showing his childlike teeth. What is his true name, is it Jean-Claude? Is it Ranier? He laughs. Yes, he says. One must have a name, yes? Any name will do. All names will do. His accent is less distinctive tonight, Kristine thinks. Less musical. Possibly it's midwestern. Mid-southern. He tells Kristine he gets restless if he stays too long in one place. If someone tries to keep him. Can't breathe, can't sleep. Can't dream. That's why the great ocean calls to him: it's ever changing, unpredictable. Beautiful and yet capable of such destruction.

Yes, he admits to Kristine, he was a dancer. As a boy.

A beautiful boy, his elders called him. But this was long ago.

Kristine wants to say you're still beautiful. You must know that.

He injured himself; he was sixteen. The Achilles tendon in his left leg. An ugly accident that changed his life . . . From which he has never recovered.

"Now I limp. You've seen. I will always limp. It's to remind me of my mortality."

Kristine wants to protest, she hasn't seen. But of course she has. He knows.

Kristine confides in her lover: she, too, was injured as a dancer. A girl of thirteen. She'd had a number of minor injuries, the cumulative effect made continuing impossible. And so her life, too, was altered. She'd wanted to die . . .

Kristine tells Jean-Claude that she wasn't really talented. Not truly talented. Not like (she guesses) him.

Jean-Claude shrugs. Maybe.

He begins making love to her another time. Overhead the quarter moon slips in and out of shreds of cloud. Like illuminated cobwebs. The surf has quieted; the tide is out. Slapping, pulsing waves. He's sucking at her breasts that feel to her sensitive, milk-filled. He's making love to her, no longer aware of her: her name, her face. And Kristine ceases thinking of Jean-Claude. The "translator." The young man who limps. Who is ashamed of his infirmity.

Kristine cries aloud. Her fingers are shut tight in his hair. *This. Like this . . . I love you.*

No: Kristine is a realistic woman. A mother, a wife. She vows not to be deluded. Not to fall in love with this beautiful young man. As a married woman she has never had a lover. Hasn't wanted a lover. Hasn't been tempted to be unfaithful—

whatever, precisely, that word means. If she doesn't love Jean-Claude, if she has no intention of falling in love with Jean-Claude or continuing to see him after she leaves Rocky Harbor, how is she unfaithful to her husband? No more than she's unfaithful to Ceci. This overpowering feeling she has for Jean-Claude has nothing to do with anyone except Jean-Claude and herself.

Kristine has seized Jean-Claude's hair. In a delirium shutting her fists in his tough, springy hair.

It's been so long since Kristine has felt like this. That sensation flaring up like flame. Yet higher. Higher.

"Oh. God."

It's a powerful pleasure, but a mournful one.

Remaining with Kristine for the rest of the night. Keeping her awake, restless—*he's too young for me, of course*—after Kristine has returned quietly to her room in the sprawling oceanside house of her aunt and uncle. Windows open to the chilly sea breeze. To the fading quarter moon. *I know, I understand. He won't even remember my name.* After she's shaken the sand from her sandals and clothing, out of her hair. After she's showered to rid herself of the musty-sweet odor of lovemaking. Her lover's briny cologne smell. She pushes open the door to Ceci's room, adjacent to hers, and listens to the child's even breathing. Her love for Ceci seems more intense after her lovemaking with Jean-Claude. *The risk. I can't bear the risk. If I lost Ceci . . .* Parker would demand custody. Morally, Parker would have the right to demand custody. If Kristine were exposed as an unfit mother, *an adulteress.*

Kristine lies in bed, open-eyed. Why is she thinking such

thoughts? There will be no divorce, Parker will never know. No one will know. She and Ceci will be leaving Rocky Harbor within a few days, and the relationship with Jean-Claude will end. *It's Parker I love. My husband.* She's dreamy, very tired; still the dull-throbbing pleasure remains with her, deep in her womb. Like mourning.

12.

"Moira, did you hear? Such good news!"

Betsey's telephone voice is hushed, thrilled. Kristine, entering the kitchen in search of freshly brewed coffee, pauses to listen to her aunt's good news. She reasons that good news, unlike bad, is meant to be shared.

"Janet Feldman just called to say that police arrested Austin DiParma's lover last night at the Canadian border. He was headed for Montreal with 'friends.' I don't know any details, yet. Maybe they were accomplices. It's no surprise to me; I always thought that young man might be capable of . . . well, anything." There's a pause. Betsey says, sighing, "It's a terrible thing, yes, but such a relief to us that the murderer has been caught. Now we can all breathe a little more . . ."

Kristine realizes she's trembling. But she's smiling, too. *I knew. Of course, it was never Jean-Claude.*

As Aunt Betsey continues speaking on the phone, she waves at Kristine and points to the coffeepot on the stove. This is good news, yes! And this is a good morning: a clear sky like polished glass, lacy waves slap-slap-slapping against the shore like music.

In two days, Kristine and Ceci will be home in Boston, with Parker. Kristine, too, will be safe.

13.

The third time. Their meeting, their lovemaking.

"Jean-Claude! You're so beautiful."

"*You* are the beautiful one, Kristine."

This is a playful exchange. It's meant to be playful. Jean-Claude pronounces Kristine's name "Krees-*tine*" in his low caressing voice that will echo in Kristine's memory for hours.

Kristine bites her lower lip to keep from crying out. She doesn't want to love this man . . . She isn't going to love him, she's sure.

But she's beginning to be frightened, just a little, by the intensity of the passion she feels for him.

Absurd! Only a physical sensation, Kristine tells herself sternly.

She's a woman who has given birth to a child. *That* physical sensation, and the subsequent sensation of nursing, are the most memorable of her life.

She hasn't yet told Jean-Claude that she and Ceci are leaving soon. Maybe she won't tell him at all . . . She's concerned that she might break down. Reveal too much. Alarm and embarrass him. And her thirty-four-year-old face, contorted by weeping, will be ugly. *I can't risk that. None of it!*

How strong, Jean-Claude's arms. The hard, compact muscles of his thighs and legs. His back that's smooth-skinned except for the startling feel of the rib cage beneath, the taut skeleton. And, when they draw back to look at each other, his long-lashed eyes with their marble sheen.

"*You* are the beautiful one, Kristine."

Almost, Kristine will believe him.

14.

I can't. Can't risk the emotion.

Their last meeting isn't lovemaking, isn't even private. Of course, Jean-Claude doesn't know this is to be the last meeting.

Kristine descends to the beach below the Robbinses' house, where Jean-Claude is sitting in the sand, playing with Ceci. Jean-Claude, his long springy hair tied back in a pony-tail. He's removed his T-shirt. His black swim trunks fit his narrow hips tightly, bulging at the groin; there's a boyish innocence about Jean-Claude—he can make his own sexuality appear accidental, even inconsequential.

Kristine is uneasy, seeing Jean-Claude and Ceci together: these past several days, Ceci has clearly become captivated by the handsome, sweet-natured young man with the "sideways walk." (Ceci is old enough to know not to speak of such a thing in Jean-Claude's presence; she's acutely sensitive to physical impairments and social embarrassments of any kind. Kristine hasn't given any precise name to Jean-Claude's way of walking, his slight favoring of his left leg; she doesn't want to use the term "limp." It's too crude to apply to an individual of Jean-Claude's sophistication. *And he would be deeply wounded if he knew.*)

Ceci squeals with laughter. What an elaborate sand castle she and Jean-Claude are building! Kristine is impressed, and perhaps surprised, at the childlike concentration Jean-Claude brings to the task; his tender, scrupulous patience. He has pronounced himself *enchanté* with Ceci, which is flattering to Kristine but worrisome: for Ceci may be upset, at least initially, leaving her newfound friend Jean-Claude . . .

Jean-Claude glances up as Kristine approaches, while Ceci scoops up damp sand with a plastic play shovel. No one else is around: the Robbinses are elsewhere. Jean-Claude's gaze on Kristine is bold, intimate, hungry. There's a new air of ease, almost of proprietary ease, in his manner. He's a favorite of Betsey Robbins's and of other summer residents of the Cape; Kristine knows there's competition for his presence at parties. She stumbles a little in the sand. She's wearing a straw hat over her bobbed blond hair and an unbuttoned shift over a white bathing suit. She supposes she's a beautiful woman if not directly competing with younger, dazzlingly beautiful women or girls. "Hel-lo," Jean-Claude calls softly, in his inflected voice. Hel-*lo*. Kristine notes the sinewy tendons in her lover's sprawled legs. His narrow upper body that's covered in a wiry dark pelt, the hairs thicker and more prominent on his chest, forearms, legs. She feels a stir, a stab, of sexual desire. In the bright sunshine she feels faint. She knows she has made a mistake but she would not unmake it, not now. Not yet.

She and Ceci will be leaving the next day.

Jean-Claude is smiling suggestively at Kristine as she continues to descend the hill, now on the beach, approaching lover and daughter. The knowledge of their lovemaking of the previous night is in that smile. The knowledge of Kristine's sexual yearning, her cries, tears, desperation, is in that smile. Jean-Claude laughs.

"Kris-tine, *chérie*! Come join us, eh?"

Chérie. Kristine feels her face flush. Ceci can't know what *chérie* means, and yet Ceci will have heard, for an alert five-year-old enraptured with a new acquaintance hears every syllable that passes from his lips.

With a sly smile Jean-Claude pats the warm sand beside Ceci, in the crook of his spread legs, close beside his groin.

15.

He has other lovers. I mean nothing to him.

Kristine decides to leave Rocky Harbor without saying good-bye to Jean-Claude. Without leaving him an address, a phone number.

That way she won't have to know. Whether he would want to see her again . . . How he feels about her.

She's badly shaken by her behavior. Nothing in her life has prepared her for it. Standing on the redwood deck overlooking the beach, the ocean, staring into the distance where she'd first seen Jean-Claude emerge limping out of the mist. At her feet there's something moving; she gives a little cry and moves away. A small sand crab? A large hard-shelled beetle? Ceci runs to investigate. "Oh, Mommy. He's *hurt*."

Kristine sees it's a black roachlike beetle with numerous legs. Something has happened to it; its nerve center has been cut and its legs wriggle frantically.

Revulsed, Kristine kicks it over the edge of the deck onto the sand ten feet below. Ceci repeats, "Oh, Mommy. He was *hurt!*"

A mistake. But it's over now.

And so, relieved, Kristine brings Ceci back to Boston after their fifteen days on the Cape. Only fifteen. It has seemed much longer.

The large white brick colonial on Washburn Avenue. Her husband, Parker Culver, who has placed long-stemmed red roses in nearly every room to celebrate "my girls" returning. Kristine is so moved, she bursts into tears. She hugs Parker— "Oh, darling. We missed *you.*"

Next morning, walking through the rooms of the house, upstairs and down. Gratified at how beautifully furnished it is. How comfortable, tasteful, safe, her life is.

Is this it? This? The rest of my life?

She sees a large insect, a spider or a beetle, at the corner of a high ceiling; she's shocked and disgusted until she comes closer and see it's just a strand of cobweb, overlooked by her cleaning woman.

For the first few days Ceci is fretful, restless. She misses the ocean, the beach, a wading pool in the village where she played with other children. Daddy pulls her onto his lap, kisses her warm flushed cheeks, asks again if she missed him, and Ceci says, Yes Daddy, oh yes, Daddy, giggling, squirming out of his arms, and crying as she ducks away, "I miss where we were, too, Daddy! I miss Jean-Claude."

Ceci pronounces the name "J'nnn Claw."

Parker inquires, who's this "J'nnn Claw"? Kristine frowns as if trying to recall. She's tempted to say he was a neighbor child, or even a dog, but Parker and she will be seeing the Robbinses in the fall; she might be tripped up in a lie. She says, "'Jean-Claude.' Some Frenchman. One of my aunt's friends. She has so *many*."

16.

Kristine telephones her aunt in Rocky Harbor. To thank Betsey Robbins for her hospitality another time.

Kristine, vivacious and articulate as her aunt remembers her, inquires after a number of the people she met on the Cape. Casually she asks about Jean-Claude — "your translator friend."

Betsey says she hasn't seen much of Jean-Claude lately. He'd been staying with a friend in Rocky Harbor; now he's with another friend in Provincetown. "You know how they are. Men like that."

Kristine asks, "Men like — what?"

"Gay men."

But Jean-Claude isn't gay.

Kristine hears herself ask innocently, "Is Jean-Claude *gay*? I hadn't known."

Betsey says, laughing, "Yes, dear, of course Jean-Claude is gay. But possibly he's bisexual, too. Is that the word? — 'bisexual.' It's all very esoteric to people like Douglas and me, but it's a way of life, I suppose, with them."

Kristine would like to break off this conversation. But she can't, so abruptly.

Betsey continues, lowering her voice, "Now poor Austin DiParma was certainly *gay*. His former lover, this despicable Trim, is said to be *bisexual*. What a terrible death, to be strangled! To be strangled by someone you've loved." Betsey pauses, sighing. "This Trim is in jail, thank God. He denies everything of course. His friends insist he was with them at the time of the murder; he has an alibi. But he's failed a lie detector test. He's a heroin addict, I've heard. He's considered a flight risk: his bail is $500,000 and no one will pay it. Police are having trouble finding evidence to link him to the murder, though. We're all thinking they should call in more experienced detectives. We're anxious he might go free like so many murderers, and none of us will be safe."

Kristine manages to say, "But a man like that would never hurt you, Aunt Betsey. He doesn't love *you*."

When Kristine hangs up, she feels emptied out, depressed.

And how beautiful a woman she'd been, only the previous week.

17.

Kristine tells herself, *I love him.*

The man she married, the father of her daughter whom she adores. He's a good man, a kindly man . . . He seems to be making, as always, a good deal of money for himself and others. (When Ceci was born, Parker insured himself, in an extravagant gesture, for $2 million.) And he loves *her*.

Kristine often speaks to Parker about her two weeks on the Cape. She doesn't want to arouse his suspicions, but she can't resist recalling it. How she and Ceci had missed him and how it can't be good for him to work so obsessively. Though it's September now, maybe he could take a few days off and they could return to Rocky Harbor? . . . Parker says, to placate her, "Well, maybe. If it means so much to you." Kristine says, "Maybe what?" Parker says, "Maybe I'll take a break. When business settles down in a few weeks."

You let me go alone. It's your fault. You've caused this.

Kristine tries to feel desire for Parker. Sexual desire. Now she's returned to the white brick colonial on Washburn Avenue she feels as if she has never left. As if her body, entombed, has never left.

Thinking of the starving cats. Hurrying to their pie tins of food, pushing one another aside in their hunger, appetite. Eating swiftly, ravenously, without pleasure. But eating.

It's a fact that Parker Culver, too, is a man of some mystery. He hasn't cared to tell Kristine much about his previous, disastrous, marriage. He has never spoken at length about his heartbreak over his emotionally unstable son, though Kristine knows that he speaks with the boy, or with the boy's doctors, frequently. (Parker never visits his institutionalized son, however. The boy doesn't want to see him, becomes too emotional, violent.) The former wife, too, is a mystery. "Just a mistake, Kristine. The two of us married too young. I hadn't yet met *you*." Kristine doesn't want to think that her husband is humoring her, as he often humors Ceci.

He wants to protect me. I should leave it at that.

Yet there's a tough, unexpectedly stubborn side to Parker. He's courteous and courtly in company, especially with

women, but very different, Kristine knows, as a businessman.
And when they were newly in love, living together in a Bea-
con Street brownstone, Parker was mugged one night outside
the Boston train station, returning from a day trip to Washing-
ton; he'd refused to surrender his briefcase, a gift from Kristine: struck on the head by two young men, fallen and
bleeding on a snowy sidewalk, he'd held on to the briefcase
with both hands even as his assailants dragged him several
yards before giving up and running away.

When Kristine learned this, she was incredulous. "Parker,
how could you? Bartering your life for a *briefcase.*" Head
swathed in bandages, Parker protested, "Darling, it was a principle, not a briefcase." Kristine told him she'd buy him all the
briefcases he needed. "Please never behave so recklessly
again."

Parker promised Kristine, yes. Well maybe.

But after the mugging, Parker acquired a licensed hand-
gun for "home protection." Kristine was frightened of it: a
small .22-caliber pistol with a polished wood handle, which
she shrank from touching, still less holding. Parker said, chiding her, "Someday if you're home alone, honey, and someone
breaks in or tries to, you'll be damned grateful for a weapon.
And I'll be grateful you have it." He kept the pistol loaded. He
showed her how to click the safety mechanism on and off. The
gun was kept in a drawer of their bedside table; rarely did they
speak of it. From time to time with a kind of childlike fascination Kristine opened the drawer to see if it was still there, but
never once did she pick up the pistol.

Yet she believed she could use it, if required. If Parker's or
her life were at risk.

After Ceci was born, they moved to this residential neighborhood where there are far fewer break-ins and burglaries. Assaults, rapes, murders, are virtually unknown. All the houses are large, and all are protected by electronic surveillance and by private security guards. In these new quarters, the .22-caliber pistol has been relocated to a locked cabinet in the master bedroom, so there's no possibility of Ceci ever discovering it. By this time the Boston mugging has been nearly forgotten.

In fact Kristine hasn't seen the gun in years. She hopes that Parker has quietly gotten rid of it, but she doesn't intend to unlock the cabinet to find out.

Why is Kristine so frightened of the pistol? She has no idea.

If ever it's used. There must be a victim. There must be someone who pulls the trigger. Who?

Trying not to think of Jean-Claude.

Such long days. At last a week. Ten days since she and Ceci have returned from Rock Harbor. Soon Ceci will start school again: first grade. *That* will preoccupy Kristine.

Sometimes she sees Parker glancing at her quizzically. Maybe he has asked her a question she hasn't heard. Or she has said something to him he hasn't quite heard.

Parker has aged this summer, clearly. As if Kristine's betrayal has sucked at his energy. Unknowing, he's been ravaged. His white hair is less thick and healthy than it was only a few months ago; his ruddy face is more deeply lined, softening about the eyes, jowls. Kristine, staring at him, feels a stab of horror, suddenly seeing Jean-Claude's beautiful young face. The tight taut skin, the deep-set eyes fixed slyly upon her.

Chérie! *Come join us, eh?*

18.

In early September, twelve days after Kristine has returned home, what she hasn't anticipated happens.

The doorbell rings. *It's him.*

She's alone in the house. She has no choice but to open the door. Kristine stares at the tensely smiling young man for a long stunned moment before she reaches for him blindly as if to pull him inside before anyone sees him, and in the same instant he steps quickly forward, shutting the door behind him and gripping Kristine's shoulders so tight she winces with pain, as he begins to kiss her.

Not a friendly kiss—a kiss that hurts.

A kiss that, in myriad variation, will continue for hours.

"You didn't say good-bye, Kristine. Did you think you could just walk away? From *me*?"

Kristine apologizes, faltering. Her words are faint, weak, unconvincing. Jean-Claude laughs at her, on his feet and stretching. That luxuriant stretching of his supple, naked body. He prowls the bedroom as Kristine lies spent on the rumpled, dampened bed, in the lavender linen sheets, staring at him. Her lover. *I have a lover. Is this possible?* Kristine would not have thought she could respond sexually to Jean-Claude in such circumstances, but of course she did. *It can't be possible.* With a part of her mind she's thinking of course: she knew he would come for her, she has been summoning him, can't bear her life without him; with another part of her mind she's concerned that Ceci will be home soon from school, within forty minutes.

Jean-Claude has said that he wants to see Ceci again, but Kristine doesn't think that's a good idea.

"Didn't you miss me? You and the little one?"

"Jean-Claude, of course. Ceci talks about you all the time. But . . ."

"*He* would not have to know."

Like a dancer Jean-Claude moves restlessly about the bedroom. He's admiring of the furnishings, curious about what's in this closet (Kristine's things) and what's in that closet (Parker's things). He selects a necktie of Parker's, gazes at himself in a full-length mirror, boldly admiring himself, the tie draped around his neck. "I thank you for this, *chérie.*"

Kristine wonders if he's joking. "I don't think that's a good idea, Jean-Claude. Parker will . . ."

"Parker *won't.* Parker has more than enough neckties."

Jean-Claude tosses the tie, a silk striped blue, in the direction of his scattered clothing.

Kristine wants to protest but laughs instead.

It's true, Parker will never miss the tie. It was a gift of Kristine's, one of many.

Next, Jean-Claude tries the locked cabinet. Kristine tells him it's a Chinese antique, from Parker's family; it's permanently locked, the key lost. He asks about the rug; yes, it's another Chinese antique. He digs his bare toes into it, like a big lithe cat flexing its claws. "This house. This life. Weren't you going to invite me, Mrs. Culver?" But he isn't angry, he isn't even sulky; he's suffused with well-being. His angular young face glows. His hair is loose past his shoulders, wildly wavy, scintillant in slatted sunshine. The hair on his thin body glistens, his penis glistens, his skin is rosy, thrumming with blood. He has been moving about the bedroom and Kristine has been watching without comprehending at first that he isn't favoring his left leg.

Naively Kristine stammers, "Jean-Claude, your leg is — healed? The dance injury — ?"

Jean-Claude laughs. "Chérie, these things come and go. You didn't think Jean-Claude was a cripple for life, did you?"

He winks at her. He has spoken in a flat, mockingly lockjawed Boston accent. With a swagger he enters Parker's bathroom and doesn't trouble to shut the door completely as, with boisterous abandon, he urinates into the bowl.

It's then that Kristine thinks, *I've made the worst mistake of my life.* Like a many-legged beetle whose nerve center has been cut, the paralysis is multiplied with so many legs.

And later, after Jean-Claude has departed and Ceci has returned and Kristine is trying to concentrate on her daughter's eager recitation of her school day, Kristine thinks, sickened, *O God help me to make things right.*

19.

She won't, can't. Will not see him again.

Saying, in a faltering voice, "Yes, of course, Jean-Claude. I want to see you again, too. But . . ."

"And Ceci. I wish to see her, too."

Over the phone he's stubborn, childlike. He tells her he

knows where Ceci's school is; he has watched from his car, at the curb.

Kristine swallows hard. She tells herself this isn't a threat. Only just a remark, a statement. Maybe it isn't true. Jean-Claude seems harried, less sure of himself.

In another room Ceci is chattering with her father who has just arrived home. Kristine keeps her voice low. "I can't arrange for that, Jean-Claude. How can I ... My life ..."

"What of *my* life, Kristine? I won't be shut out."

Jean-Claude is staying on the Cape through September, he says. He has the use of a house near Provincetown while the owner is in Italy; a car, a Jaguar, is at his disposal. This remarkable information Jean-Claude tells Kristine negligently, as if it's of little worth. Whoever his friend and benefactor is, female or male, Jean-Claude doesn't indicate.

A *lover*, Kristine thinks. *Or lovers.*

She has to wonder, but she will not ask whether Jean-Claude was a lover of the murdered man.

He's saying impatiently, "We must be together, *chérie.* You want it, too."

Kristine protests, "I can't come out to the Cape. It's hours away. Now that Ceci is in school, my life is —"

"So, take her out of school for a day. I'll come to you there."

"Not here. Not in this house."

There's a pause. Jean-Claude is very quiet.

Of course in that house. If he wishes.

But Jean-Claude says, "Where, then?"

Kristine stammers the name of a hotel. One of the luxury Boston hotels on the Common.

———

I won't. He must be made to understand.

My life isn't my own now. Even to throw away.

Yet there is Kristine in dark glasses, a cloche disguising her hair, stepping into the lobby of the Four Seasons. Registering at the desk. Not daring to pay for the room with her Visa card: to her chagrin she has to pay cash.

The nature of a love affair bluntly defines itself when you understand that you're the one to pay.

But this will work. It's practical, pragmatic. Lovers meet in hotels. Luxury hotels. If luxury, then their lovemaking isn't sordid. Sumptuous pillows, satin quilt coverlets, gleaming white bathrooms ringed in lights like Christmas bulbs.

Kristine arrives first; Jean-Claude an hour later. She has thought she feared and disliked him, yet how hungrily they fall upon each other. Kristine thinks of the feral cats rushing to their food. Then she ceases thinking.

I do love him. It's hopeless.

After the first session of lovemaking, when Jean-Claude goes to use the bathroom, it's Kristine who belatedly double-locks the door and attaches the safety chain.

Again Jean-Claude walks with no sign of a limp. His nakedness is frank and un-self-conscious as that of a child.

Kristine decides she's being ridiculous. *He can't be a murderer, a strangler. Not Jean-Claude.*

His fingers at her throat. Tracing the blue artery below her jaw. They've shared a joint Jean-Claude brought from Province-town, a golden-glowing high, they're giddy as teenagers truant from school. Kristine shudders with pleasure as Jean-Claude settles his weight upon her, roughly. As they ease into each other. She feels her body opening to him. She's laughing though she's frightened, she's terrified and yet: her hands caress and clutch at the man's lean back, his sides. Slow-pumping buttocks. She wraps her legs around him; she's squeezing with her thighs. Lifting her head to kiss. Her face is strained, contorted, ugly with desire. Her mouth presses greedily against his, their tongues in each other's mouths. Gently at first his fingers close about her throat. Then more forcibly, and then gently again when she begins to choke, to fight him. *You know what I can do. If I want. What I can do, you can't prevent.* Kristine's back begins to arch like a bow. She's in a state of terror, of ecstasy. She wants it never to stop; she's thinking how if she had no one else in her life to claim her, no other man, if her husband were to disappear she might have this always, she might love Jean-Claude always, like this, every night like this.

On the brink of delirium Kristine feels hot tears spring like acid.

Not that afternoon in the Four Seasons. Nor next time, in the Marriott. But the following week in the Swissôtel Boston. After lovemaking, after finishing most of a bottle of champagne from the minibar, Jean-Claude leans on his elbow above Kristine and places the flat of his hand against her throat as if to calm an overly excited animal, saying, "How much is he worth, *chérie*? Your 'Parker.'"

20.

Now Jean-Claude is always in Kristine's thoughts.

In this drunken-balmy warmly humid September in

Boston. Even when Kristine is speaking to others, it's Jean-Claude to whom she speaks. Even when she gives every impression of being "normal," "herself"—smiling, talking, listening, concentrating—it's Jean-Claude with whom she's preoccupied. Like a woman with a secret pregnancy.

How much is the man worth, his estate, his life insurance?

Jean-Claude, I don't know.

Then make a guess, chérie!

Driving Ceci to school in the morning, she's distracted thinking of Jean-Claude. Of this conversation. Of what he's asking, demanding. Like a dream it unfolds, yet Kristine isn't the dreamer. Kristine is in the dream, helpless. A man's slow caressing hands, his fingers at her throat, the deep shuddering pleasure of his lovemaking. She answers Ceci vaguely, mechanically. "Yes, honey. No. I don't know." She has seen, or imagines she has seen, the bottle-green sleek Jaguar in the rearview mirror of her car, following a half block behind.

More than once, Kristine has seen this car. Or imagines she has.

It isn't a threat, though. She doesn't think so. Jean-Claude would never wish to hurt her and Ceci.

She has not told Jean-Claude that Parker is insured for $2 million. She has said she doesn't know such things. She isn't one to know such things. She doesn't want to know such things.

Then find out, Kristine. We need to know.

It's true: if something happened to Parker, if Kristine were free, a young widow . . . Ceci adores Jean-Claude, still asks after him. *J'nnn Claw.* Ceci loves her father, too, but (as Jean-Claude has said) children are adaptable, adjust themselves to change more readily than adults; when Jean-Claude's father disappeared from his life, Jean-Claude simply ceased after a while to miss him.

But what could possibly happen to Parker Culver? Kristine loves him, refuses to think of him hurt . . . injured—dead.

Even to please her rapacious lover. *Even to please herself.*

A mugging, maybe. A botched mugging. The mugger shoots his victim and flees.

Another possibility. Kristine and Parker are alone together at the shore, at Rocky Harbor, or anywhere in an isolated area; they're approached by a stranger and there's an attack of some kind: Parker is attacked; Parker is fatally injured, Kristine is the terrified witness; Kristine survives. The weapon might be a knife, a heavy rock. (Gloved) hands.

Kristine can't absorb what she has heard.

Hands? Do you mean . . . your hands, Jean-Claude?

Don't you love my hands, chérie? *I think so.*

Like a mischievous boy, Jean-Claude lifted his hands to be examined, admired. Stretching the long fingers. For the first time Kristine saw how disproportionately long his fingers were; how large his hands, like his feet, almost ungainly, ugly.

"No. This is impossible. *No.*"

Kristine has spoken aloud. She's forgotten where she is, who is sitting close beside her in the car.

In a frightened voice, Ceci says, "Mommy, what? Mommy *what?*"

21.

Yes. You will see me again, Kristine. Many times.

I'm a married woman, a mother. I love my family . . .

of passion. "Are you distracted by something, Kristine?" Parker asks, more hurt than annoyed. Kristine murmurs no, no! Parker is out of breath, very warm. Kristine squirms uncomfortably beneath his weight. He's so much heavier than Jean-Claude. And clumsier. Kristine places the flat of her hand against his fleshy chest, feels the accelerated beat of his heart.

He's old. An old man. My lover is young.

Kristine bursts into tears.

"Kristine, what is it? Tell me."

And so, in Parker's arms, Kristine tells.

Hears herself tell him that she misses the ocean . . . She misses the wild beauty of the Cape . . . She feels cheated of what might have been an idyllic time with him last month, while he'd stayed away in Boston, obsessed with his work. No break for months. "As if we aren't multimillionaires already!" Kristine says. Parker strokes her shoulders, her hair. He's taken by surprise by Kristine's emotion. She has never spoken to him in quite this way. Kristine tells him that Ceci misses him, too. Ceci rarely sees him. Their time in Rocky Harbor was shadowed for Ceci because her father hadn't been there. The more Kristine speaks, the more convinced she is of the truth of her words. In fact, she's angry with Parker. Furious with Parker. *If you'd been with us — if you'd watched over your family — none of this would have happened; I wouldn't have fallen in love with a dangerous man.* Yet how girlish is Kristine's enthusiasm, how innocently she speaks: "In the early morning Ceci and I hiked along the beach, I could hardly hold her back! You know what she's like. But sometimes I hiked alone, for miles, north along the shore, and inland in the dunes, and I found myself thinking of you, darling. Of our marriage. How much I love you. How much I owe you. Yes, I worry about you sometimes: your health, your overwork. I wanted you in Rocky Harbor with me; I was so lonely." Parker is deeply moved. He holds her tight; he murmurs, "Kristine, darling. I had no idea."

Kristine shuts her eyes. This man's comforting arms! She will be protected by him, saved by him.

Seeing herself hiking along the edge of the shore. Her bare feet sink sensuously into the damp sand. Wind whips her hair. She's breathless with excitement, apprehension. In the near distance, partially obscured by mist and sea spray, a figure appears: a male figure in silhouette. A young or youngish man, with a slight limp. Long-haired, a stranger. At least, no one Kristine has yet met. He's carrying something over his shoulder, a backpack? For the first time Kristine wonders what is in that backpack.

Now the young man squats in the lapping surf. Washing hands, forearms, face. Kristine wonders what he is washing off.

Parker is saying, eagerly, "Why don't we go back to the Cape for a weekend, darling? I feel guilty as hell, and a fool, what you've been telling me. I'll take next Friday off; we'll have three days. The three of us. It's after Labor Day now, it's the off-season. I'd rather not stay with your relatives this time — why don't we stay at an inn? I'll book us into an ocean-side place in Provincetown. How does that sound, darling? Romantic?"

Kristine's lips move numbly. "Oh, Parker. Yes. I can't think of anything more romantic."

23.

God help me to make things right.

So it happens that Kristine, Ceci, and Parker have come to Cape Cod in the last week of September. So it happens that, at dusk of their second night, Kristine has talked Parker into a hike along the shore, before dinner; they'd had a late leisurely lunch in Provincetown, where they're staying at a small bed-and-breakfast inn overlooking the Atlantic.

Though they declined to stay with the Robbinses, the older couple is babysitting Ceci for the night so that Kristine and Parker can have a romantic evening alone.

Walking hand in hand like young lovers. In this gusty, wet air.

Seeing them, you might wonder: A trim, vigorous-looking older man with his daughter?

Kristine walks briskly; Kristine smiles. Yet she's a sleep-walker. She has seen by her watch what time it was when they left the inn; she won't glance again at her watch.

It's the aftermath of a shower. The air is chilly but wonderfully fresh. This beautiful wild landscape. The choppy, white-capped waves. Parker in khakis, denim jacket, cap, is marveling at the Cape Cod landscape, how good it is to be alive. How happy he is he's come here after all. How grateful to Kristine for suggesting it.

I'll take care of this, chérie.

You know it's what you want, too.

In a pocket of Kristine's jacket she has hidden the .22-caliber pistol. How small the weapon is, how compact. And heavy. Kristine found the key, unlocked the Chinese cabinet, and there it was.

Someday you'll be damned grateful for a weapon. And I'll be grateful you have it.

Kristine examined the gun, turning it in her shaky fingers. Was it loaded? Would it fire? It hasn't been fired, so far as she knew, in years.

It's a chance she will have to take. For she has no choice.

She will say, afterward, in stammering explanation: she'd been anxious about being mugged on this trip to Cape Cod, such an isolated place in the off-season. She will say she has been thinking of the yet-unsolved murder of a Rocky Harbor resident. She will say that Parker bought the gun after he was attacked nine years ago in Boston and she's never quite forgotten the incident, the shock. She will say that Parker hadn't known she was bringing the gun with them; he would have objected. He would have thought her anxiety groundless.

That afternoon they'd had lunch in a seafood restaurant on a Provincetown wharf. The three of them. The Culver family.

Parker in a sentimental mood, drinking wine to celebrate the occasion. "Kristine, Ceci. My beautiful girls. Y'know— you have made me so happy."

Kristine laughed, blushing. Ceci, embarrassed, hid her face and peered at Daddy through her fingers.

Now Ceci is with her doting great-aunt Betsey and great-uncle Douglas. At about this time she's probably watching a children's video with one or both of them, or reading aloud one of her talking-cat books. Or maybe they're having a light supper in the dining room overlooking the beach. When Kristine told Jean-Claude she was arranging for Ceci to stay with the Robbinses on the crucial night, he told her he'd had the same thought exactly, what to do with Ceci that night. *You see, we think alike,* chérie, *eh?* Spoken in Jean-Claude's flat mock–New England accent.

Kristine hasn't had to urge Parker to come out for this walk. He seems to be thriving in the brisk cold air. Gripping her hand tight in his. *I'll be waiting. Bring him. Then stand back. Don't speak. When it's over, you'll know.* In the shadows of the dunes there are scurrying furry creatures. Parker thinks they might be rats, but Kristine says, "No, those are feral cats. There's a colony; they live around here. Some of them are very beautiful."

Ahead is what appears to be a deserted beach. Wet, hard-packed sand. Frothy surf. The sky is marred with bruised-looking rain clouds. Large waves crash against the shore, spray flies over boulders like an explosion. Tears streak Kristine's cheeks.

Parker says, "You're cold, darling. We'd better turn back."

"No," Kristine says. "We can't turn back."

Tell Me You Forgive Me?

1.   The Elms ElderCare Center, Yewville, NY. October 2000.

October 16, 2000.
To my Dear Daughter Mary Lynda who I hope will forgive me,

I am writting this because it has been 40 yrs ago this day, I saw by the calender, that I sent you down into that place of horror & ugliness. I did not mean to injure you, Darling. I could not foresee. I was an ignorant & blind woman then, a drinker. I know you are well now & recovered for yrs. but I am writting to ask for your forgiveness?

Darling, I know you are smiling & shaking your head as you do. When your Mother worries too much. I know you're saying there is nothing to forgive, Mother!

Maybe that is not so, Darling.

Tho' I am fearful of explaining. & maybe cant find the words to explain, what was so clear 40 yrs. ago & <u>had to be done</u>.

Its strange for me to write this, & to know that when you read it, these words one by one that take me so long to write,

I will be "gone." I am asking Billy (the big Jamaican girl with cornrow hair) to abide by my wishes & save this letter for you & I believe she will, Billy is one of the few to be trusted here.

If you wanted to speak to me after reading this, tho', you could not. This seems wrong.

You have forgiven me for that terrible time, Mary Lynda, I suppose. You have never blamed me as another daughter might.

No one ever accused me, I think. Not to my face?

(Except your father of course. & all the Donaldsons. I'm sorry, Mary Lynda, you bear that name yourself, I know! But you are more your Mother's daughter than his, everybody has always said how Mary Lynda takes after Elsie. Our eyes & hair & our way of speaking.)

(I think of your father sometimes. Its strange, I did injury to Dr. Donaldson also, yet it never worried me. I thought— He is a man, he can take care of himself. I'm not proud that when I was young if I ceased loving a man or caring for a woman friend, I seemed almost to forget them overnight. I'm not proud of this, Darling, but its your Mother's way.)

So many times this past year, since I have been moved to this wing of the Center, tho' its only across the lawn from the other place—I wanted to take your hand, Darling, and tell you the truth in my heart. Not what you have forgiven me for but something more. Something nobody has guessed at, all these years! But I did not, for I feared you would not love me then. That was why I was so quiet sometimes, after the chemo especially. When I was sick, & so tired. Yet to be forgiven, I must confess to you. So I am writting in this way. A coward's way I know, after I am "gone."

There are things you say in quiet you cant say face to face. I am not going to live much longer, and so it is time.

Last year I think it was April, when the Eagle House was razed, & you came to visit & were "not yourself"—upset & crying—I wanted to tell you then, Darling. & explain about Hiram Jones. (Is that a name you remember?) But I saw you needed comfort from your Mother, not "truth." Not just then.

After 40 yrs.! I have not been downtown to see South Main Street since coming to this place. Since my surgery etc. That part of old Yewville was meant to be "renewed"—but the state money gave out, I heard. So there's vacant lots & weeds between buildings, rubble & dust. The Lafayette Hotel & Midland Trust & the library & post office are still there, but the Eagle House is gone, & the rest of that block.

So I try to picture it in my head. Its only 3 miles from here, but I will never see it, I think.

I know its a childish way to think, he is buried beneath rubble. & his bones are in that debris.

The Elms is a good place for me, I think. I'm grateful to you, Darling, for helping me to live here. God knows where I would be living with just Medicare & Social Security! I don't complain like the other "oldsters." Tho' I am only 70, the youngest in this cottage. The oldest is that poor thing Mrs. N. you've seen, blind & with no teeth, "deaf & can't hear" etc. Lately they haven't brought Mrs. N. into the sun room even, which is a pity for her, but a relief to us. She is 99 yrs. old & everybody is hoping she will live to 100—except Mrs. N., she has no idea how old she is or even her name. There are 3 or 4 of us who are "progressing" (as the doctors call it, but this means the disease not us!) & those of us who are "just plain old." I am out of my time element here, because I am still young (in my mind) but the body has worn out, I know Darling its sad for you to see me, your Mother who used to be "beautiful" & vain of it.

Now I am vain of you, Darling. My M.D. daughter I can boast of to these other old women, the ones who are my friends.

I love the pretty straw hat you brought for me to cover my head, & the bluebird scarf.

Are dead people lonely I wonder?

I have been writting—writing?—this damn letter for a week & it gets harder. Like trying to see into the darkness when you are in the light. The future when I will be "gone" is strange to me though I know its coming. When some other sick woman will have my room here & my bed.

You'd be surprised, we dont talk much of God here. You'd think so, but no. Its hard to believe in a universe inside these walls & lasting beyond a few days' time. Do I have a fear of God's judgment for my sins, somebody might ask. No Darling, I do not. Remember your Grandaddy Kenelly who laughed when God was spoken of. It was all just b.s. invented to keep weak people in line, Daddy believed.

Hell, God better believe in me. I'm a man, he'd say.

By that Daddy meant that man is more important than God because it was man who invented God, not the other way around.

Only just I wish I had more courage.

Daddy has been dead a long time but to me he's more real than the people in this place. I talk to him & hear his voice in my head. Since 1959! Thank God, Daddy never lived to be an old man here in The Elms. Imagine your Grandaddy 100 yrs. old, deaf & blind & not knowing his own name or where the hell he is. He was only 55 when he died — thats <u>young</u>. How Time plays tricks on us. My handsome Daddy always older than me, now he'd be younger. When he died, I mean. I dont think of these things if I can.

Billy says I should not pass away with secrets in my heart. So I am trying, Darling.

Is Hiram Jones a name you remember, Darling? Maybe I have asked you this already.

However you were told your Grandaddy died, its best to think it was an accident like a roll of the dice. Nothing more.

Wish I could undo the bad thing that happened to <u>you</u>, Darling.

You were only 10 yrs. old. I cant think why I would send you into that terrible place like I did, to see where that terrible man had got to. I was drinking in those days & missing my father & that caused me to forget my duties as a Mother.

Now its a later time. You are a M.D. like Dr. Donaldson & so you know about my case, more than I would know myself. Tho' oncology is not your field. (I hate that word, its ugly!) But this is why I am not afraid of dying: when I had my surgery & my mind went out, it was OUT. Like a lightbulb switched OFF. When I had you, Darling, I was very young & ignorant & believed I was healthy & went into labor not guessing what it would be, 18 hrs. of it, but afterward I "forgot" as they say but I knew what true pain was & would not wish to relive it. But this, when you're OUT, is different. The 3 times I was operated on, each time it was like Elsie Kenelly ceased to exist.

So if your dead and theres no pain you cease to exist. If theres no pain theres nothing to fear.

Darling, I am a coward I guess. Too fearful of telling you what I have wished to, to beg your forgiveness. I'm sorry.

But in this envelope I am leaving a surprise for you. These ivory dice, remember? From your Grandaddy you didn't know too well. These dice he'd keep in his pocket & take out & roll "to see what they have to tell me"—he'd say. They were Daddy's Good Luck Dice he'd got in Okinowa—Okinawa?—that island in the Pacific where the U.S. soldiers were waiting to be shipped to Japan to fight & a lot of them would have died (Daddy always said) except the war ended with the A-bomb. So Daddy said these were Good Luck Dice for him. He'd toss away his medals but not these. At the Eagle House he'd roll his friends for drinks. 7 times out of 10 he'd win, I swear. The other men didnt know how the hell Willie Kenelly did it but the dice werent fixed, as you will see. Yet Daddy would snap his fingers & sometimes it seemed the dice would obey him, who knows why.

After my mother died we had some happy years, your Grandaddy & me. Maybe Daddy had a drinking problem but thats not the only thing in life, believe me.

Theres something about dice being tossed, if they're classy dice, it makes my backbone shiver even now. As soon as the dice fly out of your hand & its an important bet, & everybody watching. I hope you will put away these dice for safekeeping, Mary Lynda. They're pure ivory which is why they've changed color. Daddy & I would roll them for fun, & one night he pressed them in my hand (in June 1959, I will always remember) & I knew this must be a sign of something but could not have guessed that Daddy would be dead in 5 weeks.

& Bud Beechum would be dead in a little over a year.

& Hiram Jones (maybe this is a name you dont remember) would be dead in a few years.

Well! Its too late now, Darling. For any of this, I guess. Even for feeling sorry. Like your Grandaddy said theres nothing to do with dice except "toss 'em."

Your loving Mother,
Elsie Kenelly

2.   Yewville, NY. April 11, 1999.

A fire. It looked like a fire: not flames but smoke.

Clouds of pale dust-colored smoke drifting skyward in erratic surges, like expelled breaths. In the downtown area of Yewville, just across the river, it looked like.

She was driving to visit her mother in the nursing home. She'd delayed the visit for weeks. Poor Elsie who'd once been a beautiful, vain woman, with that wavy shoulder-length dark blond hair, now she was a chemo patient, the hair gone, and what sprouted from her scalp was fuzzy gray like down or mold you had an instinct to wipe off with a damp cloth.

Mary Lynda, no: I don't mind.

I'm lucky to be alive, see?

Mary Lynda, the daughter, wasn't so sure. She was a doctor, and she knew what was in store for her mother, and she wasn't so sure.

She'd had a driver's license for more than thirty years but the fact was, which she could never have explained to anyone, in all those years she'd never once driven in downtown Yewville. She'd managed to avoid South Main Street—the

historic district—on the western bank of the Yewville River.
Not that it was a phobia; it was a conscious choice. (Or maybe,
yes, it was a phobia, and it soothed her vanity to tell herself
it was a conscious choice.) There were circuitous routes to
bring her to other parts of Yewville and its suburbs without any
need to navigate the blocks closest to the river; though, from
childhood, with the vividness of impressions formed in childhood, she could instantly recall the look of South Main Street:
the grandiose Lafayette Hotel with its sandstone facade and
many gleaming windows; Franklin Brothers, once Yewville's
premiere department store, with its brass flagpole and fluttering American flag; the old stone city hall, for decades the
downtown branch of the Yewville Public Library; Mohawk
Smoke Shop, King's Café, Ella's Ladies' Apparel, Midland
Trust, Yewville Savings & Loan with its luminous clock tower;
the Old Eagle House Tavern, gray stone, cavelike inside, with
its faded sign in the shape of a bald eagle in flight, wings out-
spread, talons ready to grip prey . . . She hadn't seen this sign
in forty years but could see it now, swift as a headache. She
could hear the sign creaking in the wind.

OLD EAGLE HOUSE TAVERN, EST. 1819.

For some reason, she was going to drive through the
downtown, today. The historic district. Why not? She was curious about the smoke, and what South Main Street looked
like after so many years.

She'd been there last in 1960. Now it was 1999.

The bridge over the river had been totally changed, of
course. Now four lanes, reasonably modern. Her car's tires
hummed on the steel grate surface. There didn't seem to be
any fire, though. No fire trucks or sirens. Main Street traffic

was being diverted into a single slow-moving lane overseen by burly men shouting through megaphones. CONSTRUCTION AHEAD. DEMOLITION WARNING. She smelled a powdery-gritty dust; her eyes smarted. *Damn*—jackhammers. She hated jackhammers. Her heartbeat began to quicken in panic; such loud noises upset her. What was she trying to prove, driving here, when there was no one to prove it to, no witness. She vowed she wasn't going to mention this to Elsie.

I'm not that girl. She was someone else.

The girl had been ten at the time. When she'd gone down into the cellar of the Eagle House that smelled of beer, mildew, dirt. The stink of urine from the men's room. She'd been sent by Momma to see where the proprietor Bud Beechum "had got to."

Now, she was forty-nine years old. She hadn't lived in Yewville for decades. She'd graduated, valedictorian of her high school class, in 1968. She'd gone to college in Rochester and medical school in New York City. She was Dr. Donaldson—she had a general practice in Montclair, New Jersey. She was fully an adult; it was ridiculous that Yewville should reduce her to trembling like a child.

In her life away from Yewville, Mary Lynda was a name she rarely heard. Among friends and colleagues she was simply Mary. An old-fashioned name, a name so classic it was almost impersonal, like a title. She liked the formality of Dr. Donaldson though it was her (deceased) father's name, too. Both her parents had called her Mary Lynda while she was growing up. Never had she had the courage to tell them how much she hated it.

Mary Lynda! Born in 1950, you could guess by the name.

Sweet and simpering in gingham, like June Allyson. Crinkly crinoline skirts and pin curls, weirdly dark lipstick. Don't hurt me; please just love me, I am so good.

Mary Donaldson visited her mother in Yewville two or three times a year. They spoke often on the phone. Or fairly often. Until just recently Elsie had lived by herself, but she'd had a run of bad luck in her midsixties—health problems, financial problems—so she'd allowed Mary to persuade her to move into The Elms Retirement Village, which was a condominium complex for senior citizens in a semirural suburb of Yewville; when Elsie's health began to deteriorate, she moved into a nursing home on the premises. ("Next move," Elsie quipped, "is out the door, feet first." Mary winced, pretending not to hear.) When Elsie had been younger and in better health, Mary bought her a plane ticket once or twice a year so that she could come visit her in Montclair; they went to matinees and museums in New York; they were judged to be "more like sisters than mother and daughter," as Mary's friends liked to say, as if this remark might be flattering to Mary. Of course it wasn't true: Mary looked nothing like Elsie, who was an intensely feminine woman with a full, shapely body carried upright as a candle, dark blond hair that bobbed enticingly, flirty eyes, and a throaty voice. ("Don't be deceived by Mother's 'personality,'" Mary said. "Mother is a dominatrix." Her friends laughed; no one believed her for an instant.) Well into her midsixties Elsie could pass for a youthful fifty. Though she'd been a heavy smoker and drinker, her skin was relatively unlined. She'd had only two husbands—Mary's father was the first—but numerous lovers who'd treated her, on the whole, as Elsie said, not too badly. But now, at last, life was catching up with her. Her childhood girlfriends were white-haired, wrinkled grandmothers; her boyfriends were elderly, shrunken, or dead. In her late sixties things began to go wrong with Elsie. She had varicose vein surgery on her legs. She had surgery to remove ovarian cysts. Arthritis in her lower spine, bronchitis that lasted for weeks in the cold damply windy climate of upstate New York. For much of her adult life she'd been a drinker, joined Alcoholics Anonymous in her early thirties and quit smoking at about the same time. ("I must have thought I'd live forever," Elsie said ruefully. "Now look!") In fact, Mary was in awe that her mother who'd taken such indifferent care of herself, who'd avoided doctors for decades, was in such relatively good health for a woman of her generation and had managed even to keep her bright upbeat temperament. *Not a dominatrix: a seductress. Her power is more insidious.*

Driving with maddening slowness on Main Street, Mary thought of these things. And of the past, coiled snaky and waiting (for her? that wasn't likely) beyond the facades of these old, now shabby, buildings. The Lafayette Hotel; the ugly discount store that had once been classy Franklin Brothers; the old city hall which hadn't changed much, at least on the outside; the Mohawk Smoke Shop, still in business, though with a sign in its window— ADULT X-RATED VIDEOS; the old Yewville Savings & Loan with the clock tower that had always seemed gigantic, a proud glowing clock face to be seen for miles, though in fact, as Mary now saw, to her surprise, the granite tower was no higher than the second floor of the bank building.

But where was Ella's, and where was King's Café, and where was . . . the Eagle House Tavern?

Mary stared, confused. Half the block was being razed. Only the shells of some buildings remained. Stone and brick. Rubble in heaps. Like an earthquake. A bombing. She was tasting dust, swallowing dust; she steeled herself against the noise of jackhammers that made her heart race as if with amphetamine. There came a wrecking ball swinging through air like a deranged pendulum and at once a wall of weatherworn stone collapsed in an explosion of dust.

Go look for him, honey. I'll wait out here.

Mommy, why? I don't want to.

Because I'm asking you, Mary Lynda.

I don't want to, Mommy. I'm afraid . . .

Go on, I said! Damn you! Just see where that bastard has got to.

Mommy's face was bright and hard and her mouth twisted in that way Mary Lynda knew. Her mother had been drinking; it was like fire inside her that could leap out at you—and burn.

Mommy wanted to know where Bud Beechum was, exactly. For he wasn't in the tavern when they went inside. When Mommy pushed Mary Lynda inside. Bud Beechum owned the Eagle House. He'd been a friend of Grandaddy Kenelly when Grandaddy was alive, and he was a friend of Mary Lynda's mother, too. Somehow, the families were friendly. Beechums, Kenellys. Bud Beechum's wife was Elsie's cousin. They'd all been "wild" together in high school. Just to remember those times, they'd start laughing, shaking their heads. The child Mary Lynda was uneasy around Beechum. He had a way of looking at you, smirking and rubbing at his teeth with the tip of his tongue.

Mary Lynda was uneasy around most adult men, except her father and the Donaldsons: they were different. They were soft-spoken, "nice." When Elsie divorced Timothy Donaldson, she was given custody of Mary Lynda and so Mary Lynda saw her father only on weekends.

Bud Beechum had been dead now for almost forty years. Yet you could imagine his big chunky bones in the cellar of that old building. His broken-in skull the size of a bucket amid the rubble and suffocating dust.

Mommy, no. Mommy, don't make me.

Mary Lynda, do as you're told.

Mommy's voice was scared, too. And Mommy's fingers gripping Mary Lynda's narrow shoulders, pushing her forward.

It was now that Mary did the unexpected thing: as soon as she was safely past the traffic congestion on South Main, she turned left on a street called Post, and drove back toward the river and, with an air of adventure, a sense of recklessness, parked in the lot, now mostly deserted and weedy, behind the old Franklin Brothers store.

Dr. Donaldson, why? This is crazy.

She wasn't a woman of impulse, usually. She was a woman who guarded her actions as she guarded her emotions. Not for Mary Donaldson the dice-tossing habits of her charming old drunk of a grandfather Kenelly.

And so it was strange that in her good Italian shoes, in her taupe linen pantsuit (Ann Taylor), her hair stylishly scissor-cut, she was parking in downtown Yewville and hurrying to join a small crowd of people gathered to stare at the destruction of a few old, ugly buildings. Coughing from the dust — and maybe there was asbestos in that dust—yet she was compelled by curiosity, like the others, most of whom were elderly retired men, with here and there some women shoppers, some teenagers and children. (Thank God, no one who seemed to recognize Mary Lynda Donaldson.)

His bones in that rubble. Ashes.

Toxic to inhale!

Of course this was ridiculous. Bud Beechum had been properly buried. Forty years ago.

The Eagle House was being razed, spectacularly. The very earth shook as the wrecking ball struck. "Wow! *Fan-tas-tic.*" A teenaged boy with spiky hair spoke approvingly. His girl snuggled against him, wriggling her taut little bottom as if the demolition of the Eagle House had a private, salacious meaning. Mary saw that the girl was hardly more than fourteen, her brown hair streaked in maroon and green, one nostril and one eyebrow pierced. She was pale, wanly pretty, though looking like a pincushion. Very thin. One of her tiny breasts, the size and color of an oyster, was virtually exposed, her tank top hung so slack on her skinny torso. She wore faded jeans and, in this place of litter and broken glass, was barefoot.

That afternoon, Elsie had picked up Mary Lynda from school. She'd driven here. She'd parked her car, the yellow Chevy, in this lot, though closer to the rear of the Eagle House. *Why are we here, Mommy?* Mary Lynda asked. *Because that bastard owes me. He owed your Grandaddy; he's got to pay.* Mary Lynda knew the symptoms: her mother's eyes were dilated; her hair hung lank in her face. When she hiccupped, Mary Lynda could smell her sweetish-sour breath.

———

"What's happening here?" Mary asked in the bright, friendly voice of a visitor to Yewville who'd just wandered over from the Lafayette Hotel. The boy with the spiky hair said, with an air of civic pride, "They're tearing these old dumps down. They're gonna build something new." His girl said, smirking, "About time, huh?" Mary had to press her fingers against her ears, the jackhammer was so loud. Such noises enter the soul and may do permanent damage. She saw that beyond the adjacent lot was an unpaved alley that led toward the river. This was the lot in which her mother had parked that day. Debris was piled on both sides of the alley, some of it Styrofoam of the white glaring hue of exposed bone. Mary was smiling, or trying to smile, but something was wrong with her mouth. "Ma'am? You okay?" The teenagers were suddenly alert, responsible. You could guess they had mothers for whom they were sometimes concerned. They helped Mary sit down—for suddenly Mary's knees were weak, her strength was gone like water rapidly draining away—on a twisted guardrail. The deafening jackhammer made her bones vibrate as she sat dazed, confused, breathing through her mouth. Her legs were clumsily spread, thank God for the trousers. She was wiping her nose with her fingers. Was she crying? Saying earnestly, "A man was found dead in that building, a long time ago. A little girl found him. Now I can tell her the cellar is gone."

3. Rochester, NY. 1968/Barnegat, NJ. 1974.

For years she would see a male figure, not fallen but "resting"—prone on the floor, for instance—inside a room she was passing; in the blurry corner of her eye she saw this figure but had no sense that the figure meant death. Because when she looked, there was no figure, of course. One night in Rochester, working late in the university library, she was swiftly passing a dimly lit lounge and though it had been eight years since she'd seen Beechum's body in that cellar and she'd rarely thought of it since, now suddenly she was seeing it again, in terrifying detail, more clearly than she'd seen it at the time. *He's here. How'd he come to be here?* Always a logical young woman, even in her panic, she reasoned that if Bud Beechum's body was actually here in the University of Rochester library, so long as there was no link between the body and Mary Lynda Donaldson, a premed student, she could not be blamed.

Her instinct was to stop dead in her tracks and stare into the room; yet since she knew (she knew perfectly well) that no one was lying there on the carpet, she averted her eyes and fled.

No. Don't look. Nothing!

She believed it was an act of simple discipline, fighting off madness. As an adult you took responsibility for your life; you were no-nonsense. High grades at the university, always high grades. She was premed after all. Ignore the politics of the era. Assassinations, the Vietnam War, the despairing effort of her generation to "bring the war home." For always in history there have been wars and destruction and people dying to no purpose, if not here then elsewhere, if not elsewhere then (possibly) here. Count your blessings, Mary Lynda, her mother often consoled her—or maybe it was a mother's simple command—and it made sense. (Elsie had joined AA; Elsie hadn't had a drink stronger than sweet apple cider in years, laughing, *Can you believe it?*) So private madness seemed to Mary Lynda the worst nonsense. Stupid and self-hurtful as dropping acid or laughing like a hyena (that belly laugh of Bud Beechum's, how she'd hated it) at someone's funeral, or tearing off your clothes and running in the street when you didn't even look good, small breasts and soft hips and tummy, naked. Fighting off madness seemed to Mary Lynda like beating out a fire with a heavy blanket or canvas — "Something anybody could do if they tried."

It was her opinion that both Kennedys could have prevented being assassinated if they'd been more prudent in their behavior. Martin Luther King, too. But she kept this opinion to herself.

One of the men she'd loved, and would live with intermittently for several years in her late twenties, she'd seen lying in the sun in khaki shorts, bare-chested, amid sand and scrub grass at the Jersey shore. She was an intern at Columbia Presbyterian and lived a life far from Yewville and from her mother. Seeing the boy sleeping in the sun, sprawled on the sand, she stared, like one under a spell. She went to him, knelt over him, stroked his hair. The boy was, in fact, a young man, her age, with long pale lashes and long lank hair women called moon-colored. At Mary's touch he opened his eyes that were sleepy but sharpened immediately when he saw who she was: another man's girl. And when he realized what Mary was doing in her trancelike state, where her hand crept, he came fully awake and pulled her down on top of him, his hands gripping her head. His kisses were hard, hungry. Mary shut her eyes that hurt from the sun; she would see what came of this.

4. Yewville, NY. 1960–1963.

Those years of Elsie chiding, frightened. *Mary Lynda, talk to me! This is just some sort of game you're playing isn't it!*

At first they believed her inability to speak might have something to do with her breathing patterns. She breathed rapidly, usually through her mouth. This precipitated hyperventilation. (Elsie learned to enunciate this carefully: *"Hy-per-ven-ti-lation."*) Mary felt dizzy; her eyes sparked. Her throat shut up tight. If she managed to choke out words they were only a sound, a shuddering stammer like drowning. "Is your daughter a little deaf-mute girl?" a woman dared ask Elsie at the clinic.

For approximately ten months after October 16, 1960, Mary Lynda was mute. And what relief when finally she wasn't expected to speak. They let you alone if you don't talk; they seem to think you're deaf, too. Except for some of the kids teasing her at school, it was a time of peace. She'd never been very afraid of children, even of the loud-yelling older boys, only just adults frightened her. Their size, their sudden voices. The mystery of their moods and their motives. The grip of their fingers on your shoulders even in love. *Mary Lynda, I love you, honey! Say something. I know you can talk if you want to.*

But mostly this was a time of peace. No one would question her words as the police had questioned her, for she had no words. Because she'd ceased speaking, she was surrounded by quiet. Like inside a glass bubble. She carried it with her everywhere, inviolable.

In school where she was *Mary Lynda Donaldson* she occupied her own space. Her teacher Miss Doehler with the watery eyes was very kind to her, always Mary Lynda's desk was just in front of Miss Doehler's desk in fifth and sixth grades. She was *the little girl who'd found the dead man. The dead man!* The man who'd owned the Eagle House Tavern by the river. With the soaring eagle sign that creaked in the wind. When Bud Beechum was killed, his picture was printed in the Yewville paper: the first time in Bud's life, people said. Poor bastard, he'd have liked the attention.

TAVERN OWNER, 35, KILLED IN ROBBERY.

Strange that, in Bud Beechum's picture, he was young looking, without his whiskers, and smiling. Like he had no idea what would happen to him.

Strange that, when Mary Lynda's throat shut up the way it did, she felt safe. Like somebody was hugging her so tight she couldn't move. Sometimes in the night her throat came open, like ice melting, and then she began to groan, and whimper like a baby, and call "Momma! Mom-ma!" in her sleep. If Elsie was home and if Elsie heard, she might come staggering into Mary Lynda's room, groggy and scolding. "Oh Mary Lynda, what? What is it *now*?" If Elsie wasn't home or wasn't wakened, Mary Lynda woke herself up and tried to sleep sitting up, which was a safe way, generally. Not to put your head down on a pillow. Not to be so unprotected. She stared at the walls of her room (which was a small room, hardly more than a closet) to keep them from closing in.

Always in one of the walls there was a door. As long as the door was shut, she was safe. But the door might open. It might be pushed open. It might glide open. On the other side of the door there might be steep steps leading down, and she had no choice but to approach these steps, for something was pressing her forward, like a hand against her back. A gentle hand, but it could turn hard. A hard firm adult hand on her back. And she would see her own hand switching on a light, and she would see suddenly down into the cellar into the dark. That was her mistake.

5.   Yewville, NY. October 1960–March 1965.

The boy was a Negro, as blacks were then called, with an IQ of 84. This was not "severe retardation" (it would be argued by prosecutors); this was not a case of "not knowing right from wrong." Though the boy was seventeen, he'd dropped out of school in fifth grade and could not read, still less write, except to shakily sign his name to a confession later to be recanted, with a protestation of his court-appointed attorney of "extreme police coercion." The case would receive the most publicity any murder case had ever received in Eden County. In some quarters it was believed to be a race murder—the boy, Hiram Jones, had brutally killed and robbed Bud Beechum because Beechum was a white man. In other quarters, the case was believed to be a race issue—Hiram Jones was being prosecuted because he was a Negro. Because his IQ was 84. Because he lived in that part of Yewville known as Lowertown, a place of makeshift wood-frame shanties with tin roofs. Because the testimony of his family that Hiram had been home at the probable time of the murder was dismissed as lies. Because when he'd been arrested by police he had in his possession Bud Beechum's wallet, containing twenty-eight dollars; he was wearing Bud Beechum's favorite leather belt with the silver medallion buckle; Bud Beechum's shoes were hidden in a shed behind Hiram Jones's family's house. These items, Hiram claimed he'd found while fishing on the riverbank, less than a mile from the Eagle House. Yet when police came into Lowertown to arrest him, having been tipped off by a (Negro) informant, Hiram Jones had "acted guilty" by trying to run. He'd made things worse by "resisting arrest." Police had had to overpower him, and he'd been hurt and hospitalized: his nose and eye sockets broken, ribs cracked, windpipe crushed by someone's boot. He would speak in a hoarse cracked whisper like wind rattling newspaper for the remainder of his life.

Always Hiram Jones would deny he'd killed the white man. He would not remember the white man's name or how exactly he'd been charged with killing him, but he would deny it. He would deny he'd ever been in the Eagle House. No Negroes in Yewville patronized the Eagle House. He would be tried as an adult and found guilty of second-degree murder and robbery; he would be incarcerated while his case was appealed to the state supreme court where a new trial would be ordered, but by this time Hiram Jones was diagnosed as "mentally deficient"—"unable to participate in his own trial"—so he was transferred to a state mental hospital in Port Oriskany where, in March 1965, he would die after a severe beating by fellow inmates.

6. The Eagle House Tavern, Yewville, NY. October 16, 1960.

At the bottom of the wooden steps there was a man lying on his side. Like he was floating in the dark. Like he was sleeping and floating. His arms sprawled. Maybe it was a joke, or a trick? Bud Beechum was always joking. *Hey, I'm kidding, kid,* Bud Beechum would say, in reproach. *Where's your sense of humor?* If he saw you were frightened of him, he'd press in closer. He smelled of beer and cigarette smoke and his own body. His stomach rode his big-buckled belt like a pumpkin. He had hot moist smiling eyes and the skin beside those eyes crinkled. He'd been in the Korean War. He boasted of things he'd done there with his bayonet. He refused to serve Negroes in the Eagle House because, as he said, he owed it to his white customers who didn't want to drink out of glasses that Negroes drank out of, or use the men's room if a Negro had used it. His wife was Momma's cousin Joanie, who smelled of talcum. Once at the Beechums' in the old hay barn where kids were leaping into hay and screaming like crazy, bare arms and legs, Bud Beechum laughed at Mary Lynda for being so shy and fearful—"Not like your momma who's *hot.*" Because Mary Lynda didn't want to run and jump with the others into the hayloft. Bud Beechum teased her pretending to grab at her between the legs with his big thumb and forefinger. *Uh-oh! Watch out the crab's gonna getcha!* It was just a joke though. Bud Beechum's face was flushed and happy-seeming. So maybe now, lying at the foot of the steps, in this nasty-smelling place with the bare lightbulb that hurt her eyes, maybe this was a joke, too. Bud Beechum's head that was big as a bucket twisted to one side like he was trying to look over his shoulder. Something glistened on his head—was it blood? Mary Lynda was fearful of blood. She began to breathe in a quick light funny way like the breath couldn't get past her mouth. Was Mr. Beechum breathing? Or holding his breath? His mouth was gaping in surprise and something glistened there, too.

There was a smell—Mary Lynda's nostrils pinched—like he'd soiled his pants. A grown man! Mary Lynda wanted to run away but could not move. Nor had she any words to utter. Never had she spoken to Momma's man friend Bud Beechum except shyly in response to a teasing query and that only side-long, out of the corner of her mouth, eyes averted. You could not. You did not. She stood paralyzed, unable to breathe. She could not have said why she was in this place. Or where exactly this place was. A dungeon? Like in a movie? A cave? It made her think of bats: she was terrified of bats; bats got into little girls' hair. Of the Yewville taverns where Momma went when she was feeling lonely, Momma's favorite was the Eagle House because that had been Grandaddy Kenelly's favorite, too. There, Mary Lynda was allowed to play the jukebox. Nickel after nickel. Sometimes men at the bar gave her nickels. Like they bought drinks for Momma. Bud Beechum, too—"This one's on the house." Mary Lynda drank sugary Cokes until her tummy bloated and she had to pee so bad it hurt. If Momma stayed late she slept in one of the sticky black vinyl booths. All the men liked Momma, you could tell. Momma so pretty with her long wavy dark blond hair and her way of dancing alone, turning and lifting her arms like a woman in a dream.

Mary Lynda had overheard her parents quarreling. Her father's voice, then her mother's voice rising to a scream. *Because you bore the shit out of me, that's why.*

Such words, Mary Lynda wasn't allowed to hear.

Why was this afternoon special? Mary Lynda didn't know. Momma had come to pick her up at school, which wasn't Momma's custom. Saying she didn't have to take the damned school bus. They'd come here and parked in the next-door lot. It would turn out—it would say so in the newspaper—that the front door of the Eagle House was locked; only the back door was open. There were no customers in the bar because it was early: not yet four o'clock. Momma talked excitedly explaining (to Mary Lynda?) that she was in no mood to see Bud Beechum's face. "Just tell him I'm out here, and waiting." Momma repeated this several times. It wasn't clear why Momma didn't want to see Bud Beechum's face yet wanted Mary Lynda to find him, to ask him to come outside so that Momma could talk to him. For wouldn't she have to see his face then? But this was Momma's way when she'd been drinking. One minute she'd grab Mary Lynda's head and kiss her wetly on the mouth, calling her "my beautiful baby daughter," the next minute she'd be scolding. Only fragments of the afternoon of October 16, 1960, would be clear in Mary Lynda's memory. For possibly much of it had been a dream or would be dreamed. Her throat began to shut up tight as soon as she'd entered the barroom looking for Bud Beechum, who was always behind the bar except now he wasn't. She'd have to look back in the kitchen, Momma said. She wanted to leave, but Momma said no. *See where that bastard has got to. I know he's here somewhere.* Mary Lynda saw Bud Beechum, and the thought came to her—*He's dead.* She giggled and pressed her knuckles against her mouth. The day before, Momma had kept her home from school with an "ear infection"—a "fever." When you have a fever, Momma said, you might become "delirious." You might have wild, bad dreams when you weren't even asleep and you couldn't trust what you saw, or thought you saw. So she'd called Mary Lynda's school and made her excuse. Yet, yesterday, it had seemed to Mary Lynda that Momma kept her home because she was nervous about something. She was edgy and distracted. When the telephone rang, she wouldn't answer it. She wouldn't let Mary Lynda answer it. After a while, she left the receiver off the hook. She made sure every blind in the house was drawn and the lights were out in most of the rooms except upstairs. When Mary Lynda asked what was wrong, Momma told her to hush.

Already, yesterday was a long time ago.

Mary Lynda was crouched at the top of the steps staring down to where Bud Beechum was lying. Looking like he was asleep. *No—he's dead.* Still, Bud Beechum was tricky; he might wake up at any moment. Maybe it was a trick he was playing on Momma, too. You couldn't trust him. Mary Lynda stood there on the steps so long, not able to move, not able to breathe, at last Momma came to see where she was.

Soft as a whisper coming up behind Mary Lynda.

"Honey? Is something wrong?"

7. The Eagle House Tavern, Yewville, NY. October 16, 1960.

He told her to come to the Eagle House at noon; he wanted to see her. He'd leave the rear door unlocked. He was pissed as hell at her not answering the phone, he'd almost come over there and broken down the door and the hell with her little girl or any other witness. So she came by. She saw she had no choice. She parked the Chevy on Front Street, by the Lafayette Hotel. A dead-end street. She wasn't seen walking to the Eagle House through the alley. She wore a raincoat and a scarf tied tight around her head and she walked swiftly, in a way unusual for Elsie Kenelly. She entered by the rear door. At this time of day no one was around. There was a raw, egg-white look to the day. High clouds were spitting rain cold enough to be ice. The clouds would be blown away, and the sky would open into patches of bright blue, by the time she left. The Eagle House wasn't open for lunch; it opened, most days, around 4 P.M. and it closed at 2 A.M. Beechum was waiting for her just inside. "About time, Elsie." He was angry, but relieved. She'd come as he had commanded: the woman had done his bidding. He grabbed at her. She pushed him off, laughing nervously. She'd washed her hair and put on crimson lipstick. Perfume that made her nostrils pinch. She'd brought a steak knife, one of that set her mother-in-law Maudie Donaldson had given them, in her handbag but she knew she wasn't brave enough to use a knife. She was terrified of blood, terrified of the possibility of Bud Beechum wrenching the knife out of her fingers. He was strong, and for a man of his size, he was quick. She knew he was quick. And he was shrewd. She would have to say the right things to him, to placate him. Because he was pissed from last night, she knew that. She told him that Mary Lynda had been sick, an ear infection. She told him she was sorry. He squeezed her breasts, always there was something mean in this man's touch. And when he kissed her, there was meanness in his kiss. His beery breath, his ridiculous thrusting tongue like an eel. His teeth that needed brushing. The wire whiskers she'd come to hate though at one time (had she been crazy?) she'd thought they were sexy, and Bud Beechum was "sexy—sort of." She'd always been curious about this guy married to her cousin Joanie, even back in high school it was said all the Beechum men were built like horses, which was fine if you liked horses. Drunk, she'd thought just maybe she might. But only part drunk, then stone cold sober, she'd had other thoughts.

Mary Lynda was at school. She'd be at school until 3:15. "Look. I got kids, too. You think I don't have my own kids?"

Now he was blaming her for—what? Mary Lynda? The bastard.

There was the doorway to the cellar. Like a dream doorway. *Pass through to an adventure! But you must be brave.* She wrenched her mouth free of his and laughed. She was breathing quickly as if she'd been running. She lifted her heavy dark blond hair in both her hands and let it sift through her fingers as it fell, in that way he liked. She could see his eyes dilate with desire. He led her urgently toward the cellar steps, where a bare lightbulb was screwed into a ceiling fixture filmy with cobweb. It was both too bright here and smudged seeming. It smelled of piss from the men's room in the back hall and of damp dark earth. All the cellars in these old historic buildings were earthen. Things died in these cellars and rotted away. Beechum was talking excitedly, laughing, that warning edge to his voice. He was sexually charged up like a battery. But he didn't like tricky women; he wanted her to know that. He'd hinted at things about her old man she wouldn't want generally known in Yewville. She'd got that, right? He was leading her down the steps, ahead of her, to this place they'd gone before—this was the third time in fact; she was disgusted and ashamed and she pushed him, suddenly pushed him hard, and he lost his balance and fell forward. Elsie's fingers with the painted nails, which were strong fingers, you'd better believe they were strong, at the small of the man's fattish back, and he fell.

He fell hard. He fell onto the wooden steps, limp and lumpy as a sack of potatoes, sliding down. Horrible to watch, and fascinating, the big man's body helpless, thumping against the steps that swayed dangerously with his weight. Beechum was six feet three, weighed two hundred twenty pounds at least. Yet now, falling, he was helpless as a giant baby. He lay on the earthen floor, stunned. A groan of utter astonishment escaped his throat. If Beechum wasn't seriously hurt, if he got hold of Elsie now, he'd kill her. He'd beat her to death with his fists. She'd seen a pipe amid a pile of debris. Beechum was writhing, groaning—possibly the bastard had injured his back in the fall, maybe his spine or his neck was broken, maybe the bastard was dying, but Elsie hadn't faith this could be so easy. Almost, she was willing—she was wanting—to work a little harder. Her father Willie Kenelly had killed men in Okinawa, gunfire and bayonet, he hadn't boasted of it, he'd said it was goddamned dirty work, it was hard work: killing was hard work, nothing to be proud of but not ashamed, either. That had been his job, and they'd given him medals for it, but in his own mind he'd just done his job. *Do it right, girl, or not at all. Don't screw up.*

She knew. She'd known, making up her mind to drive over here.

Afterward, she wrapped the pipe in newspaper. It was bloody, and there were hairs on it. But nothing had splattered onto her. She would bathe anyway. For the second time that day. She wiped the dead man's mouth roughly, thoroughly, removing all traces of crimson lipstick. She took his wallet, stuffed with small bills. She unbuckled his belt and removed it. She unlaced his shoes. She was feverish yet calm. Whispering aloud, "Now. I want this. These. One, two. The shoe. Three, four. Shut the door. *Don't screw up.*" In a paper bag she carried Beechum's things to her car parked on Front Street beside the Lafayette Hotel. This had been an ideal place to park: a side street above the river, a dead-end used mainly by delivery trucks. No one had seen her, and no one would see her. It wasn't yet 1 P.M. The sky was clearing rapidly. Each morning, as winter neared, the sky was thick with clouds like broken concrete, but the wind from Lake Ontario usually dislodged them by midday; patches of bright blue glared like neon. Elsie drove north along the River Road humming the theme from "Moulin Rouge." It had snagged in her brain and would recur through her life, reminding her of this day, this hour. She surprised herself, so calm. *You're doing good, girl. That's my girl.* Why she would behave so strangely within a few hours, bringing her daughter Mary Lynda to the death scene—as if to ascertain yes, yes the man was dead, yes it had really happened, yes she could not possibly be to blame if her own daughter was the one to discover the corpse—she would not know. She would not wish to think. *That's right, girl. Never look back.*

She drove the Chevy bump-bump-bumping along a sandy access road to the river, where fishermen parked, but today there were no fishermen. Scrub willow grew thick on the riverbank here; no one would see her. She was a doctor's wife, not a woman you'd suspect of murder. She threw the bloodied pipe out into the river, about twenty feet from shore. It sank immediately, never to be recovered. Beechum's fat, frayed pigskin wallet Elsie hadn't glanced into, not wanting the bastard's money, the leather belt he'd been so proud of, like the oversized silver buckle was meant to be his cock, and his shoes, his size twelve smelly brown fake-leather shoes, these items of Bud Beechum's she left on the riverbank for someone unknown to find.

"Like Halloween," she said. "Trick or treat, in reverse."

8. Yewville, NY. 1959–1960.

She was just so lonely, couldn't help herself. Missing him.

Crying till she was sick. Lost so much weight her clothes hung loose on her. Even her bras. And her eyes bruised, bloodshot.

At first, her husband was sympathetic. In his arms she lay stiff in the terror of a death she'd never somehow believed could happen. *Can't believe it. I can't believe he's gone. I wake up, and it's like it never happened.*

Couldn't help herself, she began dropping by the Eagle House though he wasn't there. Because, each time she entered, pushing through the rear door which was the door by which he'd entered, she told herself, *It might not have happened yet.* She told herself maybe he was there, at the bar. Waiting.

The other men, his friends, were there. Most were older than Willie Kenelly had been. Yet they were there, they were living, still. Glancing around at her when she entered the barroom, the only woman. And Bud Beechum behind the bar, staring at her. Elsie Kenelly! Willie Kenelly's girl, who'd married the doctor.

God, they'd loved Willie Kenelly: nobody like him.

Except he'd left without saying good-bye.

Short of breath, sometimes. The heel of his big callused hand against his chest. And that faraway look in his eyes. She'd asked her father what was wrong, and he hadn't heard her. She asked again, and he turned his gaze upon her, close-up, those faded-blue eyes, and laughed at her. *What's wrong with what? The world? Plenty.*

Except he'd given Elsie, one evening at the bar of the Eagle House, those worn ivory dice he liked to play with, he'd brought back from Okinawa. His Good Luck Dice he called them.

"Don't lose 'em, honey."

That had been a clear sign, hadn't it? That he was saying good-bye. But Elsie hadn't caught on.

No one would speak of how Willie Kenelly died. One of the papers, not the Yewville paper, printed he'd "stepped or fallen" off the girder of a bridge being repaired upriver at Tintern Falls; there was water in his lungs, yet he'd died of "cardiac arrest." In any case Willie Kenelly's death was ruled "accidental." But Elsie knew better; her father wasn't a man to do anything by accident.

In the Eagle House that summer, she drank. Few women came alone into Yewville taverns, and never any woman who was a doctor's wife and lived in one of the handsome brick houses on Church Street. Yet Elsie was Willie Kenelly's daughter long before she'd become Dr. Donaldson's wife. She'd gone to Yewville High School; everyone knew her in the neighborhood. But Beechum leaned his high, hard belly against the edge of the bar, talking with her. Listening sympathetically. Beechum, greasy thinning dark hair worn like he was still in high school, sideburns like Presley's and something of Presley's sullen expression. And those eyes, deep-socketed, black and moist and intense. Elsie had always thought Bud Beechum was an attractive guy, in his way. By Yewville standards. She remembered him in his dress-up G.I. uniform. He'd been lean then. He'd had good posture then. He'd been fox-faced, sexy. They'd kissed, once. A long time ago in somebody's backyard. A beer party. A picnic. When?

Bud Beechum had liked her father. He'd "really admired" Willie Kenelly, he said. Elsie's father was a guy "totally lacking in bullshit," he said. Elsie's father had been in World War II, as it was called, and Beechum in the Korean War. They had that in common: a hatred of the army, of officers, of anybody telling them what to do. And Willie Kenelly hadn't had a son. When Beechum wiped at his eyes with his fist, Elsie felt her heart pierced.

It was hard for men to speak of loss. Of grief. Of what scared them. Better not to try; it always came out clumsy, crude.

But Elsie could tell Beechum, and her father's friends, that he'd been her best friend, not just her father. He'd loved her without wanting anything from her and without judging her. That had always been his way. Maybe she hadn't deserved it, but it was so. She'd seen his body at the funeral director's, and she'd seen his coffin lowered into the ground, and she saw his death reflected in others' eyes as in the draining of color during a solar eclipse, yet still it wasn't real to her. So she found herself drifting to the places he'd gone, especially in the late afternoon as fall and winter came on, as the sun turned the western sky hazy, rust-red, reflected in somber ripples on the Yewville River. Never would Elsie drive to Tintern Falls; never would she cross over that bridge. Never again in her lifetime. And this time, the melancholy time, dusk: never would she not think of him, waiting at the Eagle House for her. She should have been home with Mary Lynda, her daughter. She should have been preparing supper for her husband. She should have been a wife and a mother, not a daughter any longer.

This was the dangerous time.

Possibly Dr. Donaldson wasn't so sympathetic with his wife's grief as people thought, when they were alone. Between him and the older man there'd been rivalry. Donaldson disapproved of Kenelly's business practices. Kenelly had owned a lumberyard in Yewville, but it hadn't been very prosperous. He gave customers credit and rarely collected. The tarpaper roofs of his sheds leaked; his lumber warped and rotted. When customers came to buy single planks, a handful of spikes, he'd say airily, "Oh hell, just take 'em." His son-in-law Tim Donaldson was a very different kind of man, and after Willie Kenelly's death Elsie began to hate him. Her husband! His teeth-brushing, his bathroom noises, his sighs, his chewing, his frowns, his querying of Mary Lynda: "Did you and Mommy go out in the car today? Did you go shopping? Where?" Tim Donaldson never spoke meanly. Always, Dr. Donaldson spoke pleasantly. As he did at his office with his nurse-assistant and with his patients, the majority of whom were women. His sand-colored hair was trimmed neatly every two weeks and he was a dignified, intelligent man, yet after Willie Kenelly's death his jealousy of the old man quickened. Worse, Kenelly had left several thousand dollars to Elsie and Mary Lynda, without so much as mentioning him in the will. And he'd married Elsie, who hadn't been a virgin! Who'd had a certain reputation in Yewville, as a girl. He'd thought the old man would be grateful to him for that, at least.

One night when he touched Elsie in their bedroom, she shrank from him with a look of undisguised dislike. She began crying, not in grief but in anger. *Leave me alone — you disgust me. I don't love you; I love him.*

Next day, in the dusk of an early autumn, Elsie dropped by the Eagle House for just a single drink. She would stay only a few minutes. But Bud Beechum was alone there, waiting. Seeing her face as she entered the barroom, her eyes snatching at the place where her father should have been. "Elsie! Hey." Beechum spoke almost gently. Elsie saw his eyes on her; she saw how he wanted her.

That first time, she'd been drunk. Beechum shut up the Eagle House early. Running his hands over her, greedy and excited and a little scared. Murmuring, "Oh baby, baby." Like he couldn't believe his good luck. Like he was fearful he'd explode, too soon. He led Elsie down into the cellar. A bare lightbulb shone in her eyes, screwed into a ceiling fixture amid cobwebs. There was a smell here of stale beer, a stink of cigarettes. She was sexually aroused as she hadn't been in months. What a strange, dirty thing to do; what a wicked thing to do, instead of preparing supper for a hardworking, hungry husband and a sweet little daughter. Elsie and Bud Beechum laughed like kids and pulled at each other's clothing. This was high school behavior, this was teen rock music, oh God how they'd been missing it, these years of being adults. Somehow it hadn't taken with either of them, adulthood. Beechum was grunting, leaning over Elsie on a broken-springed sofa with a nubby surface that chafed her skin and managing to enter her, that hot hairy opening between the woman's fleshy thighs, always an astonishment to realize that it's there, inside the clothing, no matter the woman, and Bud Beechum groaned and shuddered and came violently, as if he'd been struck a killing blow at the base of his spine, and Elsie was cursing him, laughing and cursing, "Damn you. Fuck. You fucker," pulling his greasy hair and squirming and writhing against him, the dumb bulk of him, as if sex, too, was something she'd learned to do for herself: you can't depend upon the man, so learn to do what's needed yourself, and be grateful.

Afterward she had to concede she felt good. Dreamy-lazy, and good. As she hadn't felt in a long, long time. Not wanting to think now she'd feel tenderness for Beechum, and she was afraid of Beechum. And she didn't want to feel tenderness for any man again in her life.

And yet, next afternoon she returned to the Eagle House, to Beechum's hot staring eyes, telling herself it's only for a single beer, only so she'd feel less lonely, and she'd explain to Bud Beechum why yesterday had been a mistake: she'd been drinking and not thinking clearly, and she hoped he wouldn't disrespect her . . . but somehow it happened this time, too, Bud Beechum led Elsie down the unsteady wooden steps into the cellar, to the filthy sofa she recognized as a castoff from her cousin Joanie's living room. "Bud, no. I can't, Bud. I . . ." Elsie heard her voice, plausible and alarmed, and yet there she was kissing him, mashing her mouth against his, the two of them clutching at each other, crazy. *It's just I'm so lonely.*

So it happened that, when Elsie changed her mind about seeing Beechum again, Beechum laughed at her, and said,

"Elsie. C'mon. I was there. I remember how it was." He knew and she knew, he'd felt her thrashing against him, her legs around him, he'd seen her contorted face, and her tears. Elsie was crazy for him! And so when she stayed away from the Eagle House, naturally he was pissed. A man would be pissed. He began to telephone her at home. "Hey Elsie, c'mon. Don't play hard to get. This is me, Bud. *I know you.*" When she hung up the receiver he began to drive past the handsome brick house on Church Street. Elsie shouldn't have been surprised; she knew who Beechum was, yet somehow she couldn't believe it, couldn't believe what was happening, spinning out of her control. *I made a mistake, I guess. Oh Daddy.*

When she drove to the grocery store, with Mary Lynda, and she glanced up to see Beechum's car in her rearview mirror, she knew—she'd made a serious mistake.

One evening Elsie stopped her car at the Sunoco station. And Beechum stopped his. And they talked together at the edge of the pavement, Elsie brushing her wind-whipped hair out of her eyes, Beechum hunching close in a zip-up jacket, bareheaded. Elsie was talking quickly now. There was a smile she had, a smile girls cultivated, for such circumstances, desperate, not quite begging, and Elsie smiled this smile and told Beechum she'd changed her mind about "seeing him": the mistake had been hers. "See? I'd been drinking. I was drunk." Beechum stared at Elsie, not hearing. She understood that the man was sexually aroused, even now. Her breathy words mean nothing to him, only his arousal had meaning, concentrated in his groin but suffused through his tense, quivering body. She saw it in his eyes, angry and triumphant. For the first time she realized that Bud Beechum, her cousin Joanie's tavern-owner husband, might be dangerous. Like Willie Kenelly, he'd killed men in combat. He'd had the power to kill in his hands, and that power had been sweet. Hoping to placate him, to soften the expression on his flushed, sullen face, Elsie said, almost shyly, "Bud, I just feel wrong, doing this to Joanie. If—" "Fuck 'Joanie,'" Beechum said savagely. "This has got nothing to do with 'Joanie.'" Beechum's lips twisted, pronouncing his wife's name. Elsie was shocked at the hatred in his voice. For Joanie? She tried to move away, but Beechum caught her by the arm. His fingers were powerful as hooks. "Your father told me some things, baby," Beechum said suggestively. His breath was warm and beery. "What things?" Elsie asked uneasily. "Things you wouldn't want known," Beechum said, smirking, as if Elsie and her deceased father were coconspirators in some shame. Elsie asked, "About—what? What?" Beechum said, "How your old man felt about—things. Like, wanting to step in front of a train, or off a bridge. This time he told me—" Elsie lost control and slapped Beechum. The bastard's smug fat face! She was too upset even to scream, and when Beechum tried to grab her, she wrenched free of him and ran back to her car. Driving away she trembled with rage and panic at what was happening to her. *Maligning the dead! Beechum would pay.*

9. Yewville, NY. July 12, 1959.

The call came late at night: 2:20 A.M. Naturally you'd think it was one of Dr. Donaldson's patients.

Through a haze of sleep, resentfully, Elsie heard her husband's calm condescending voice. He loved such late-night calls, obviously; if he didn't, he could leave the damned phone off the hook. (The Donaldsons were sleeping, at this time, in the same bed of course. Technically, at that time, in the summer of 1959, they were still man and wife, with all that implies of marital intimacy and obligation.) Then Donaldson's voice sharpened, in surprise. "When? *How?*" Elsie was fully awake in an instant. This was something personal, urgent. And yet there was a thrill to her husband's voice, a quavering she knew meant triumph of a kind, vindication. And when Donaldson put the palm of his hand over the receiver and said gently, as if he were speaking not to his wife but to his nine-year-old daughter, "Elsie, I'm afraid there's bad news. Your father—in Tintern Falls—" Already Elsie was out of bed and backing away from him, clumsy as a frightened cow in her aqua nylon nightgown with the lacy straps and bodice, shaking her head. *I already knew. Nothing could hurt me, after this.*

10. Yewville, NY. March 29, 1957.

This call, Elsie had been expecting.

"Honey? Your mother has"—there was a moment's pause, delicate as her father's fingers touching her wrist in that way he had, as if to steady her, or caution her, or simply to alert her that something crucial was being communicated—"passed away."

Elsie surprised herself, beginning to cry. The tears, the childish sobs, burst from her.

Elsie's father disliked women crying, on principle. But he didn't interrupt Elsie. He let her cry for a while, then told her he was at the hospital if she wanted to come by.

Elsie tasted panic. No, no! She didn't want to see her mother's dead, wasted body, her skin the color of yellowed ivory, any more than she'd wanted to see her mother while the woman was alive and disapproving of her. "Daddy, I can't. I just can't. I'll come by the house, later."

"Suit yourself, Elsie." Her father laughed; she could imagine him rubbing at his nose, a brisk upward gesture with his right forefinger that signaled the end of a conversation he felt had gone on long enough.

11. Yewville, NY. 1946–1957.

Elsie and her mother hadn't gotten along. It happened in Yewville sometimes, a girl and her mother, living too close, recoiled from each other, hurt and unforgiving.

Elsie's mother hadn't approved of her. Even her marriage to Dr. Donaldson's son Timothy (as Tim was known at that time in Yewville). Mrs. Kenelly had been furious and disgusted with her youngest daughter since she'd caught Elsie, aged seventeen, with her boyfriend Duane Cadmon, in Elsie's attic bedroom, the two of them squirming partly undressed in each other's arms, French-kissing on Elsie's rumpled bed beneath the eaves. Never would Mrs. Kenelly forgive her for such behavior: being cheap, "easy," soiling her reputation, bringing "disgrace" into the Kenelly household. Elsie, who'd had reason to think her mother would be gone from the house for hours, lay pretzel-sprawled in Duane's grip, in a thrumming erotic haze like drowning, and her eyes sprang open in horror to see, past Duane's flushed face, her pinch-faced mother staring at her with ice-pick eyes. In that instant, Mrs.

Kenelly slammed the door, hard enough to make Duane wince. Later, they would have it out. Mrs. Kenelly and Elsie. (Where was Willie Kenelly at such times? Nowhere near. Keeping his distance. He never intervened in such female matters.) Elsie's mother spoke bitterly and sarcastically to her, or refused to speak to her at all, even to look at her, as if the sight of Elsie disgusted her; Elsie slammed around the house, sullen, trembling with rage. "How'd anybody get born, Momma, for Christ's sake," Elsie said, her voice rising dangerously so the neighbors might hear. "You act like people don't do things like Duane and I were doing, well god*damn*, Momma, here's news for you: people *do*."

You didn't talk to your mother like this in Yewville in those days. If you did, you were trailer trash. But here was Elsie Kenelly screaming at her mother. And Mrs. Kenelly screaming back, calling Elsie "tramp," "slut," telling her "no decent boy" would respect her, or marry her.

Elsie brooded for weeks, months. Years.

Even after Elsie was married to Tim Donaldson, who'd gone away to medical school in Albany, and was eight years older than Elsie; even after she'd married, not just some high school boyfriend, or a guy from the neighborhood, but a "family physician" with a good income who brought her to live with him on Church Street, still Mrs. Kenelly withheld her approval, as she withheld her love. For that was a mother's sole power: to withhold love. And Elsie recoiled with yet more resentment.

Goddamn, Momma! I married a man of a higher class than you did so maybe you're jealous. My husband's a doctor not a lumberyard owner, see?

She didn't love Timothy Donaldson. But she took pride in being Dr. Donaldson's wife.

After Mary Lynda was born, and Elsie's mother had a beautiful baby granddaughter she wished to see and to hold and to fuss over, then Elsie realized her power: to exclude her mother from as much of her life as she could. (Of course, Elsie's father was always welcome in the Church Street house. Invited to drop by after work. Anytime!) Though in public, when it couldn't be avoided, Elsie and her mother hugged stiffly and managed to kiss each other's cheek, in Mrs. Kenelly's presence Elsie was light-headed, giddy. She laughed loudly. She drank too much. *Momma, I hate you. Momma why don't you die.*

12. Wolf's Head Lake, NY. Summer 1946.

Those evenings at the lake. Where Yewville families went for picnics in the summer. Some of the men fished, but not Willie Kenelly who thought fishing was boring— "Almost as bad as the army. Almost as bad as life." He laughed his deep belly laugh that made anybody who listened laugh with him.

Elsie was proud of her dad who'd returned home from the war with burn scars and medals to show for his bravery, though he dismissed it all as bullshit and rarely spoke of it with anyone except other veterans. And at such times the men spoke in a way that excluded others. They were profane, obscene. They shouted with laughter. Summer nights, they liked most just to sit drinking beer and ale on the deck of the Lakeside Tavern. Often they played cards (poker, euchre) or craps.

These could get to be rowdy, raucous times. The sun set late
in summer and so, toward dusk, when the sky was bleeding
out into night, red-streaked, bruised-looking clouds, serrated
and rough-seeming as a cat's tongue, and the surface of the
lake had grown calm except for erratic, nervelike shivers and
an occasional leap of a fish, the men would have been drinking for hours, ignoring their wives' pleas to come eat supper.
"Daddy, can I?" There was Elsie Kenelly on the deck at her
father's elbow, teasing him for sips of ale from his glass or a
puff of his cigarette, asking could she play his hand at cards,
just once. Could she take his turn at craps, just once. Elsie in
her new white two-piece swimsuit with the halter top, ponytailed dark blond hair and long tanned legs, nails painted frost
pink to match her lipstick: Elsie was sixteen that summer and
very pretty, lounging boldly on the deck against the railing by
the men's table, liking the attention her dad gave her, and the
other men, which meant more to her than the attention she
got from boys her own age. Elsie regarded her good-looking
father with pride: how muscled his bare shoulders and his bare
heavy torso, covered in a pelt of hair, mysteriously tattooed
and scarred. She was his girl for life. She blushed and squealed
with laughter if he teased her. She bit her lip and came close
to crying if he spoke harshly to her. Always it was a risk, hanging by her father; you couldn't predict when Willie Kenelly
might speak sarcastically or suddenly lose patience. He'd
come back from the war with an air of speechless rage, like a
permanent twitch or tic somewhere in his body you couldn't
detect, though you knew it was there. You felt it if you touched
him. Yet you had to touch him.

"Sure, honey—toss 'em."

Willie Kenelly spoke negligently, handing his daughter the ivory dice, as if fate were nothing more than the crudest, meanest chance requiring no human skill. Always she would remember those ivory dice! As the men's eyes move over her young eager body in the white swimsuit, taking in her snub-nosed profile, the graceful fall of her ponytail partway down her back, Elsie is laughing self-consciously, her heart swelling with happiness, and the excitement of the moment as the dice are released from her hand to tumble, roll, come to rest on the sticky tabletop, and there's that anxious moment before you dare look to see what, as your dad says, the dice have to tell you.

Angel of Wrath

And seeing her for the first time *I knew.*

How she crossed the park pushing a baby stroller and I had been called to that place quick before the church bell ceased its tolling as it was rare that any sign called to me now that I am grown — *Go! Go where you are needed, Gilead* — and in a patch of hot sunshine where the elm trees had been sawed down she lifted her hand to shield her eyes frowning and squinting and the movement alerted me to see her and our eyes met and she smiled at me knowing I could not be a stranger.

I did not follow her then. Never did I follow her but was drawn in her wake like a scrap of paper in the wind. My head bowed, I continued through the shabby park. Patriot Park it is called. Stricken with shyness and joy, I cast my eyes down in the comfort of knowing we would meet again; always we would know each other.

And seeing her the next day *I knew.*

At the sandstone steps of the library where they are crumbling, she hesitated, trying to lift the front of the stroller, as others passed by not seeming to notice the young mother, and soundless as a cat I came beside her and aided her bare slender arms in lifting the stroller and she glanced up at me startled and grateful—"Thank you!" And the baby in the stroller stared up at me, blue eyes widened in recognition. *He knows. He, too.* I did not speak for the hurt in my throat. I did not look at her close-up for I did not dare. Nor smile with the ease of others for I could not trust my mouth, which twitches and twists like an alive thing. And I am so tall and clumsy looming over her and the baby, what if I slipped, stumbled, and injured them somehow? So like a blind man (knowing my face was ugly in blotches and burning), I entered the library before her and walked quickly away not glancing back. My breathing like a dog's that has been running. I was staring at a display of audiobooks and young adult books and there was a shelf of books in shiny new jackets and their words mocked me for these were words I could not speak aloud. And there was a roaring in my ears. For the librarians in this place might know me. I had not entered such a place since grade school when we were made to go. Women of that kind staring at me. They were my teachers, staring in dislike. Before my voice was taken from me, even then I was shy. *You are not trying, Gilead.* Because once I held the book to my face but my eyes were shut tight and teeth clenched and bared.

If you don't try how can you read?
If you don't read how can you grow up?
If you don't grow up how can you be?

Three women, and three knives. In a dream I came to them. The knife handles were carved of a hard dark wood and inside the wood a small heart beat. These handles that when you closed your fingers around them a terrible thrill of strength poured through your arms and into your heart.

Gilead I was named, for a holy place.

Gilead I was named by my mother whose face was bright-blinding as the sun.

Gilead, you must never tell, my mother had no need to command me and so I did not, and will not.

On my head a gray baseball cap and on the cap a Happy Face button.

It's a yellow round face like a sun with just dots for eyes but a big wide smile. It makes you smile to see it. Dr. Cotton praises me for "optimism." But next time I saw the woman in Patriot Park she did not smile at me as before but turned away. Pushing the baby stroller quickly away. You don't tell I *love you* to one who has turned from you. You don't tell I *have come to protect you.* Or I *am Gilead who loves you.*

Next door to the brick row house where she lived was a barking dog. A heavy breed, looking like a mix of German shepherd and doberman. Its collar was tied to a chain that slid along a clothesline so the dog could rush one way and the other, furious to break free and do injury to the mother and her baby as they passed on the walk to their door. From across Seneca Street in an alley I observed. I felt wrath rising in me, to see such a sight. I was working then at the post office (at the rear, where the trucks come in) and my shift ended at five, and during those hours loading and unloading I thought

of her and what it meant she had lifted her hand to greet me
in the park: she had smiled at me that first time, in the joy of
recognition.

Later she would seem to forget. But I knew better.

In the night in my bed she would come to me not in sin
stroking my body as some women and girls have done but to
watch over me as I slept. Sometimes she held her baby cradled
in her arms and would open her clothes to nurse it but I
couldn't see then; a blindness came over me. For it was forbidden for me to see. And I could not move but must lie still.
There was a murmur — *Gilead, Gilead* — but no words passed
between us.

Yet in the day when she saw me she would not smile and her
eyes were dimmed now with fear and dislike of me. These
words sprang from her lips so shocking almost I could not
comprehend.

What do you want with me

Are you following me

Leave me alone *please*

I am asking you — *leave me alone*

Beautiful eyes they were but ringed with shadow. And the
skin of her face like bruised fruit. Crossing a street and I followed (at a distance, not close) and she stumbled at the curb
and I watched after her to see that no harm came to her but
did not follow her for I understood it was the wrong time. She
was alone without the baby. It excited me to see her alone and
to know that she was a mother who nursed her baby; inside
her clothes was the woman's body, her breasts beautiful and
hidden from the world except not from me. The clothes were

men's clothes. She wore a shirt and jeans and a backpack. She entered one of the old granite buildings that belong now to the community college. On her feet were sandals that slapped against the steps. Her oak-colored hair was tied back in a pony-tail that swept her shoulders. Her face turned from me in a fiery blur. She looked young as a schoolgirl, though a grown woman and a mother, and I wished to call after her as you'd call after a child to tease and comfort. *Fear of me, of Gilead—why?*

GRADY was the name on the mailbox. But I was cautious to say this name aloud, not knowing if it was a man's name, a hus-band's name, and not hers. Saying aloud the name of one who is beloved, or saying aloud the name of one who is my enemy. I could not know.

She is a small-boned woman but not a weak woman. No! Strong in her will as in her limbs. When I was close to her on the library steps she came hardly to my shoulder. And weigh-ing maybe a hundred pounds less than me.

A big boy Gilead has been called. Young in the face and in the heart. My hair that falls into my eyes, the color of corn silk it's been called (by women). And my eyes the bluest blue. (That was why her baby smiled at me, recognizing me.) So sometimes in the street girls turned to watch me, and smile. I have the use of a pickup truck and if I'm driving, a girl will stick out her thumb to hitchhike as a joke, but I never stop. A flame passes over my face, but I never stop. And when I first came to County Health Services and to Dr. Cotton's office I saw her surprised eyes on me in a way you don't expect for a woman of her age, beyond forty or even fifty.

It was a family court judge who ruled I must put myself

"under the care" of Dr. Cotton "in lieu of incarceration" at Red Bank State Facility for Men. Dr. Cotton is my friend, I believe. Calling me *Gilead* in a calming voice as you might speak to a nervous horse, not wishing it to buck or to bolt. A horse that has been hurt and is capable of giving hurt. Never would Dr. Cotton touch me to soothe me if I became agitated but there is a wish in her eyes to touch me, my long hair, my skin that flares up in rashes, my fingers with dirt-ridged nails that drum drum drum on the edge of her metal desk.

My appointment with Dr. Cotton is every other Monday in the county building. Five-thirty to 6 P.M. Upstairs past social service, public assistance, tax assessor, county clerk, death certificates, marriage licenses, rodent and insect control. Seven more months assigned to Dr. Cotton who speaks of "trauma" — "adjustment" — "restorative surgery" — and to this I make myself smile politely but say nothing. For never will Gilead enter any hospital (where I can't remember being taken, by ambulance it's said) again in my life and be "put to sleep" and my throat cut with a knife another time. *I will never.*

Gilead, when will you speak to me of your mother? Dr. Cotton asks; it has been years now and that woman can't hurt you anymore. A hot stabbing anger goes through me that this ugly old bitch would speak of my mother in such a way as if she knew my mother and had the right and my fingernails are drumming hard on the edge of the metal desk so I won't rise from my chair to grip her bony shoulders and *shake! shake! shake!* until her eyes roll in their sockets and her neck is snapped. You need to speak of your mother, of what she did to you, Dr. Cotton says, to get beyond it. Gilead?

I am smiling like the Happy Face. I duck my head like I don't understand. For never have I said who it was that did this to me, and there is no way of them knowing truly if I never speak. And I will not speak, because it would give a false impression of my mother who loved her son and wished to protect him. It would confuse the person she was that single time with the person she was truly, in her soul.

Gilead, are you listening? Dr. Cotton asks frowning. Her face like a wrinkled glove. You are twenty-three years old. You are no child now.

The scarred flesh and cartilage in my throat is a knot that won't let me speak. When I'm excited, my mouth twists like an alive thing. My head and shoulders twitch. Boys would laugh at me, my age, but never girls. Girls and women would shrink from me. But there was pity in their eyes too. It was believed I might suffer from "epilepsy"—"brain seizure"—"asthma." There were "chemical toxins" in my blood. My mother believed I'd inherited a curse of the blood from her and from her people and now she has passed away that secret has passed with her.

Sure I have seen Gilead in the mirror, red-faced and trying to speak, a spectacle of pity and ugliness. I have never blamed anyone for shrinking from such a spectacle. *But I am not angry*, I would wish to explain. *Gilead is not angry not ever.*

But I am angry on the part of others. Of the innocent and the cast down. I am the Angel of Wrath protecting the one I love.

> Please don't follow me
> I will call the police if
> I've seen you following me—*please don't*

This time I was downtown and saw her and could not prevent following her it was an accident, I swear. But when she saw me she stopped as if she'd been struck by a blow and called to me in a voice hoarse like something scraped, asking what did I want from her, why the hell was I following her, I'd better stop, I'd better stop or she'd call the police, she was angry now and I shrank back, pulling my cap low over my forehead for I was ashamed that she should deny me. She knew me, yet she would deny me. Why? *Gilead, I am Gilead, you know me.* Like there was blindness in her eyes. I could not comprehend. She'd run into the five and dime store and I came through the alley to the rear and when she appeared there leaving by the back door (but everybody knows there is a back door) she stopped again, staring at me like a hunted rabbit, and I tried to smile to comfort her, I tried to speak to explain but she began to scream saying she'd call the police, goddamn me, she'd have them arrest me, so I backed away, my face blotched and burning in shame.

Little Mother! Yet she was exhausted sometimes from the baby. The baby's father was nowhere near and she was alone with the baby and sang to the baby sometimes until the baby fell into a doze, but at other times the baby would not sleep but cried, cried. And my heart went out to her: *Little Mother, I am here to help you. Don't turn me away.*

Where the shade was unevenly pulled and did not come to the windowsill or where there was a rip in the shade like a lightning flash, there I could observe. Smiling to see her and to know she could not see me where for hours in the alley behind her house I watched over her. I was sleepless, I did not require sleep. She lived in a first-floor apartment at 929 Seneca Street in a row house of weatherworn dark brick. I had reason to think she had moved there only recently for there were unpacked cartons in all the rooms I could see and not much furniture. For a while there was a telephone on a bare floor, and a stool beside it. She would make calls from this phone but rarely would it ring. Sometimes talking on the phone she would begin to cry and strike her thigh with her fist and I wanted to stop her from hurting herself and give comfort to her but I dared not.

In the house next door were two men and these were the owners of the dog that barked so much and lunged and snapped its teeth at anyone who passed by. These were men a few years older than Gilead who treated their dog cruelly and would not keep it inside when they were gone. And they were often gone.

By day it happened I observed how she pushed the baby out in his stroller trying to move quietly and quickly so the dog would not be wakened but the dog would wake and bark in fury with glistening bared teeth, and later when she returned she would take care to approach her house from the other side yet the dog would be waiting and like a maddened creature sniffing blood it would bark, bark, bark and throw itself against its chain to terrify her and to make the baby cry. And calmly Gilead thought, *The angel of wrath is required.*

Thirty-five hours later the dog lay dead.

It had been killed by night and its bloodied, motionless body discovered by its owners in the early morning. Around its neck the frayed collar, and attached to the collar the chain.

Already in the early heat of the day a swarm of blue-glittering flies had gathered. The dog's eyes were open, glassy. Its skull had been crushed and brains and blood leaked out onto the grassless soil.

A first blow struck to the dog's bony head must have been so powerful no one heard a death cry. No one heard a struggle. A succession of blows struck with a heavy weapon like a tire iron. Or so the policeman who came to investigate believed.

This weapon was not found. Whoever had crushed the dog's skull was not found. The dog owners were youngish bearded men with tattoos on their forearms and wary eyes and in the neighborhood it was believed that they dealt in drugs and that they killed their own dog out of disgust with its crazed barking and a wish not to continue to feed it.

In her mailbox I left a Happy Face card. Inside the envelope some dog hairs, coarse and bristly.

Dr. Cotton smiled to see me so happy. For I was whistling, and I had washed my hair and combed it back from my forehead to fall in two wings streaked with flame beside my face. And I had shaved. Gilead, how handsome you look, Dr. Cotton said. Yet there was trouble with my job at the post office; they reported to Dr. Cotton I had been missing some hours. I pulled my baseball cap down onto my forehead feeling shamed in this woman's eyes. As if she might read my thoughts and would know of the dog and I would have to hurt her to destroy that knowledge. I did not want to hurt Dr. Cotton: she's an old woman who has been good to me.

By grunts and gestures then, pointing to my mouth, my nose, my throat, I told Dr. Cotton that I had been sick, a bad cold. I coughed and made a sneezing noise and Dr. Cotton said she would call them but I was angry to be forced by her to lie because *Gilead is a man of truth.*

I would quit that job and get another loading and unloading at Sears.

It was never hard for me to get jobs. I was strong, and just to look at me you'd know. Eager to obey and not minding hard work if I was spoken to kindly and what I had to do was explained.

The Sears job would pay twenty cents more an hour than the post office. The Sears near Seneca Street. I would take this for a sign.

Because of the dog I had reason to believe she would be kindly to me now. I had reason to believe that she would ask me to come to her house, to the door openly, and she would allow me inside. And the baby would laugh to see me, and play with my fingers. Blue-eyed baby, Gilead's own. (I did dream of this. In the daytime I would begin to remember.) But when I dialed her number from a pay phone in the bus station it was not what I expected.

By this time I knew that GRADY was not a husband's name. There was no man who came to the house at 929 Seneca Street in the hours I had observed. Her first name was Katrina, I'd learned. I'd practiced speaking this name—"Ka-*treen*-ah"—shaping my lips with care, before the mirror. Instead when the phone was lifted by her, a voice came—"Marsh?" A voice hopeful and eager as a young girl's. "Marsh? Is that you?"

I drew breath to say her name—"Ka-*treen*-ah"—but my throat closed up and she knew it was not "Marsh" and could not be anyone other than Gilead who'd killed for her and loved her. And I could hear her breathing sharp and ragged and in the background the baby was fretting and it was a shock to me how suddenly Katrina began to sob—"Leave me alone, why are you doing this, I didn't ask you to h-hurt that poor dog, how could you do such a thing, you're crazy, leave me alone! *I will call the police*"—and this was so surprising to me, even to beg forgiveness of her, I could not speak except in choked sounds like drowning *Uh-uh-uhhh K'tree-ah*, and she slammed down the receiver hard as if wishing to break it.

Yet I did not consider that Katrina was ungrateful to me. I did not believe she'd fail to love me. I'd seen her face in the park that day. For it was only a matter of time, I would be patient. *Little Mother*, my thoughts flew to her, *I love you. I have come into the world as Gilead to love you.*

And I would wonder of "Marsh." Again and again I would hear her voice lifted, eager and hopeful—"Marsh."

"Marsh"—the baby's father (?).

"Marsh"—"Marsh"—this name I spoke aloud again, again, again, until the very sound of it was harsh as glass breaking and stirred my wrath. Wishing the man stood before me like the vicious craven dog trapped by its chain and nowhere to hide.

Through the summer I waited for her to summon me and she did not and always I kept at a distance waiting for a sign, and so it was a shock to me: one day she called the police and they came and I knew this to be a fact, that she'd called, they informed me, blunt and mocking in my face. They called me Gilead twisting their mouths so the sound of that name was ugly. She'd taken the baby to the Lots-of-Tots Day Care Center in the church basement on Cicero Street as she did on Mondays and Wednesdays in the early afternoon and rode the South Ave. bus to downtown (to the community college, I knew, though I did not follow her that day for I had to work at Sears for all that day) and when at 6 P.M. I was waiting on the church steps out of the rain sitting with my knees to my chest and my head turned to the side resting on my knees (for I was tired, that day) there came suddenly before me two policemen in uniforms, and spoke sternly with me demanding to know my last name and to see my ID and telling me there was a complaint by a woman that I was "stalking" her and calling her on the phone and this must stop or I would be arrested. I was surprised and did not put up any resistance. You don't put up resistance to the police; they have weapons and will beat you bloody-headed and kick your ribs and between your legs. I had not time to think of Katrina, why she would call the police knowing that I loved her and would never mean harm to her, and I tried to speak to explain but the sounds that came from my mouth were strange and garbled and I saw in the policemen's faces that look of pity and disgust. Trying to say *I love Katrina, Katrina knows me, I would never hurt Katrina*, but all that came out were ugly choking noises. I began to twitch and shake like palsy and one of the policemen said Whoaa! What's wrong here. They put their hands on me and steadied me and walked me down the steps, forcing my legs to move like a puppet. I was strong, but two policemen together as tall as me and heavier than me were stronger and I did not resist when they slammed me against the side of the police car for I believed that Katrina would be watching and her heart would go out to me in sorrow. In the back of the car I tried to explain: *She would not do this*, I told the policeman who turned to watch me through the wire divider, *She's my friend*. I believed this policeman understood; he seemed ashamed to have hurt me, but with the other beside him he laughed at me saying the woman wanted nothing to do with me—"N-O: no-thing"—and if I wasn't careful I'd be put away behind bars with the other crazies so better mind my own business, okay, keep away from the woman and don't call her, okay? See, Gilead, you're not the kind. Okay?

Hung my head and smiled, okay.

Immediately I telephoned her from the pay phone to whisper just *I love you, I'm sorry, Katrina* and quickly hang up before she could speak.

For she had not told the police of the dog killed by Gilead for her sake. That was the secret between us, and the sign.

And for three days and three nights I stayed away from 929 Seneca as the police commanded and I did not see Katrina Grady to follow her, though the need to see her was so strong, almost I could not breathe. For I was fearful that something bad would happen to her and the baby and I would not be there to protect her. Gilead, what has happened to you? Dr. Cotton was surprised to see my appearance, unwashed and unshaven, and my work clothes soiled; she knew of "the complaint" as she called it, and a knife blade turned in my heart that there could be no secret from this woman; the police and social workers and therapists share their information; there's nowhere to hide in this county. She wanted to talk about "the complaint" — "the young woman" — "the police" — whether there was some misunderstanding, and quickly I nodded my head yes, yes there was some misunderstanding; I felt tears of hurt and rage spring into my eyes. *I was not to blame.* Dr. Cotton said carefully that if a young woman did not want me to speak with her, follow her, telephone her, of course I must not. Gilead is not that kind of person, to behave rudely to any woman, Dr. Cotton said. I shut my eyes recalling my mother and how my mother knew always what Gilead was capable of, nothing of Gilead could surprise her, she would not be surprised now that the police had come for me, my belly and ribs were covered in ugly yellow bruises from where they'd slammed me against their car. No explanation was required for my mother to act, and never was there any explanation. Dr. Cotton did not comprehend this. My mother would have scorned her. In my chair I was hunched over, pulling my baseball cap down low on my head to hide my eyes that were bloodshot and shamed, but I told her yes, I knew.

I did not tell her that Katrina Grady and I had known each other long before this lifetime. That Katrina knew this fact in her heart but had forgotten. But she would know again, one day.

I did not tell Dr. Cotton any of these things. For I would not wish to harm her, yet might harm her if she knew. If she knew what she had no right to know. I would not tell her about my mother and the knife and what it did to me because she had no right to know. It was for Dr. Cotton's protection. I am a vessel of mercy as well as wrath. I am one who respects and protects women. I would not harm a woman. I would not frighten a woman. Not a lady like Dr. Cotton, and one her age. But if something went wrong, it would not be my fault. I would drive a spike through her forehead to stop her mouth chattering. I would take hold of her wrinkled old throat in both my hands and squeeze, squeeze, squeeze, till her doctor brains seeped out at one end and her guts at the other. I would use the tire iron to crush that skull like a flowerpot beneath the thin crinkly dyed-dark hair and I would dig the heel of my boot into the hairy hole between her legs, hard. This would be to cease her words like yellow bile in my ears. It would be for no other reason. For I knew that Dr. Cotton was my friend. And so to prevent the bad things happening, I held myself in my chair to keep from rocking side to side as my teachers had scolded me for doing when I was a boy and I told her, yes, yes, Dr. Cotton. Yes, you are right.

Dialing the number I had memorized. Waiting for the phone to be lifted! I was trembling; my breath came short. But the phone rang and rang. I hung up and dialed again and the phone rang and no one answered and this would be a time when Katrina Grady would be home, I believed. Another time I tried, and later. And no answer. And so I went to Seneca Street and stood across from the house for a long time, staring at the darkened windows. A sickness came into my heart: *she was not there.*

And the next day, and the next she was gone. At the rear of the house in the alley I stood to look into the windows, seeing no one. But no sign that she had departed. For there were things of hers and the baby's scattered about and the cartons only just part unpacked from her moving in. So I believed she had not moved away to another place, though there was the danger of that, I had not comprehended until now. I was sick with fear that I would lose her, out of cowardice. And if she was returned to me it would be a sign I must not lose her a second time out of cowardice. Never again.

Had there been any woman like this in Gilead's life before? No there had not. A woman for which Gilead would die and would kill to protect. There'd been girls and some women who had smiled at him, and pursued *him*. Not believing or not minding that Gilead is "slow" — "strange." For they saw in me a gentleness and goodness and a strength to protect and my hair burnished like the sun and my eyes and heavy jaw, and at church sometimes in the pew the ray of sunshine would fall upon me, like a blessing of God you could not mistake. And my hurt throat. The piteousness of my speech. Gilead would never speak cruelly of anyone, for Gilead can't speak. And Gilead can't write, or read. A pure child of God you'd think him.

Some of them, they'd touch my wrist. And some would stroke my hair or brush it off my face and I would hold myself very still, stricken in shyness.

At last she returned after six days and six nights' absence and I gave thanks to God on my knees she was returned to me, and safe. And the baby. Gilead's baby, you could see by the eyes. There was no mistaking this. Never would she leave me again, I vowed. I believed she'd gone away to seek out another man but now she was returned to me. My heart was filled with tenderness and forgiveness for Katrina Grady who'd come back of her own free will to me.

After the police spoke with me I behaved with more caution. I'd been a hunter as a boy sometimes. I knew the caution of the hunter not to be seen or smelled. And so if Katrina called the police seeing me or believing she saw me, I was not there on Seneca Street when they arrived, or on any street close by. And if sometimes she called the police in the night hearing a sound like the wind rattling the house or noise from next door or somebody in the alley outside, believing it was Gilead, and it was not Gilead, but I was in my own bed (where the police would find me if they came by my address), then it would begin to happen that the police would not always trouble to come, not each time she called them.

So it was in the fall and the early winter of the year. For it became clear to them that Gilead was no threat. Not the kind to do harm, the kind you'd call "harmless." And in time, Katrina would cease to call the police. There was a futility in calling the police. She would change her telephone number and each time it would be "unlisted" and yet somehow after a week or some days Gilead would discover the new number and would call her just to hear her voice uplifted in hope before fear entered it, and dread, and she'd curse — "Damn you, *leave me alone*" — and slam down the receiver. I came then to see she didn't mean this so I took no offense by it, or hurt. Recalling how my mother had hurt me but out of a definite purpose and love. Knowing that there would come the hour when Katrina understood *Gilead loves me, and the baby. He has come into the world to love us.*

I was patient — I would wait. All Gilead's life until now has been waiting.

———

That winter was the time of change in Katrina. When before she'd run from me or hide or complain to others about me, now seeing me (on the street, in the park, in a parking lot or store) she would stop to stare at me, and sometimes her mouth would twist in a strange smile. A smile of mockery, scorn. Her mouth was pale like skin worn raw. Her eyes were not beautiful eyes now—though to Gilead, they would always be beautiful as on that first day in Patriot Park—but hollow in their sockets. Her hair was long and tattered and needed washing. Sometimes she would stamp at the ground as you'd stamp to drive away an unwanted dog. She would laugh, a harsh sound like a shovel scraping stones. "You! Think I'm blind I don't see you, I *do*. I know your name Gilead, you pathetic fucker. I'm telling you—*leave me alone or I'll kill you.*"

She would clench her fist and strike her own thigh, saying these terrible words. And I would blush for her, her blindness.

One evening in the 7-Eleven parking lot in almost a quiet voice, coming to stand about ten feet from me where I stood unmoving, my hands in my Windbreaker pockets, and my cap pulled low on my head, she said, "I'm going to be frank with you, Gilead. You're stalking me, and I don't like it. Trying to say you 'love' me when you don't know me. You don't! Don't know the first thing about me. See, asshole, if you knew me you'd feel fucking sorry for me. I'm a mess, that's what I am. I'm nobody a guy would want to stalk unless he's a real loser. Got it? Am I getting through to that dimwit brain of yours? My baby's father can't stand the sight of me. He sure as hell isn't stalking me. He told me under no circumstances you're gonna have this baby, and when I said I would, he said okay count me out. So I did. I have. So go to hell, you. You're a worse joke than I am, got it? Asshole."

Bursting into tears, and running into the store before I could speak.

Then in December, she shot me in the leg.

And I fell from the back stoop of her house, in the alley, moaning like a hurt dog, and right away she came outside crying "Oh God, oh God" — "I'm sorry, oh God" — and I grabbed on to the railing to pull myself up, staring at the dark blood seeping through my work pants; the bullet had grazed the calf of my right leg and torn the flesh. It was a small revolver she had, she would show me later, a .22-caliber that can do some wicked harm close up. A bullet doesn't hurt but slams into you like a hammer, that's the surprise of it. The shock. The actual pain will come later, so quickly I told Katrina I was okay, tried to tell her, the words mangled and choked and yet, this was the wondrous thing, Katrina seemed to comprehend them. For the first time she comprehended me, and I could feel the warmth of her hands on me. *Katrina Grady was beside me, and touching me.* She helped me to stand, to lean on her. She was saying she would call an ambulance to take me to the hospital, she was terrified I would bleed to death, but I told her no, I was not hurt bad, I was okay. She was ashamed, she said. She'd been drinking and now the police would know it and she'd be sent to jail and lose her baby. She'd been drinking and now she was sober and scared what would happen. The gun wasn't registered, she'd bought it on the street. Oh God she was scared shitless she would be arrested and her baby taken from her.

She begged me not to tell, and I told her no, I would never tell.

I told her I loved her, I would never tell.

She brought me into her kitchen where the air was warmed by an opened oven. We rolled up my pants leg and Katrina washed the wound and tied a towel around it, tight. There was no bullet in the flesh, the bullet had gone into the ground outside. Oh God, oh God, she was murmuring. Like a woman in her sleep praying. She gave me a beer to drink and she was drinking from a can herself. She gave me three aspirins to swallow down, and she swallowed two herself. We were shivering and trembling and staring at each other, not knowing what had happened exactly, that Gilead had been shot, standing on Katrina's back porch he'd been shot, shot through a window, but was now in this warm kitchen drinking a Coors and his wound being bound. Wild! You had to marvel, and to smile. This was worth any amount of blood and pain to come. And the blue-eyed baby that had slept through it all was still sleeping in the next room. After about five minutes a squad car came along Seneca Street. Police were knocking at doors asking about gunshots. Somebody had called police reporting gunshots. Katrina threw on a raincoat over her blood-splashed nightgown and went to the front door when they pounded on it and I was in the kitchen not daring to breathe, hearing her voice scared as a young girl's — "Gunshots? You mean just now? Oh God, I hear gunshots all the time. In this neighborhood. I almost don't listen anymore. But I didn't hear any tonight. I mean, I don't think I did. I've been asleep. My baby is asleep. I wish I could help you, officers, but I guess I can't."

Soon after that, Katrina sent me away. Back through the alley where I'd come. Now there was pain but I didn't feel it; my heart was filled with joy that God had sent such an unexpected blessing to me. I could forgive this woman I loved.

"I shot you, don't you hate me? Gilead? Don't you hate me? I shot you." She spoke wistfully and in wonder. We would examine the moist wound in my leg, that scabbed over in days. Like a wound made with a serrated knife it seemed to me. I didn't mind the pain, you can take pain inside you like freezing air, to warm.

She said, "I would expect you to hate me. I don't understand you, I guess."

I cast my eyes down, a hot flush came into my face. Almost I could not move, in the holiness of the moment.

That night Katrina fed me supper. She hadn't told me to come around but I came to the front of the house this time, and stood on the cracked front walk until, shading her eyes by a window, she saw me.

She spooned onto my plate a cheese-and-macaroni casserole with tiny hotdogs in it that I removed, carefully, with my fork. For I don't eat meat any longer. I'd worked in a slaughterhouse in Port Oriskany for three months when I was eighteen. Katrina watched me saying, "There's a purity in you, Gilead. After I shot you, coming back to me."

She gave me beer from the refrigerator. We would drink together. In his baby chair, blue-eyed Reuben stared blinking at us, waving his pudgy hands. He was a hungry baby; Katrina fed him many times a day. He was growing fast she said. He was all her happiness.

His father had wished him to die she said. In the womb, to be sucked out and disposed of like trash.

Katrina said, "Maybe I don't deserve this baby. I don't deserve to live. Maybe."

I didn't like to hear such words. No! I told her.

She said, "Except for Reuben. I think, what would happen to my baby if I died, and I know for sure I am not going to die. Not for a long fucking time."

It was then I spoke with her, as God might speak with her. The words came to me then. Not easily, but they came. Patiently she listened as I shaped these words with my mouth, trying not to stammer or twitch my neck. "God is a spirit, Katrina. In you, and in me. And in Reuben."

Laughing she said, "Oh Gilead, bullshit. That's sweet but bullshit. I know it, and you know it."

"I don't know it. No."

In Katrina's kitchen there were dazed flies on the ceiling and windowpanes. Waking up, in midwinter, to crawl out of the windowsills. "These damn flies, is God in them?"

I could not reply to her mockery. I sat silent, eating.

She would speak in this way, and open another can of beer. She would eat a little and push her plate from her. She would lift the baby from his chair and take him to change his diaper and when she returned her face showed surprise that Gilead was there in her kitchen.

She laughed, and her eyes were bloodshot and set deep in her face. Tears glistened on her cheeks, I leaned across the table to wipe them with my fingertips and Katrina meant to shrink from me quick like a cat, but not quick enough.

———

There was a time I would help with the baby at last.

Katrina trusted me to hold him. My big hands cupping Reuben's head and lower body in such gentleness, his blue eyes drowsy and sinking to sleep, his mouth wet with spittle, and a light shone up from his face onto mine, and I heard Katrina suck in her breath seeing us. Wanting to speak but she could not.

And there was a time Katrina took my wrist, that was so much bigger than she could wrap her fingers around, and led me into the kitchen to seat me, and said in a voice that trembled in excitement, "Gilead. You could help me."

I bent my head closer. Katrina would know, any word she said to me I would obey.

"There's a man. Who hurt me. And wanted to hurt Reuben. He deserves punishment."

Yes, I said. Tell me his name.

Katrina was laying out snapshots on the table. Most were of her smiling and a man with nickel-colored eyes, a face that looked baked like clay, wavy dark hair worn long past his collar and a dark mustache, smiling and not smiling. The man's arm was heavy around Katrina's slender shoulders. In one snapshot this man was posed alone in tinted glasses, a cigarette in his mouth, exhaling a cloud of pale blue smoke. At once I saw that this was the father of Reuben who had wished to destroy him in his mother's womb. And Katrina showed me the necklace of scars beneath her jaw like tiny stitches in the skin. From when he'd knocked her down, and a glass-topped table had shattered and cut her.

Katrina's fingers touched my scarred throat. The knot in my throat.

I waited for her to ask who did this to you, Gilead. Like Dr. Cotton eager to learn any evil of another. But seeing the look in my eyes she did not.

"You've suffered, too. You know."

Katrina printed out his name — *Marshall Hagan* — and his address which was in a town twelve miles away. The university town it is called and "Marsh" lived near the campus where Katrina said he'd been an adult student studying business. My heart was filled with wrath for this man; I took up the address and those snapshots of him in which he stood alone for (I reasoned) if something happened I would not wish Katrina to be involved.

Katrina told me not to do anything I did not truly wish to do, she would not send me on any mission contrary to my own heart, but already I was restless to leave. I knew what I would do: I had the tire iron, and I had the use of a pickup. I would act swiftly as always and be back to my home this night.

Katrina walked with me to the doorway and I was breathing quick and excited and my heart beating in my chest like a fist thudding there and Katrina laughed to feel it, touching my chest, her eyes lifting to mine wide and scared like a girl's, but she laughed saying, "Gilead, I will give you my blessing." On her tiptoes standing to touch my cheeks with her fingertips, and her lips.

The Angel of Wrath. Though acting quick and unerring and without emotion as you'd wield a shovel or an ax performing a necessary task. Raising the tire iron in gloved hands to bring it down on the man's head, shoulders, his uplifted feeble hands and arms, that could not block such blows. That face I knew to hate with the righteousness of the Lord. A handsome face broken at once like an eggshell gushing blood. Break, and break, and break, the skull, and the neck, and the backbone shattered beneath the soiled T-shirt and Gilead was covered in a film of itchy sweat and breathing heavily but did not speak. From the man who'd hurt Katrina Grady and had wished to destroy her baby there came a cry of hurt, surprise, astonishment at first, but quickly there was no sound from him except low groans and whimpers and neighbors in the building would not hear for a TV was turned up and Gilead would leave by a back outdoor stairs as in stealth he'd come in the night, bearing the bloodied tire iron wrapped in newspaper and carefully he would wash it before returning to his home. For there would be a time when such an instrument of wrath would be required again, and Gilead would wish to be prepared.

Never would Katrina speak of that occasion. Never would Katrina ask. Taking Gilead's big hands in her small trembling hands and staring up into his face knowing that Gilead would never speak of it either.

That secret lodged deep between us like scar tissue.

"Gilead. You must be cold. You must be famished."

Yet I wondered, would she bring me to her bed? As other girls and women have done, or tried. But I had not loved them as I love this woman now.

That evening she would nurse the baby who sucked hungrily at her breast. A milky-pale fat breast with pale blue veins that tore at my heart, to see for the first time. Like a young girl Katrina laughed at me, at the clumsiness in my face. She instructed me to sit down, to sit across from the bed, to come no nearer, not to move nor to speak, and so I sat very still on a stool leaning forward on my haunches, watching. If you'd asked me what had been executed for the sake of such a vision I would not know how to answer, all was gone from my mind like a scrap of paper blown in the wind.

Around my head a fly buzzed groggy from waking in December, my hand brushed it away not knowing what it was.

Angel of Mercy

In the Kingdom of Stroke & Tumor
We prescribe a Sense of Humor.

1.

Angel of Mercy she died in April 1974 and beside her body, curled and composed as in sleep, there would be discovered a hospital syringe containing traces of the powerful muscle relaxant succinylcholine.

Angel of Mercy she has sometimes been sighted in the early hours of morning, predominantly between 4 A.M. and 6 A.M., at the far end of the eleventh-floor fluorescent-lit corridor where walls dissolve in shadow as into the hazy urban horizon outside the hospital.

Angel of Mercy she has been glimpsed even by medical workers new to the neuropsychiatric floor who have never heard of her, sometimes no more than an upright vapor, a constellation of mist like the exhalation of a mysterious breath, and sometimes she is walking firmly yet seeming to glide in a blurred silence in her crisp white nylon uniform in the style of nurses' uniforms of the 1950s. Not trousers and smock we mostly wear now, no matter our age or rank, but a dress, belted, with a skirt falling modestly to midcalf. And her starched white nurse's cap pert on her head, hairpinned to her hair. And spotless white laced-up orthopedic-looking shoes, rubber-soled to aid in this gliding in silence into patients' rooms, smiling and eager as any young 1951 graduate of Mount Saint Joseph's Nursing School. In sheer white stockings that cause her fleshy upper thighs to rub together in a friction that leaves her breathless . . .

Angel of Mercy of the neuropsychiatric floor of the revered old city hospital overlooking the notorious midwestern river that once, in that long-ago era, saturated with chemical pollutants, burst into oily flames rising to a height of thirty feet.

Well, things are better now. It's nearly fifty years later. Sure, people laugh at us, this rust belt city they call it, like the inhabitants are to blame for the recession; it's cruel as blaming victims of climate changes or war or cancer for disasters visited upon them. But the river burning is ancient history. And hospital conditions are much improved; staff morale is improved now that we're unionized. Yes, we will always be underpaid, some say exploited, but, over all, things are definitely improved. I don't believe personally that there was any Agnes. I mean, an individual nurse who committed those acts. Or whoever committed them. Have I seen the Angel of Mercy? No I have not. When you're exhausted and practically out on your feet on the night shift you might imagine you see things by the elevators or by the storage closet where allegedly she died, but that does not mean

*such things exist. It means only that you are exhausted, and you
are vulnerable. Because the recovery rate is nil on this floor,
there's so many deaths of even younger patients, you can get
kind of depressed, and you can get kind of spooked. But definitely things have improved since the 1950s. The river may still
be polluted, but it doesn't stink like formaldehyde and it doesn't
actually burn. Won't explode in your face if you toss a cigarette
into it. And they say there are some species of fish returning, or
mollusks, some kind of hardy marine life definitely it's returning. From somewhere.*

2.

The first time you'd think would be the hardest, wouldn't you?
But it was not. When it happened (she would realize afterward with the astonishment of one who has peered over the
edge of the world like the terrified black mongrel dog of
Goya), it was like slapping a mosquito . . .

A reflex. Pity, the scourge of mankind.

3.

Nurse R——, April 1999. A recent graduate of Mount Saint
Joseph's Nursing School, summa cum laude. A striking blond
girl in nylon white trousers and shirt, static electricity at elbows and thighs. And her hair crackling beneath the crisp
white cap. R——'s task this morning is bathing flaccid flesh,
runny bedsores, tenderly in peroxide solution (ugh, the smell!),

and gently shampooing stiff hair-quills or scaly scalps or, saddest of all, as in this case following weeks of radiation therapy after brain surgery, fuzzy down, like that of an unfledged baby bird blown from its nest. The patient groans, shivers. R— murmurs, *Too hot? Too cold? Am I being too rough? Am I hurting you? Here, this should be better.* The patient is, or used to be, a middle-aged, attractive Caucasian female. Now blinking, confused, unable to recall what words are. R— thinks, *Words: how could you explain?*

Impossible. You can't.

The older nurses in the City of the Damned (as the eleventh floor is called by its staff) observe R— with approval. Do your job, follow instructions, never question authority. Not for the youngest nurse on the floor to question authority.

In the City of the Damned, the gods Stroke & Tumor reign. Fatherly gods gone bad.

Many of the patients are incontinent. (R— wonders: Is the opposite of *incontinent, continent?* What do such words mean?) Dr. C— tells R— that after speech impairments go bodily functions: brain cells degenerate. No recovery with degenerative disease like Alzheimer's, for instance: the brain is encrusted with senile plaque, deposits of protein, neurofibrillary tangles. Nothing to be done. Stem research isn't going to help these patients; brain cells don't regenerate—turn to mush. No reversing the clock. You forget what you learned when you were toilet trained: easiest thing in the world to forget; what's miraculous is memory. And you can forget how to eat, too.

R— is subdued, listening, though reluctant to hear. Dr. C— is a second-year resident, only three or four years older than R——. Leaning in, telling her that Alzheimer's patients lose the ability to eat; place food in their mouths, it lies inert on their tongues. They've forgotten what to do with it.

R—— knows about such things, of course. She's a nurse: she doesn't need to be told. Not liking the drift of Dr. C——'s remarks, meant to make her uneasy, vulnerable, susceptible to seduction, yet she hears herself laugh nervously. Despite the hospital chill she feels her cheeks warm; she supposes she is attractive to Dr. C—— without intending it. Murmuring, How can anyone forget how to eat?—you'd think it must be an instinct like a baby's, not requiring memory. And Dr. C—— says, his breath like rubber bands in her face, Stick around the City of the Damned long enough, you'll know.

R—— vows she will not. She will not become hard, cynical, depressed, like the others.

4.

Angel of Mercy she was called, Agnes O'Dwyer. After her death would be discovered her nurse's diary, in a code never satisfactorily broken by investigators.

March 1959

In this 8th yr of service I have begun.
At last I know my way, that has been destined.
෨ is the sign.

Acts of Mercy encoded in cuneiform.
In my Nurses Diary.

No I dont believe that these Acts will be discovered.
I harbor no fear that any Court of Law will "try" me for
I am blameless.
It is Mercy perpetrated upon innocent victims of
another's Evil

(G——D whose terrible name cannot be uttered.)

A.

5.

Dr. C—— jokes, *Many are blind but few are chosen.*

In the Kingdom of Stroke & Tumor in this rainy spring
2001 beside the rust river among the beds of the stricken you
move upright as a flame. Healthy and defiant and bristling
with nylon-static sex-electricity. Not only Dr. C—— but others observe you closely, with admiration. With envy.

So young.

But she won't be young forever.

You have heard tales of the Angel of Mercy; you scorn
such tales as the most ridiculous superstition. You are a Christian girl, in a vague benevolent way, not a believer in super-
stitions and not a fanatic. You are R——, proud of your job.
R—— at whose fresh, glowing face the brain-stricken of the
City of the Damned stare, if their eyes can function. Good
morning, good morning, good morning! Always in the City of
the Damned there is at least one elderly fellow with snowy
Santa Claus hair and whiskers you want to feel kindly toward,
no matter that this elderly fellow is ninety-three and a barely
breathing stroke victim mummy you must shift, turn, turn,

shift, in his stale-smelling bed in the (futile) hope of alleviating bedsores. Always in the City of the Damned there is at least one elderly woman to remind you of the grandmother you adored, in this case a brain cancer patient with dazed eyes that snag upon you and move with you in raw yearning. *Who are you, are you my daughter, will you take me home?* Stroke & Tumor & Senile Plaque are the gods of this kingdom.

That ripe-banana/curdled-milk odor of the sickest patients you have come to dread inhaling, in terror that the odor will permeate your skin, your scalp and hair. Unmistakable odor of bacteria gleefully breeding in the mouths of doomed men and women.

Your warm flesh, another's chill fingers. It's B——, the nearly blind sixteen-year-old afflicted with severe chorea, twitching, jabbering, shivering in his wheelchair. *Help me goddamn you, help me,* B—— pleads, except his mouth works wetly without the ability to speak, and with a smile of infinite regret you disengage the chill fingers from your wrist.

Afterward, in secret, you examine the marks of those desperate fingers. Faint flushed-red impressions like love welts in your flesh.

Stroke is swift and spontaneous as lightning. Stroke is the brain's lightning. *A painless way to die, if only.* Except there follow aphasia, dementia, paralysis, and not death. Until at last the brain mechanism is extinguished; the "patient" is gone. The body may remain; the "patient" is gone. And finally death? *The horror that washes over you. Take no heed, shake yourself free of such thoughts like a young dog shaking droplets of water from his coat.*

Then there are tumors. Tumors sly, proliferating like cockroaches in the old hospital beside the river. Cut them out, often they reappear, like cockroaches, metastasizing where they will. From the colon, for instance, to the cerebral cortex. From the prostate to the liver. From the breast to the lungs. Cancer of the esophagus, cancer of the cerebellum. On the eleventh floor of the hospital make your way at this early hour among the tumor-ridden spastics with flurried eyes, catatonics oozing ashy sweat, palsied Parkinson's victims, honeycomb brains split neatly in half so that, as earnestly smiling young R—— moves from one side of the patient's bed to the other, she disappears into a void.

Nurse? Nurse where have you gone?

6.

Angel of Mercy our red-haired Agnes O'Dwyer drifting in and out of such voids. Angel of Mercy she will not come when summoned and will come when you least expect her.

For if you see Agnes, in the next instant you don't. If you don't see Agnes, in the next instant you might.

Is it only those whom we see, who exist?

7.

It was a spectacular smashup. It was the very best of entertainment tragedy. Luridly featured on the front pages of newspapers and on TV newscasts through the Midwest, at this time starved for entertainment tragedies. A twenty-nine-year-old man in a $75,000 Porsche sports car racing with the driver of a Dodge Dakota pickup on the nighttime expressway lost control of his car, skidded, crashed into a concrete wall, and had to be lifted from the wreckage; his broken body, fractured skull, injured brain, delivered to the hospital on the river by ambulance. There followed hours of brain surgery. Days of intensive care. And now, in room 1104. R—— stares at the motionless figure in the bed. *I would not fall in love with any patient. And not such a patient. A nurse avoids emotion. Personal attachments. I have been praised as a "born nurse."*

And R—— could not approve of this man. His *lifestyle.* There was the class thing. You resent people like this. R——'s father had been a utility company worker for forty years. Wages, union dues. A pension frozen five years before his retirement. R——'s father, whom she loved, now in his midseventies and afflicted with emphysema and Parkinson's.

No. R—— could not approve.

Yet seeing the man's photo in the papers. On TV. Hearing his name repeated. At the time of the crash, he'd been driving his Porsche at ninety miles an hour. He'd passed the Dodge pickup, left the other driver behind. These facts and others about Marcus Roper, R—— had learned before Roper was her patient. Before there was any thought of Roper being her patient.

"Marcus Roper."

Not that he was, any longer. You could see that. This was a figure of indeterminate sex, race, age, swathed in gauze and bandages and motionless as a bundle of laundry. There were broken legs, useless now, fated to shrink, shrivel. Unless consciousness was soon resumed, and where had consciousness gone? Beneath the bandages, there was rumored to be one-third

of the swarthy face missing. The left ear was gone; only a stub
of raw meat remained. For seventy-two hours following neuro-
surgery the patient's head was swathed in bandages and twin
pint-sized plastic containers dangled beside his head like an insect's cartoon antennae, filling up with draining blood from the
sawn-open, lacerated, multistitched scalp, which brackish
blood R—— was obligated to remove. There were vital functions that persevered grimly, despite the trauma. There were
bravely quivering eyelids and twitches of the mutilated mouth
that seemed to respond to words, stimuli. Sometimes.

Days passed. R—— returned to an empty room; the patient
had been stricken with a hospital infection and was back in intensive care. A fever of 103 degrees, near collapse of vital functions. Yet the heart was strong and did not cease its beating.

Another day, R—— returned to room 1104. Marcus Roper
was back.

*When my shadow fell over him, his eyelids quivered, his
blind eyes lifted to my face, and a shudder passed through his
body as if in that instant he knew me as I knew him.*

8.

August 1964

These Acts of Mercy ↷ in this Diary.
Of the 6 not one detected.
For Nurse Agnes is cautious, & acts out of Love.

Masses for the dead. I kneel & say the rosary to Our
Lady. Saint Mary, a nurse like me.

Mary pray for my soul.
Pray G——D does not hear.

A.

November 1967

(The radiation room is leaking its rays,
that is why I have been sent in. I protect
myself with double layers of underwear,
stockings. Beneath my cap a knitted cap.
I am aware that certain others are laughing
at me but I give no sign.)

Ꮐ for Thanksgiving this lonely time.

A.

June 1969

Ꮐ Ꮐ Ꮐ

Pity is mankinds scourge.
Pity breeds like bacteria in open sores.
Nurse Agnes make yr. heart harder!
G——D does not know pity.

A.

9.

Agnes O'Dwyer. Wan homely, saintly freckled face of the sort
common to the 1940s and 1950s, in either sex but mostly

female. And deft hands, strong back. A clumsy look to Agnes like a female calf on its hind legs and so you were surprised how capable Agnes was in her work, yes, and how graceful. For there is a kind of grace even in clumsiness, in some female workers.

They said of Agnes O'Dwyer she'd never been kissed. Not true!

They said of Agnes O'Dwyer she died a virgin at the age of forty-nine. True.

A plain stolid Girl Scout girl even into her forties. Rarely complaining, given to silences, yet not at all sullen while executing the nastiest of nurse chores (peroxide sponge baths, smelly bedsores, sudden hemorrhages, vomiting spasms, adult diapers, etc.). Fated never to marry. Devoted to her aging, ailing, clinging parents all of her adult life and uncomplaining here, too. *Some of us asked couldn't her married sisters help out more at home, what about her CPA brother, why'd he move to San Diego, does that seem fair?* But Agnes would only laugh, blush, look away stricken with embarrassment.

There are matters of the heart of which you cannot speak.

You lack the vocabulary, you cannot speak.

You can act. But not speak.

Older staff physicians liked Agnes O'Dwyer, whom they knew simply as Agnes. Younger doctors were apt to forget her name, with the passage of years. Male hospital workers took notice of her red hair and ruddy flesh until she passed the age of thirty-two or -three, by which time it was difficult to imagine Agnes as a sexual being. For how would a man approach that awkward body, elbows, big bust, big-boned jaw? How to kiss that shy, damp, opened mouth?

Febuary 1971

O Mary its that I want to do Good
Its that simple I think
♋ is the most direct Way, giving comfort
Seeing how you help the sick,
in their eys.

A.

10.

"Mr. Roper? Marcus."

In time Mr. Roper's left eye would open, stony gray and
threaded with blood. In time both Mr. Roper's eyes would
open, though unfocused, and the left eye would drift like a vagrant thought. R—— wanted to touch the ruined face. R——
recalled the handsome face of the lurid headlines and tried to
see that face in this face, which looked as if it were stitched together out of mismatched skins. And the nose, partly collapsed. Yet the nostrils were clear enough for a breathing tube
to be inserted, initially. Now patient was breathing laboriously
but unassisted. Patient was on a diet of liquid mush running
through a tube. And the catheter threaded through the limp
penis carried liquid toxins away. From Dr. C——, R—— knew
that much of Mr. Roper's parietal lobe in his left cerebral
hemisphere was gone. Lost in the auto wreck or scraped off
the surgeon's scalpel. (Dr. C—— had observed the operation.
Six hours, forty minutes.) Often there was red froth at patient's
mouth like the remnants of a primitive language.

"Marcus."

Approaching the high hospital bed like a shrine where the man lay motionless in sleep, R—— had reason to believe she entered this sleep and was welcome.

Patient had not died. Neither had he regained anything like a stable consciousness.

Yet patient's vital organs were strong. His heart was strong. His damaged brain persevered. Dreaming what?

"Good morning!"

R—— imagined a faint flutter of the left eyelid. By this time, after so many days of intimacy, Mr. Roper recognized her voice.

Strange how quickly R—— forgot her resentment of Marcus Roper, owner of a $75,000 sports car. A spoiled young man from a well-to-do family racing with another young man on the expressway, endangering lives. Endangering his own life. He should have died in such a wreck, another would have died, yet Marcus Roper stubbornly did not die. In the City of the Damned, among the dazed, catatonic, comatose, Marcus Roper was most fascinating. *For he is not damned; he's young. He will survive.* At first, R—— had supposed that Roper would never recover in any significant sense of that word, now she was beginning to think that, yes, he might. He would. The damage to this patient's brain wasn't the result of a degenerative disease: it might be possible for him to relearn speech, motor skills . . .

R—— had saved the newspaper clippings. Marcus Roper's face before the damage would always be his face inwardly and there would be that solace. *I know. I know who you are. Marcus.* This name which R—— murmurs aloud softly, with an air of encouragement, as any nurse might do at the bedside of a sleeping patient. "Marcus. Roper." She was drawn to the four equally stressed syllables — "Marcus. Ro*per*" — as if they were poetry bearing a special, private meaning. "Mar-cus." An uncommon name, with a foreign sound. "Marcus Roper. Marcus—" Like an incantation the name was, uttered in R——'s low thrilled voice, a voice that came to her only when she was alone with the patient in room 1104 (and reasonably certain that no one — in the corridor outside? — could overhear).

Though Mr. Roper wasn't responding to R—— (yet). Though perhaps he was, and R—— must be closely attentive. His eyelids?

It had been a long exhausting vigil for the patient's relatives. In the City of the Damned such vigils were not uncommon. Such vigils often became wakes, for the living dead, the living soon-to-be-dead. Marcus Roper's relatives were of this type. Dispirited and exhausted, staring at the unconscious man with horror, anguish, dread. R——, who was sometimes obligated to enter the room at such times, noted that in the presence of these mourners Mr. Roper seemed to sink more deeply into himself. What relief he felt when they left him alone. When R—— was with him, the two of them alone together.

11.

Pray to make my heart harder. How?

Angel of Mercy the first time she'd have thought it would be the hardest but it was not. Like brushing away a fly. So Agnes would think. A mosquito. Giggling, wiping at her mouth. Her eyes. Then you see you've killed it, the mosquito. Mashed it against your skin.

Angel of Mercy it would not be determined who her first was, only Agnes knew. Therefore her second, her third. In all were there eighteen? Or, as some investigators believed, as many as twenty-three? Or more? Angel of Mercy she was called after her death but (of course) Agnes wasn't known as an angel during her lifetime, only just Agnes O'Dwyer, *a damned good nurse.*

Not during the lifetime. During what you'd call the death-time, which has been nearly thirty years now. Angel of Mercy if you believe in such things. A spirit, like a vapor. Like a hospital virus. Not a ghost.

Older nurses recall Agnes. *Couldn't have been Agnes O'Dwyer. Couldn't have been any of us. Whoever claimed to see her with a syringe. Not Agnes! We knew her; we never believed any of the accusations.*

A hospital virus, an infection. Your immune system is weak, you breathe it in, it's got you.

In the neurological intensive care unit. In the peaceful hours before dawn. Suctioning the respiratory tract of an elderly stroke victim with a snaky plastic tube passed down into the woman's throat, drawing out secretions of mucus clogging the larynx, and the odor of decay so strong the thought came to her to use this very tube to suffocate the woman; it was an act of mercy G——D would not perform. Yet unpremeditated and unnamed. And afterward it would feel like grace to the dazed young nurse who'd experienced her first intimate death to be noted assiduously ♋ in her nurse's diary. But it would not be her last.

Angel of Mercy undetected for fifteen years because unsuspected. The patients were moribund, or nearly. Always there are patients who take a turn for the worse overnight. Or within a few hours. Twenty-three years a nurse at the hospital on the river, Agnes would record ⟲ for each year, having to double up some years, of course, for she'd begun late, not until her eighth year of service, 1959. *It is something that happens. It is Good, to dispel Evil. I bring Mercy to those who suffer. I AM MERCY.*

12.

"It's a beautiful day, Mr. Roper. I wish you could see it! But you will, soon. The sky is clear, almost. Just those high fluffy white clouds—cirrus?" Outside the grime-flecked window what R—— could see of the sky was the hue of a soiled bandage, but Marcus Roper need not know. "And a wind from the southeast, up from Tennessee. From the mountains, that is. Not polluted." R—— performed her nurse rituals briskly and without apparent sentiment. She took hold of the patient's left wrist and pressed her forefinger against his pulse and counted the beat, which was erratic but strong; this beat which was displayed on a monitor both in room 1104 and at the nurses' station. Yet the beat was a signal between them, a fact of extraordinary intimacy. R—— felt a stab of happiness. For it seemed to her that she held the man's very heart in her hand. And no one could know, except Marcus Roper and R——.

The IV dripping through a tube into Mr. Roper's bruised arm had to be replenished. Pungent-smelling urine draining out of Mr. Roper's bruised groin through a tube into a plastic container beneath the bed had to be emptied, flushed away in the toilet. Such nurse tasks R—— performed with zest, enthusiasm. As if Marcus Roper were observing her. *A miracle might happen. Even in the City of the Damned.*

Saying, in her low thrilled voice, "I have to leave now. But I'll be here on the floor, and I'll be checking back. And tomorrow morning, of course. Always I'll check back, Mr. Roper. Remember!"

The eyelids quivered, the left eyelid twitched and seemed to lift a fraction of an inch. But a crescent of pale mucus was all that showed in the bruised socket of Mr. Roper's eye.

Leaving room 1104. Soundless, gliding in her rubber-soled shoes.

Leaving room 1104, her young heart beating hard. Calmly.

Of course I'm not. Not in love. Not with a patient. Not such a patient.

At the elevators at this sunless hour of early morning R— sees rippling air. It's the odor of Lysol, perhaps. Invisible proliferating death-bacteria. The heart falters yet the heart must beat, beat. R— is young, only twenty-six. R— must persevere. R— means to be a damned good nurse. Yet shutting her eyes, dazed with fatigue, refusing to see the shimmering translucent shadow at the end of the corridor.

Opening the door to the storage room where, twenty-eight years, five months, and sixteen days ago, the body of Nurse Agnes O'Dwyer was discovered by hospital workers, death attributed to self-induced cardiopulmonary arrest.

13.

December 1969. A twilit room smelling of the usual flesh she enters soundless and breathing calmly. The syringe prepared:

a new muscle relaxant, brand name Anectine. It's said to be quickly eliminated from the bloodstream, won't show up on routine blood tests, respiratory arrest, for such patients the most natural of deaths, who would suspect? In this room there are three patients. Two strokes, one post-op brain tumor. Two are elderly, the third middle-aged. Female or male little matters now. Angel of Mercy does not discriminate. Angel of Mercy these days before Christmas she is desirous of making a gift to the most deserving of sufferers yet can risk only a single ℞ for fear of being discovered. With so much work ahead, years of stealth and vigilance in the City of the Damned.

Angel of Mercy smiling upon the patient in the farthest bed. Yes, he is the one. The syringe readied, Nurse Agnes's capable fingers injecting the Anectine into the IV solution, dripping into the bruised forearm.

Here is the Mercy that G——D has forgotten. G——D has no time for the teeming multitudes of Earth though these are G——D's own creation.

14.

Ridiculous to think that R—— is in love with any patient in the City of the Damned. R—— has a lover of her own, D——. She values D——'s aloofness, his sense of himself. She values in D—— the fact that, like most individuals knowing little of the medical profession, he has virtually no awareness of mortality, still less of his own mortality. D—— knows little of the old hospital on the bank of the rust river and often brags that he has never been hospitalized, is rarely sick, even with a cold. R—— smiles at D——'s vanity. R—— believes that such vanity must be normal in the species. R—— silently pleads with D—— to love her, that R—— will be saved from what R——'s fate would be if D—— does not love her.

Ridiculous to think that R—— is in love with any patient in the City of the Damned.

15.

Meat nausea.

Abruptly it begins; you aren't prepared. Why?

Bathing flaccid flesh, suctioning respiratory tracts and the red-meaty interiors of scummy mouths. Palpitating muscle meat atrophied to the texture of Wonder bread. Suddenly R—— is nauseated and knows that something in her—her biological self, her animal self—has been permanently altered.

"Meat," her lips shape the moist ugly word. *Meat, with a chewy fibrous texture. Meat that is the body. Blood-juicy meaty-meat. The distinctive wet smell of (raw) meat. Meat in the mouth; meat particles lodged between the teeth.* R—— is weak with nausea staring at the meat on her plate she is expected to eat. Staring at D——'s mouth wetly chewing.

16.

They say of the patient in 1104, poor man, that it will take a miracle for him to wake up, even. And beyond that . . .

R—— hears, but knows her place. R—— is not a brash young nurse to contradict her seniors, knows not to question doctors. Yet she needs to say, reprovingly, so that the older nurse stares at her in surprise, "Yes but. Miracles can happen. If you have faith. Mr. Roper is young."

17.

R—— is young: only just twenty-six, having been born in July 1976.

Two years after Agnes O'Dwyer's cooling, seemingly sleeping, body was discovered curled up peacefully in a nest of towels and bedding on the floor of a storage closet in the City of the Damned.

R—— knows nothing of Agnes O'Dwyer.

R—— has never seen any photograph, any likeness, of Agnes O'Dwyer.

R—— is impatient with rumors, gossip. Superstition. She is one of those who turn aside, bemused and offended, when others allude to the Angel of Mercy. (Not just the Jamaican-born nurses' aides with their tightly cornrowed hair and glistening eyes, but certain of the older nurses as well. R—— is indignant: you'd think these women, fully certified nurses, would know better!)

R—— is a proud 1999 graduate of Mount Saint Joseph's Nursing School, one of the most highly regarded nursing schools in the state. (Agnes O'Dwyer was a 1949 graduate of the school. At Saint Joseph's, the dread name *Agnes O'Dwyer* is never spoken, even in jest.) R—— graduated summa cum laude, sixth in her class of eighty-one young women and eight young men. (Agnes O'Dwyer graduated summa cum laude, fourth in her class of sixty-six, all young women.) R—— is not a Roman Catholic (as Agnes O'Dwyer is believed to have been), but R—— considers herself a Christian: believes in the example of Jesus Christ and the redemption of sin. She believes in family life, the United States of America, and democracy, in fulfilling her job as a nurse, meeting the expectations of others. R—— inwardly seethes when well-intentioned fools ask why nursing school and not medical school? *What can you know of a nurse's life — you are ignorant.*

18.

R——'s father whom she loved. R——'s father in the decline of his manhood. The shock of certain odors lifting from his body, she recognized from the City of the Damned. *I must love him all the more. I must love him to save him.*

He's furious with his palsied hands, red-faced and choking from his coughing spells. Yet still food placates him. In old age R——'s father has become infantile in his appetites. Sugary things, ice cream and doughnuts and bread smeared with jam. And meat. Meat cut up into bite-sized pieces by his daughter R——, who loved him.

"Eat that, on your plate," he's saying suddenly. "Eat that damn meat, this is some new game of yours, eh? 'Veg-e-TAN-ism.' Bullshit."

R—— is shocked by the change in her father. His cruel crude wit. Always he'd been a taciturn man, with an air of subtly wounded dignity. A workingman, with big blunt hands. Now he's bossy, unnervingly watchful. He seems to have forgotten that R—— is an adult, R—— is a nurse with an excellent job. Pushing R——'s plate roughly toward her, as if to dump its contents in her lap. R—— tries to laugh, as if this is a joke. But can't force herself to eat the fatty pot roast, feels nauseated watching the others eat, their greasy mouths, teeth grinding like the teeth of beasts.

"Think you're too good for us, eh?" the old man sneers. "Well, you're not."

It's just his age. The illnesses. I will love him all the more. I will love him as he used to be.

19.

Angel of Mercy in shimmering white nylon grown tight at bust and hips, ankles swollen from years of service in the City of the Damned. Angel of Mercy, she has sacrificed her youth to the City of the Damned. *It's that simple I think. Giving comfort.* Angel of Mercy whose hot breathless mouth no man has wished to kiss for a decade, and more. She has difficulty some days deciphering words. Doctors' handwriting, newspapers, books. (But does Agnes O'Dwyer ever open a book?) Sometimes her thickened tongue plays tricks on her, mispronounces words Agnes knows perfectly well. She has ceased learning patients' names. She mistakes her coworkers for one another. Calls nurses and even staff doctors by the names of individuals long retired and vanished. Angel of Mercy, she stumbles sometimes even in her rubber-soled shoes. Angel of Mercy frequently distracted, clumsy. Drops things, misplaces things. Yet (who could guess? Agnes smiles to think) in secret she has become daringly random, extravagant. ⟳ as if willing (wishing?) to be caught. Acts of Mercy committed upon patients you would not expect to die so soon. Or to die at all. The not-moribund but the relatively healthy . . . *I am Mercy*, smiling upon her victims. *Do not resist Mercy.*

Over the years Agnes has perfected her technique. A death wizard she has become. Possibly it isn't always mercy, possibly sometimes it's her hands acting of their own sly volition, administering lethal doses of muscle relaxant, morphine. Air bubbles to the heart. The masterful use of the pillow. (No layman knows what the nurse knows: the pillow is the most effective of all murder weapons, and the least detectable.)

Staring then into a mirror at a grubby pale freckled-turnip face like something unearthed in the soil. Baring her teeth in a scared smile. "Do I look like someone who . . . ?" She imagines her faceless accusers as male. They would stare and stare and seeing Agnes O'Dwyer in her white nylon nurse's uniform, *they would not see her at all.*

20.

Bathing Mr. Roper in room 1104. Bathing *Marcus.*

Though no one is likely to enter the private room at this hour, R—— draws the curtain around the bed. Tenderly sponging the limp, yet strangely heavy, male body. The coarsely haired groin, the rubbery stub of a penis, testicles. Sometimes bathing this man (who's young, only twenty-nine) R—— observes his penis move as if of its own volition; and it seems to her that Mr. Roper's breath quickens too. He moans softly, with longing . . . "Mr. Roper? Marcus." R—— murmurs his name as in an incantation. During the course of his bath she will murmur it many times, as a mother might murmur to her baby. The name "Marcus Roper" fascinates R——, as if in some way she has yet to discover it's linked with her own.

From time to time, always unpredictably, this severely traumatized patient will surface to a kind of consciousness. He murmurs incoherent words. His eyes open, unfocused and yet (possibly) aware of lights, faces. The left eye wanders helplessly, but the right, once opened, exudes a "look." R—— has chanced to be present when this miracle has occurred, not once but twice; several times she's convinced that Marcus Roper has tried to communicate with her. She has declined to discuss this with others, including Dr. Roper's neurologist, for fear of being misunderstood. "Mr. Roper? I'm here. I am your nurse; I will take care of you." She hesitates, suddenly shy. "I love you, Marcus."

R——'s heart swells with happiness. There, she has said it! She has said it.

The stink of peroxide clinging to her hands despite the rubber gloves. A perverse sort of aphrodisiac. Smelling it, after her shift, she will think of this moment, this sacred time. Of him.

The scarred, burned-looking face with its mismatched skins, sunken eyes, and wounded mouth, R—— bends to kiss, brushing with her lips in a swoon of girlish daring, ecstasy. "Marcus! How cold you are. But you will be warm. Soon again. I promise."

————

Each week, fewer visitors come to see Marcus Roper. That's all they can do—see him. There has been little, perhaps no, communication with him. R—— has caught glimpses of the Roper family, their strained, exhausted faces. *How bored we are with the dying, who cling to their diminished lives like barnacles to the hull of a rotting ship.*

But R—— is never bored! Not with the patient in room 1104.

R—— is exhausted, too, sometimes. But never bored. She has postponed her vacation week explaining that, with her father unwell, it's no time to go away. "I couldn't enjoy myself; I'd be so distracted. Here, I'm never distracted. I know that I am needed."

At home, R—— is needed. But more urgently in the City of the Damned.

Gently washing, sponging, the stubby veined penis. Like a sea slug it seems to her, living yet barely sentient. Warmed by R——'s fingers, the penis stirs, seems to become conscious in a way that the man is not conscious, quite.

Though his eyelids quiver, just perceptibly.

21.

R—— wasn't drunk. She'd had a few beers. Maybe it was nerves; she'd been slipping away to the women's restroom more than usual. And afterward at D——'s apartment D—— began kissing her and she felt heat rush into her cheeks; her eyes were dreamy and half shut seeing Marcus Roper as he'd been before the accident. Avidly she kissed D——, and they

lay together on D——'s bed, and D—— began to undress
R—— who felt her body go limp as she thought of her true
love's ruined face and his secret, inward face only R—— knew.
Yet she was kissing D——, biting his lips in a kind of passion,
felt his penis hard against her belly, pushing against the wet-
ness between her legs until abruptly D—— ceased, lifting his
head from R—— as if a thought had struck him. And R——
whispered, "Is something wrong?"

One moment D—— was making love to her; the next he
eased himself from her with an expression of distaste. "That
smell."

"Smell? What smell?"

R—— was shocked. R—— would never forget this, her
shock and dismay. She'd bathed thoroughly before meeting
D—— that evening. She wanted to protest that always upon
returning from the hospital she bathed, or at least showered,
thoroughly and shampooed her hair. Rubbed her body with
lotion, dabbed it with talcum powder. Took care to apply a
fragrant, but not excessively fragrant, deodorant to her shaved
underarms. Tonight she'd made up a face so that she was
good to look at, luscious red mouth and striking eyes; she'd
smiled and winked at her mirrored reflection, that held such
promise.

Now her voice rose hurt, disbelieving. "What smell?"

22.

Agnes O'Dwyer whispered into her pillow to a faceless but aggressive lover. *Oh gosh, I don't think so. I mean, thank you for*

asking me to be your wife, but my work at the hospital is all the life I need.

September 1973

The x rays are in my bones I think,
in the night theres a radium glow
almost I can see. But I am not fearfull.
I have lived a full life.

since March 1959, 26 ↻
not one traced to A. For no one would belive
& no one at the hospitil wishes trouble.

(Didn't vote for the Union but now I'm glad
theres a Union to protect nurses!)

A.

Angel of Mercy she became anxious when patients known to her were admitted to the City of the Damned. For sometimes they knew her as Agnes O'Dwyer from the neighborhood and sometimes they recognized her but did not recall her name, and sometimes though she knew them, they did not know her, and this is frightening, like looking into a mirror and you see an individual looking back at you not knowing you. There came Bessie E. who'd been Agnes's mother's friend only a few years ago. Bessie E. from Saint Anne's parish. A soft fattish woman with a worn face and worried eyes often at 8 A.M. mass where Mrs. O'Dwyer used to go, and sometimes her daughter Agnes with her, whispering the rosary. Bessie E. had raised three children while working in a canning factory and living with the father of these children who, deranged by drink, was convinced that Bessie had betrayed him with numerous men including what he called black niggers. A sad life, yet all but one of Bessie's children had turned out reasonably well. Agnes had gone to school with the girls; they'd escaped and presumably sent money back home to Bessie though they rarely visited. Now Bessie was sixty-eight, which isn't that old, but Bessie was exhausted, skin tight across the bones of her formerly round face. Bessie had been stricken with breast cancer for years and it had metastasized to her brain and the chemo, too, was killing her, Agnes knew the symptoms. Agnes observed her mother's old friend with horror. The shrunken face, battered shapeless body, forearms and the insides of her ankles and thighs discolored from injections, IV tubes. Agnes was in terror that Bessie would know her. Bessie would speak her name. In her delirium Bessie would ask after Mrs. O'Dwyer (who had died two years before) or might confuse Agnes with Mrs. O'Dwyer; this Agnes could not bear. She must rid the City of the Damned of such a witness, she knew. Hurry, hurry! Not a syringe but a pillow Agnes used. A pillow is always chancy (because you might be observed). Two other patients in the room, so Agnes drew the curtains around Bessie's bed. The others were sedated, sleeping. But stirred and moaned in their sleep. It was only just after midnight, not yet the safe zone of the early morning hours when Angel of Mercy was most assured. *We are those G——D has forgotten. I love you Bessie.*

Alarming to Agnes when she lifted the heavy pillow, brought it against the woman's face, mashing it against her head, Agnes felt Bessie feebly struggle. Agnes had anticipated no resistance, or not much. Poor Bessie E. had lost eighty pounds at least, eaten by cancer. Agnes whispered, "No. No! Stop." Agnes pushed the pillow harder against Bessie's head, gritting her teeth. Big blunt teeth they were, a beast's teeth you might think, discolored by decades of tea drinking. Not teeth of which Agnes O'Dwyer had been proud as a girl but now (she believed) she was without vanity, such foolishness burned away forever. "No. *No.*" How to comprehend that this woman, eaten by cancer, wanted to live? It was wrong; it was a nasty thing. It was ugly. Agnes was panting, pushing the pillow. Her eyes were damp and bulging and her heart beat hard in determination knowing *This is Mercy, this is needed.*

After some minutes the struggle ceased. As all such struggles cease. Agnes carried away the only evidence, damp with the dying woman's saliva.

Afterward in the nurses' lavatory washing her flushed face and her hands and a younger nurse entered, an attractive light-skinned black woman, looking strangely at Agnes O'Dwyer but saying only hello. In the mirror, flecked with droplets of water from Agnes's energetic washing, the wan turnip face. Small lashless eyes and the teeth-baring smile. Agnes giggled as if embarrassed. "Oh gosh! So tired sometimes. Just want to curl up and sleep sometimes . . ."

After Agnes's death a few years later, the younger nurse would recall this remark, prophetic in retrospect. At the time she merely said, "Uh-huh! Don't I know it."

23.

This was the season of her life when the romance of R— and her father began to sour. Within a year of his Parkinson's diagnosis. Three years after R—'s mother's death. R— began to break down more often speaking with him. On the phone especially, Dad was difficult. He was going deaf, could not adjust to a hearing aid, became impatient, shouted. In silence R—— pleaded with him, *Daddy I love you. Daddy this isn't you.*

He had emphysema; he'd smoked three packs of cigarettes a day for thirty years and had stubbornly continued long after he'd been warned to stop. He had Parkinson's disease, palsy and tremors. He had high blood pressure. He was not an elderly man, and yet his life was unraveling. Especially he hated his tremulous hands that betrayed his illness to any shrewd eye. Crudely he joked of pissing red in the toilet. When R—— anxiously questioned him, he shrugged and refused to answer. "Daddy, please? Let me take you to" —naming the doctor of youthful middle-age her dad despised.

R—— was a health care professional. R—— knew what was in store for the angry old man. If she had not loved him so much, and in her child's heart harbored a hope that against all logic and reason he would be restored to her as he'd been only a few years ago, she would have said to him, *Daddy why do you want to live? Why cling to your wretched life? Every hour of your life is complaint now, or misery and pain. You're a rat in a trap. Time is the trap; old age is the trap. You can't even gnaw your leg off as a rat would do. Now that you are beginning to die, and your body to smell. Yet you want to live. You stuff your greasy mouth, you eat like a pig. You soil the bed—I hate you for that. Daddy why disgrace yourself? Why not die, while you are able? All those pills you have, and I can supply you with more.*

But R—— loved her father, and R—— would never utter such cruel words.

24.

April 1974

You can ask them, the patients
liked & trusted Agnes. Always I had
their best intersts at heart not like
the doctors, & the hospitil keeping
them alive like vegtables for the $.
even when they saw this nurse with a
sirnge leaning over them smiling.
even when they saw the pillow big
as a cloud lowering upon their brains
like a duststorm in the sky. even then,
they wold not belive
Agnes O'Dwyer meant them harm.

I think, of all my life, its that
I wold say I was most proud.

A.

In that rainy April in her nurse's diary she would record the
final ↻. Swift and unpremeditated and almost innocent as
the first had been so long a time ago it seemed when she was
young.

A pillow. A pillow is best. She'd come to believe so. For
when the patient is smothered, oxygen ceases to flow to the
brain and the heart races and lunges and begins to falter and
fails and will stop. And where, in the City of the Damned,
hearts are old, leaky, strained, there is a yearning to stop. And

so an ordinary pillow over the mouth and nose satisfies this yearning. And so the death pronouncement will be *cardiac arrest*. And so no physician would suspect, for why would he? Nor any nurse, mostly. Though Agnes must be alert to her sister nurses who look upon her (she has reason to think) with some suspicion. But this time, this ↻, Agnes must act swiftly. One of three post-op cancer patients, a split-brain, half the visual field sliced away as you might slice a peach in two. Male, female — scarcely mattered any longer. But for the record, male. Seventy-two years old. With a drum-tight face and sunken eyes like broken eggs. Sunken cheeks where the ill-fitting dentures had been removed. Agnes had not expected much exertion but once in the room her capable hands moved swiftly out of pity and impatience. She would tell herself she had not planned this ↻ though in fact she'd been feeling anxious, jumpy. Resentful of what, she did not know. As in the days before her menstrual cramps (which had ceased soon after her fortieth birthday). Menopause! Men joked of it, crude and cruel. As if men, too, did not suffer menopause, aging. Agnes knew to fear senility, dementia. She feared the symptoms of early mild strokes: strokes you don't know you have had, that leave you strangely cheerful, indifferent and unworried. In the City of the Damned it was understood among the older staff that such symptoms were contagious over time. Like the sepia-tinged air of the old industrial city, communicating its contagions to the yet unborn. *I will have no children at least. At least not that.* Though knowing that both her mother and father were saddened, Agnes did not marry and have babies. Waking sometimes in the night, her heart beating hard, in the silence of the row house on Caliper

Street now her parents were gone to the graveyard behind Saint Anne's, and beyond all harm and criticism of her, Agnes could not always recall her name. Panic! She could not recall the month, the year. Certainly could not name the president of the United States. (This question routinely put to confused patients in Admissions believed to have suffered mild strokes.) And so there was the old man frowning toward her out of his sunken blind-seeming eyes. And yet he seemed to see her, condemn her. His peevish little mouth jabbering what sounded like, "Y-You! *You!*" A smell of urine and feces rose from the bedpan his skinny ass had dislodged. Agnes saw her panicked hands leap out—seize a pillow on a supply cabinet—and carry it to the old man. Agnes's cracked lips murmured, "No. Not me."

For he could not see her—could he?

No screen around the old man's bed, and no time to pull the curtains though two other patients lay sedated and dazed in their beds, hooked to IVs, but the Act was upon her in a fierce sexual rush, not to be thwarted. And Agnes was disgusted with this pathetic being who wanted so badly to live, yet could not live. In a trance she pressed the pillow over his grimacing face. And pressed, and pressed. Her eyes shone, veins protruded in her forehead. She wasn't prepared for the old man's resistance. As if his life were worth preserving for even an hour, how he struggled! You could hear him moaning through the pillow. The IV needle detached from his flailing arm. The bedpan and its disgusting contents overturned into the bed. Agnes commanded "Stop. Stop. *Stop.*" The strength of desperation suffused her. The rapacious G——D in whom she did not believe came to her rescue now as by degrees the old man ceased his struggling. His claw fingers grasped at the underside of the pillow, trying to wrench it from Agnes; then suddenly these fingers relaxed their grip.

Oh, but it was midmorning: not a safe time in the hospital. Not once in her nurse's diary of fifteen years had Agnes recorded ♋ at such a dangerous time. Thinking, *This would be proof, wouldn't it; it could not be intentional. No nurse would take such a risk.*

Cautiously Agnes lifted the pillow. This could be a trick— the old man's sudden stillness. In the bed by the window someone stirred, groaned faintly. Agnes was staring at her ashen-faced victim, seeing that the face was disfigured, the nose mashed. Had she done this? A wave of cold terror washed over her. She would be detected, accused. The pillow would be seized as evidence.

Agnes fumbled for the man's pulse. In horror she felt it beat—no, it was her own heartbeat, in her fingertips.

The pillow wet from the dying man's saliva and mucus, Agnes calmly observed her hands carrying away, into the corridor and swiftly to soiled linens. For this evidence had to be removed, and was removed. The corridors of the City of the Damned were busy at this hour of midmorning yet Agnes believed that she was not seen, for in recent years she had become invisible. *A good nurse is invisible. Does her duty.* And now, where was she expected? She reentered room 1117 which was incongruously bathed in sunshine. Through the tall and not very clean windows, morning sunshine. Briskly Agnes surveyed the room: the three patients in their beds, unmoving. Another time she checked the old man's pulse and there was none. His skin that felt like bread dough, clammy to the touch, yet retained a mild warmth. "Gone! Oh my God." Agnes murmured aloud, in stunned surprise. Her eyes were widened in the innocence of one who imagines she is being observed though in fact she knows she is not being observed. Quickly then, she left the room, her glasses askew on her nose. Her face was gauzy with sweat. Another nurse saw her face. *Maybe I knew. That look of hers. Something had happened in that room.* Agnes stammered, "He has died. In there. The pulse is gone." The floor supervisor was summoned, the attending physician, the death cleanup team. There would be no autopsy, for survivors of the deceased did not wish an autopsy and had there been an autopsy what could have been noted except *cardiac arrest?*

She was not detected, yet another time. Would not be accused.

And yet how tired she was. Made her decision and returned to the hospital that night, though it wasn't her night shift, in her white nylon uniform as usual and her starched cap she was seen rinsing her face, washing her hands vigorously at a sink in the nurses' lavatory. *She looked like her usual self. She did not look any different I swear except maybe more tired. And she didn't notice me.* Sometime after 3 A.M. she filled a syringe with the powerful muscle relaxant succinylcholine. In a storage closet she prepared a comfortable nest for herself of towels and bedding, knelt, and injected the full syringe into her left arm and lay down curled up in relief soon sinking into the merciful sleep she had long provided for others. The date was April 11, 1974. The body would not be discovered until 5:25 A.M.

25.

"Mr. Roper! Marcus."

She replenished the IV antibiotics. She emptied the container beneath the bed and flushed away its pungent-smelling contents. She prepared to bathe the unconscious man. Softly she murmured his name and spoke to him of the early-morning weather, the forecast for the day. Though the sky outside the window was smudged, blank. The notorious rust-river was not visible. Swaths of fog were blown against the window-panes, like brainless and shapeless life-forms seeking entry. Mr. Roper was running a fever. Returned from another session of brain surgery he'd contracted a hospital infection. R—— felt the injustice of it: infections sweeping through the hospital, most virulent in pediatrics, oncology, and the City of the Damned.

R—— believed that, except for the fever, Marcus Roper was "progressing." His interludes of consciousness were more frequent and of longer duration. He could not yet utter coherent words, but at times he seemed to comprehend what was said to him. The neurologist had not been pessimistic though not (of course!) overly optimistic. This was the City of the Damned. R—— was shy about inquiring; it was not R——'s place to inquire. Though knowing that Mr. Roper's spinal column had been injured, poor man (as the nurses said) would be partially paralyzed from the waist down. Soon to be removed to a health care facility elsewhere in the state. "But where? Maybe I could . . . I could apply there. I could transfer." R—— sponged the yeasty-smelling flesh. R—— could not fail to notice how shallow the man's breathing was. How shrunken Marcus Roper had become, his chest collapsed upon his ribs, sallow sickly old-man flesh, and always saliva at the corners of his ruined mouth. His face would not heal, would not be restored. Perhaps R—— had thought it would be restored; now R—— knew better. As R—— bathed the man she felt the injustice, the wrongness of this situation. This patient should not be taken from her. If he could not be healed, he must be nursed, nursed permanently, why would they remove him from *her*? She saw herself pleading, arguing. She saw her application to work at the nursing home torn into pieces, ridiculed. R—— was stroking the limp stubby penis. To console the man, and to console herself. For there was consolation in such simple crude pleasures as stroking and bathing the flesh of an infant. An infant all flesh and very little brain. R—— felt in her fingertips the coursing of the other's blood. "Take me with you. I want to go with you. Marcus?" R—— was disappointed with the bruised eyelids that failed to lift, or even quiver. It was the fever ravaging his flesh. The broken mouth that could not speak. How exhausting this was, the shallow breathing. The twitching, the tremors. The IV fluid that continued to drip into shriveled veins, the liquid excrement draining from the body into a plastic container beneath the bed. "Is this our life? This can't be our life." They were meant for so much more. More life, happiness. It had been meant to be and yet it was not to be. A born nurse they'd said of her. As if this were the highest praise and not a curse. As if they were commending her and not laughing at her. And now on the floor her coworkers were apt to criticize her for being distracted, forgetful. Still she followed instructions diligently but there appeared to be something wrong: what? "It's nobody's business, Marcus and me." R—— was becoming emotional, thinking of these things. These were facts. You had to confront them. Like her father: an aging, ailing man. Who might yet live for a long time. R—— was sick with pity for both men, these broken men once so manly. She was sick with the effort of caring for them. She was sick with the effort of love. "I hate it. I would never have chosen it. I hate 'nursing.'" The futility of Marcus Roper's life swept over her, a black bitter taste in her mouth. The futility, the absurdity. Why did Marcus Roper insist upon living, and why did others, like R——, collaborate in this folly? *Into the IV. Demerol, Anectine?* She would choose Anectine. It was quickly eliminated from the patient's bloodstream, it would not be indicated in routine tests, it would cause cardiopulmonary arrest and the fever would be blamed. The Roper family would want no autopsy. R—— had long spied upon these grieving exhausted people, R—— understood how they wanted the stricken young man dead, and gone. And perhaps he would not die in this room; more likely he would be removed to intensive care and he would sink into a deep coma and perhaps be resuscitated and yet finally he would die, his heart would fail, his exhausted organs would fail. R—— was relieved to know it was time, and more than time.

R——completed the sponge bath; R—— drew the covers back up over the fevered body. "Mr. Roper! Good-bye."

26.

At the elevators she was waiting, subdued and chastened after her exhausting night shift. Thinking, *I'm not young I guess. No longer.* It was late summer 2002. Or was it autumn, or an early winter. And soon the winter solstice, and the New Year. *In the Kingdom of Stroke & Tumor/we prescribe a Sense of Humor.* She smiled to think yes, this was so. You don't want to realize, at first. When you are the youngest nurse in the City of the Damned.

She'd begun to keep a nurse's journal. Her brief entries were made in ink, in code. Asterisks, symbols, abbreviations, initials. She'd begun soon after the first death. Though the patient had not died in neuropsychiatric services, but in intensive care, under the supervision of intensive care nurses. Never had she seen Marcus Roper again, after that final sponge bath. Room 1104 was now occupied by a post-op brain tumor patient, a middle-aged man given a "fairly positive" prognosis by his surgeon.

Like an emptied syringe, R—— felt, after the night shift. Foreseeing a life of service, selflessness. There was no other life available that seemed to her worthy. She foresaw, too, that she would be living alone soon. She would mourn her father, but she would surrender him. She had to be realistic: he was an elderly man. His lungs would fail. His heart, strained from years of smoking. Parkinson's would leech away his brain, he would soon be bedridden. In his nurse-daughter's care.

R—— no longer saw D——, or any man. A revulsion passed over her at the thought of marriage: of lying together with another person, sleeping together, in a single bed. Now she knew too much, there could be no more romance of the body. All that was behind her, disdained.

Yet there were buoyant moments in R——'s life. She lived for these, and they did not fail her. Even in the City of the Damned. She knew she would never request a transfer to another floor. She would never apply for a job at another hospital. *This is my place; I belong here.* Sometimes she felt as if she'd been a nurse in the City of the Damned for an entire lifetime, recalled as in a dream. Her nurse's journal interested her greatly. It would be a ledger of secrets more real to her than her own life. In this journal she recorded moments of ecstatic insight as well as sorrow; wonders as well as horrors. The promise of new admissions on the floor, for instance. Those patients with "positive" prognoses. That morning, for instance, she'd entered room 1104 bearing a breakfast tray and there was her patient awake and hungry for orange juice, bouillon, cereal mush sucked through a straw. A lacerated and battered skull, scalp stapled together, clown bruises for eyes, yet he'd smiled at R——; he'd been ravenously hungry.

Always a thrill: that those who can eat at all, eat with appetite.

Waiting for the elevator to rise to the eleventh floor R——, who believed herself alone, felt the presence of another, at her elbow. This presence she had sometimes felt. Thinking calmly, *If I turn, no one will be there.* But she did turn, to see a patient in a wheelchair gazing up at her with an impudent grin. This was E——, nineteen years old, post-op brain cancer patient, totally bald and wearing thick glasses attached to his eggshell head by an elastic strap. At first, R—— had confused E—— with B——, who was departed from the City of the Damned. But E—— was his own person, distinctive, even aggressive. Daring to pluck at R——'s elbow, his voice hoarse and sibilant like crackling tissue paper. "Nurse? Are you the nurse? *My nurse? Nurse?*"